The
Trouble With Clouds

Kevin Cookson

en Press

First published in Great Britain by Pen Press

All paper used in the printing of this book has been made from
wood grown in managed, sustainable forests.

ISBN13: 978-1-907499-57-9

Printed and bound in the UK
Pen Press is an imprint of Indepenpress Publishing Limited
25 Eastern Place
Brighton
BN2 1GJ

A catalogue record of this book is available from
the British Library

Cover design by Jacqueline Abromeit

Acknowledgements

This book would not have been possible without the full support of my wife Christine, whom I love dearly.

The following people have also made important contributions to the making of this book: Marion Banks, Les Calvey, Emma Cookson, Sally Deford, James Donaldson, Linda Lloyd, Francesca and James Loynes, Lynne Starkey, and without him ever knowing: Gavin Pretor-Pinney.

Thanks Everyone!

Kevin Cookson B.Sc. PGCE (early years). C.Eng.

After studying for his degree in Electrical Engineering Sciences Kevin's start in industry was as a quality manager in the field of aerospace electronics. Whilst following his career, he and his wife Christine adopted and fostered children. Having had enough of moving around with the job they both decided to settle back in their hometown and, together with another couple, opened a number of children's nurseries.

An accomplished guitarist and songwriter Kevin is more used to the stage and performing than he is to writing books. Eighteen months ago he took his 'Traveler Guitar' on holiday to the Canary Islands with songwriting in mind, only to find the ambient noise was far too high for him to sit down and write music. Facing two weeks of nothing to do but sunbathe, he chose to start this book; he says he's not very good at sunbathing.

If you wish to know more then go to: kevincookson.com

Last Night I Saw The Sun Go Down

Last night I saw the sun go down
But felt no chill upon the ground
A new sun would be coming round
Come morning time

I'd seen those pictures sent from space
Showing the haze where the human race
Built its cities and growing space
When things were fine

But winter came so warm this year
The snow-caps blew away
Another day, another year
Amongst these cosmic rays

Last night I saw the sun go down
On mankind's bid to stay around
The global warming battleground
It soon was lost

Saw children ask their parents why
Saw Fathers hang their heads and cry
Saw Mothers weep so horrified
Of the holocaust

Still winter came so warm this year
The snow-caps blew away
No other day, no other year.

Last night I saw the sun go down

... Song by: K. Cookson.
(January '10)

Contents

Preface

(By the Author)

The trouble with writing a book of fiction that contains many facts is that the two types of information merge and one can easily distrust the factual information on offer. In fact, it becomes easier to assume that everything that is said in the book is fiction. This is not the case.

For example: there is a squadron called the 53rd Weather Reconnaissance Squadron and they operate from Keesler Air Force Base. But Ollie and the modification of their aircraft, for seeding purposes, are entirely fictional.

In most areas of the book this doesn't matter. There is, however, one area of the book where it does matter.

It is important to me that you, the reader, understand that the scientific data regarding temperature rises and the rate of decline of the snow fields, as quoted in this book, are not fiction. One of the main reasons for writing this novel was to give a story line for young readers, so that they could more easily understand the significance of global warming. Thus, these areas are left as facts with no exaggerations or embellishments.

- Chapter One -

Hammerhead's First Outing

On the one hand ....

Sometimes the measure of a man can't be found in how great he may have become during his lifetime, nor in how many possessions he had, nor how rich he was before he died. Sometimes it can't even be found in how generous he was while he was alive. No! Sometimes the measure of a man can only be found in his children, not in their material inheritance as such, but in the wisdom and knowledge he has imparted.

Philip Winter was such a man. The wisdom he handed down to his only child mattered much more to him than any gains he could ever have made for himself during his lifetime. And, in the end, that wisdom would come to matter to all of humanity.

Phil, as he preferred to be called, was not at all a remarkable man. He was 'the salt of the earth' type. A middle-aged family man, slim of build with his once jet-black hair starting to grey at the temples.

He'd arrived in America, from England, with his American fiancée, Martha, some fifteen years earlier and instantly fallen in love with the place. After the wedding, he'd applied for U.S. citizenship. It was, without doubt, one of the greatest days of his life when he was made a citizen of the United States of America.

Philip had met Martha at a furniture exhibition in Birmingham, England. He had a small business

1

manufacturing high quality furniture and she was temporarily working in London, as a Product Scout, for a large American department store chain.

Martha's home base was Florida and so, when they came to America, that's where they settled.

Living in Florida gave the family lots of advantages. There was the sun of course, and all the well-known theme parks, which were great for young kids. But there were other more natural attractions like the Everglades and the bay areas. Not to mention the closeness of the NASA sites.

As you would expect with Father and Son (although as we all know it's not always the case), Phil and Jack were very close. Sometimes when Phil was alone, like now, working his wood, he would reminisce about the times they had together.

"A chip off the old block," he would often call Jack. He always thought in woodworking terms and this particular thought made him smile.

He was also very proud of the fact that, compared with the rest of the kids in the neighbourhood, there was definitely a touch of Englishness about Jack.

As Jack had grown older his tastes had matured. In fact, they'd changed to such an extent that he now preferred visiting the science-based attractions to the theme parks that most youngsters enjoyed.

Martha still preferred the theme parks and really wasn't interested in visiting the other attractions. So, once a month, Phil and Jack would organise a science trip, leaving Martha at home. She had always been comfortable with this, since it gave her a little respite and allowed Jack and his Dad to have some quality time together.

Seeing the launch of an Apollo rocket was such an occasion; boy was that a sight and sound to remember! Then there was the time when they'd spent a few days in the Everglades and gone on an airboat, winding in and out of the mangrove bays. Jack was so excited to see the alligators swimming in the water or sunning themselves on the banks.

Their last trip out together was when they had gone down to Biscayne Bay to look at the ship wrecks that littered the coast there. Phil had partly organised this trip to teach his son about the dangers of the sea and the violent weather events that plagued the southern coast of the United States.

He had especially warned Jack about the power of the Hurricane. He'd exaggerated a little bit, as Fathers do, to make his point. "All these ships were wrecked and all the men lost, because of one simple fact: they didn't understand the power of the hurricane." Actually, he knew very well that wasn't really the case and many of the ships had floundered because of poor navigation but he wanted his son to be a little fearful and respectful of hurricanes and the power of the wind, especially in their neck of the woods.

Good family man that he was, you couldn't just sum up Phil Winter's life as a husband and father.

The other half of his life was his work. He was a fully trained woodworking genius and his tool shed, as he liked to call it, (in truth it was more like a small factory) was his den. A craftsman's dream with lathes, band saws, and routers ... you name it. If a tool or machine was required for the making of furniture it was in the shed.

He was currently working with his lathe, turning four non-descript pieces of oak into a set of rather beautiful legs for a table that had been ordered by one of his neighbours just a few days before.

Over the last few years Phil's hearing had been deteriorating and his doctor had advised him to use ear defenders whenever working with machinery. He never thought that wearing them would one day prove fatal.

It was a hot and sultry day and even with the air conditioning on, the ear defenders were getting a little uncomfortable to wear and a little too sweaty around the ears. Well, he'd had the ear defenders on for a good twenty minutes or so and thought he would try to keep them on until the last leg was complete; but no sooner had that thought entered his head than a large piece of timber hurtled through the side wall of the tool shed. It was at a height that would have removed Phil's head had it been just a little closer. As he stared in amazement the missile carried on straight through the opposite wall; it didn't seem to slow down at all.

He knew instinctively what had made that piece of wood puncture the walls of his shed: as he ripped the ear defenders off, the deafening roar from outside the cabin only confirmed his worst fears. He knew he was done for as the cabin started to collapse around him and the wind lifted him off the ground feet first. He just had time to shout a warning to Martha "TORNADO!"

There was no way Martha could ever have heard him. Even if she had only been a few feet from him, the noise of the tornado would have smothered his words. She had heard the noise coming, it was like a fast moving freight train and it was headed directly for her sitting room. As soon as she realised what it was, she pulled Jack away from his train set and gripping his hand tightly hurried down into the storm shelter.

What made Brandy, the Winters' dog, follow them? To this day she still didn't understand. It must have been instinct, she kept telling herself.

There was absolutely no time to look for Phil and she

knew shouting wouldn't have done any good. She was just hoping he was somewhere safe.

'Thank goodness for the shelter,' Martha thought. Phil had only built it twelve months ago and his prophetic words now rang in her brain: "Tornados and storms seem to be getting more frequent, so I think we may need it one day Martha."

To this day Martha and Jack still remember how little time they had to react to the danger. As they made it to the shelter and pulled the trap door open, the house had already started to shred around them. Martha sent Jack down the steps first. Luckily Jack had the foresight to shout and whistle after the dog. Martha was fully aware of the danger around her and would not have waited for Brandy to appear before closing the trap door. So it was lucky indeed that Brandy raced past her and down the steps as she closed and bolted the door above her head.

Within a second of the bolt being slid in place, a large object bounced off the trap door. The noise was so loud and so sudden that Martha jerked away from the door in fear. It was pitch black, which made it all the more frightening. There was no light visible through the door she had just slammed shut and there was no electricity flowing to the shelter lights.

They were in total darkness with a freight train passing over their heads, through what was once their house.

"Jack!" shouted Martha.

"Over here, Mom!"

Martha groped her way over to him and they both crouched in the corner of the room hugging each other, both of them quietly stroking the dog. They remained there without speaking until the freight train had passed overhead.

They waited for what seemed like an age before they

ventured out, yet it could only have been minutes. When Martha finally lifted the door above her head, part of her expected to be walking back into the room she had just left. But no! Instead, as she rose out of the shelter, she was greeted by bright sunlight. So bright, that for a second, it blinded her.

As they both climbed the shelter's steps the true horror of what had just happened was slowly coming into view.

Jack could see the devastation but there was something else. He felt different. It was nothing to do with the material things that lay broken and scattered all around him. In fact, at this moment, they didn't mean anything to him at all. They were totally irrelevant. He was numb and something inside was saying that his life had just changed forever. He still couldn't speak! It was as if speech itself was unimportant.

As the three of them emerged from the underground shelter their eyes fell upon a world that was totally different to the one they had left just a few minutes before.

Their house was gone. Dad's shed had gone but not only that – the neighbourhood had gone too. There wasn't an undamaged house on the street, although from what Jack could see, theirs and the house opposite were the only two buildings that had been completely demolished.

Numb and confused, he couldn't immediately take it all in. He started thinking the weirdest of thoughts: how am I going to find my way back home from school now the street doesn't look the same? I'll not be able to find my house! In his mind he was actually replying to himself: 'don't be silly, there isn't a house to find.' Where would they deliver the mail now? He'd been expecting a late birthday present from Aunty Barbara, but how would it find him now? Then, slowly but surely, he was coming out of his daze; he could hear his Mom crying and he was the one holding her hand and hugging her arm. Jack wasn't sure whether he was doing it because he needed comforting or because *she* needed comforting. He had a lump in his throat but this was not the time to cry. He needed to find Dad.

Then he noticed how deathly quiet it was. No sound of his friends and the other children running around on the streets; no birdsong either.

As his head cleared he started to realise that there *was* a noise. Yes! It was Brandy, barking in the distance.

The dog had run off and was making an almighty din right at the end of their row. A group of neighbours were running over to see what the dog was barking at. Jack let go of his Mother's hand and ran towards Brandy; he wanted to see what he was barking at too.

"Jack, come back!" cried Martha.

But Jack was too intent on doing something. He wasn't the type to just stand there feeling sorry for himself.

The neighbours reached the dog first. Old Sam Brock, with horror on his face, turned quickly to the others and shouted, "Keep the boy away!"

The neighbours responded immediately, trying to create a cordon around where the dog was, but Jack was far too quick for them.

As he reached the place were Brandy was, he looked down and saw the lifeless body of his Father.

"Dad!" He screamed, dropped to his knees and just cried, and cried, and then everything went black.

It could only have been a few minutes that Jack was out cold. He woke to see his Mother cradling him in his arms and Brandy licking his face. "Did I see Dad ... " He didn't finish the question.

"Yes Son, he's gone to a better place now."

They both sat there for a few moments, crying. Then Martha stood. "Jack, look after Brandy for a second, I just want to have a word with Sam," and with that Martha went over to the small group of neighbours that were stood close by.

After talking to them for some time Martha came back. "C'mon Jack, there's nothing left for us here now. Let's pack a few of the things we can find and we'll go and stay at Aunty Barbara's house, just for a short time."

"What about Dad?"

"Sam will look after Dad. He'll make sure everything is taken care of here. We'll come back to say goodbye to Dad in a few days time." And with that they both started crying again.

It was a long time before they could find the energy to hunt around in the ruins of what was their home, their life, for some evidence that they once existed. Mementos from their earlier existence were suddenly of great importance.

Jack's value system had changed: old photographs were now much more important than computer games.

The next few days were spent at Aunty Barbara's house. Yet today at the funeral they seemed distant. Even going to church earlier in the day seemed dream like and unreal. Yes, there were many people saying kind words about Dad but Jack wasn't interested in what other people thought of his father. He just wanted to see him again, to talk to him once more. There was an emptiness he'd never felt before, an ache he never wanted to experience again, and all the words in the world couldn't stop this feeling.

In fact, all the words he heard that day felt completely unimportant. The only words that mattered to Jack right now were his father's words.

As Philip Winter's coffin was lowered into the ground,

Jack followed his mother's example and threw soil onto his casket and swore with all his heart that he would dedicate the rest of his life to making his neighbourhood safer from such storms in the future. Dad had warned him how dangerous the weather was to seafarers and now he could see for himself how dangerous it was to everyone else.

* * *

On the other hand ....

Perspectives can be so different. For example: the child is gone. One minute he was there, the next nothing. No emotion. Just gone.

The man involved in the accident, the one that killed the child by knocking him down with his automobile, did not intend to do so. His feelings of guilt and remorse are enormous. He is so, so sorry for what has happened. It was just another day and the child ran out in front of his car!

In his rage the child's father just wants to kill the driver. How can he have killed his only son? As yet, there is no forgiveness in his heart.

Yet neither of them is a bad man and in truth they could easily be walking in each other's shoes right now.

So it is when worlds collide.

The cloud that caused Phil Winter's death was called Hammerhead. The contrast between what happened to Jack Winter's dad that day and what happened to Hammerhead couldn't have been starker.

Hammerhead was really proud of his first foray into turning himself into a thunderstorm and it looked like it may have been an event to remember. He'd only know that for sure once the Inspectors had given him their report but from where he was flying it was looking good.

The storm was a 'First Attempt' and since Cloud TV hadn't covered a first attempt for quite a few years, it was decided by those higher up that it would be a good idea to do so. They had just turned up, totally out of the blue, to cover the story. The reporter was a young cloud, a Fluffy named Dizzy.

Let me explain: the smallest clouds that humans see are called Fluffies and all of the clouds you will ever see are made up of Fluffies. Yes, I know it's hard to believe but believe it! The fiercest of storms, the strongest of tornados and the biggest hurricane you will ever see are all made up of these little individuals.

You see, when Fluffies come together they don't have hard edges like humans, so they merge. If a cloud merges with another cloud the one with the strongest mind takes over and the other cloud's mind is put into limbo. It sort of goes to sleep and we call this mind a captive; it doesn't die. In fact if the two clouds happen to separate at a later date the captive would re-awaken and the two Fluffies would go their separate ways. The captive would wonder where the heck it was and what it was doing there! But it would not have been harmed in any way. No! The result would be two perfectly good Fluffies.

The cloud mind that takes over when the two clouds merge is called the 'Head'. Thunderstorms are created because the Head gets stronger and stronger as each merger takes place and some Heads just like this feeling; they find it intoxicating. So the Head carries on gathering more and more smaller clouds, thus getting bigger and stronger all the time.

Now a Fluffy cannot move by itself. It has to have a Windlet to move it and each Fluffy has its own Windlet. Humans may think that wind is just one big thing but it isn't. The wind is made up of lots of smaller Windlets and as the Fluffies merge their Windlets, being very loyal to their Fluffies, stay with the building cloud. So the storm is not just building more cloud, it's also building stronger and stronger winds.

Eventually something beyond lots of Fluffies and Windlets is created. As the cloud and winds get stronger a metamorphosis takes place and a thunderstorm is born.

Dizzy, the reporter for Cloud TV was trying to appear knowledgeable about thunderstorms by explaining what happens during metamorphosis.

"As you know, a thunderstorm is much more than just a large collection of Fluffies: as it becomes bigger it becomes a different entity. The Head of a thunderstorm gains powers he or she never had before and soars high above other clouds. This gives the Head a feeling of absolute power over everything it sees. It gains the ability to generate electricity and this enhances its powers even further because it can then communicate over large distances and with higher beings like the Great Conveyors or the Cloud Hierarchy. Another new power is the ability to spin up tornados..." Dizzy was about to continue with her lecture when she noticed Hammerhead heading towards her, so she positioned herself in such a way that he had to brush past her. As he did so, Dizzy said quite loudly: "Well, today we have the privilege of interviewing the Head of a thunderstorm. It's his very first time and the event has just ended. Could you tell us your name Sir?"

"Hammerhead," he said, surprised at the question and that anyone was interested in talking to him. He turned to face the camera.

Dizzy continued: "It takes a lot of hard work to become a thunderstorm, so why does a normal cloud like yourself choose to do this?"

"I'd heard a lot of rumours saying how exciting it was, so I just thought I'd give it a try." He smiled quite deliberately at the camera and said "I'm old enough you know!"

"And was it as exciting as you thought it might be?"

"Well yes, it gave me a great sense of control and power. Imagine being in control of hundreds of smaller clouds that obey you at every turn. Then imagine you can spin one or two of their windlets up and up, and turn them into tornados. I know that tornados, being what they are, have a mind of their own, but they do want to obey you. You see, they always want to go faster and they need you to help them do that, so if they won't tow the line you just spin them down again."

Hammerhead had just used this exact ability to spin up the tornado that killed Jack's dad. He didn't know that he was in the shed at the time, but it wouldn't have made any difference even if he had.

"Is there any more to it than that?" Dizzy asked.

"*Of course* there is, I haven't told you about the good bits yet!"

Dizzy felt slightly intimidated by Hammerhead's forceful tone and backed off a little to ensure she didn't start being absorbed by this brute of a cloud.

"What good bits?" she said with a smile.

"Once you get to a certain height *suddenly* a metamorphosis takes place. You become something different."

"What do you mean?"

"You are soaring higher, looking down on lesser mortals. Then suddenly you are aware of the electric pulse. At first I was throwing bolts of lightening all over the place but then you learn to control it; the accidental discharges to ground reduce and you find you are able to communicate over vast distances. While I was up there I talked to one of the Great Conveyors (*humans like to call these 'Jet Streams'*). I must say he did seem to be in such a hurry though. I could never have had a decent conversation with him. Then I conversed with the Cloud Hierarchy. Well, as you can imagine, they have such a different view of the world at over twenty nine thousand feet as opposed to where we exist at a few thousand feet. It certainly opened up a completely new dimension for me; it was wonderful!"

"Well, you're obviously enthusiastic about your experience as a storm cloud but what about the darker side, like the damage you may cause? Doesn't this make you feel a little guilty at times?"

"Well no! Not when you're a storm. You don't think of the little guy at all. I mean I never liked humans anyway; they're trying to destroy the planet for goodness sake, so a few less humans is OK with me!

"But I suppose now that I can think straight again I feel a *little* sorry for the Fluffies I pulled in. Most of them just wanted a quiet life before I arrived on their scene but what the heck!" Hammerhead's tone changed noticeably. With a touch of defiance he said: "In the end they return to their boring little lives and in the long term no real harm is done to them, is it?"

"Well there are some that say it can leave the little guy, as you put it, a bit shell-shocked?"

"Nonsense!"

Dizzy decided it was time to change the direction of the conversation. She smiled directly at the camera "So do you think you'll do this again Hammerhead?"

"Well it's hard work during the generation phase but I can understand why some guys get hung up on it and do it time and time again. It *is* exhilarating ... Yes! I think I'll do it again."

"Well, there you have it viewers, straight from a

thunderstorm's mouth; after the break we'll be interviewing Princess Pearl. It's our first royal interview for over two years, so stay with us!"

* * *

The commercial break commenced on Cloud TV.

"Hello Thunderheads – are you finding it difficult to generate the sparks you used to? Do you feel your updraft is too weak? Then you need a dose of StaticF! It can help you generate fifty percent more ions than you ever thought possible. StaticF! – There's no Fiction in our Friction!"

The scene faded to what looked like a larger than average running track, where a number of twisters were whirling down the lanes. Exploding onto the screen and growing in size, so that the race behind could hardly be seen, were the words: The Twister Cup!

"Yes, its twister games time again folks! And this year 'Dead-Ringer' is competing against the likes of 'Scramble' and 'Spin-Up'. So if you don't want to miss these close encounters, come down to the White sands Arena on May 15th! You won't be disappointed – see you there!"

Accompanied by soft music and an animated picture of the rotating earth, a softer voice in a deep southern accent could now be heard:

"Do you have a loved one on the other side of the globe? Then we have the perfect way for you to keep in touch. We have constant uplinks to the Great Conveyors who are only too willing to pass your message on. Just talk to your nearest thundercloud for details – but hey! Don't get too close now, you hear!"

And with that the advertisement interlude ended.

* * *

"Welcome back Fluffies & Windlets, today we've set up a special link with The Palace – up there at thirty thousand feet – and have on the end of the line the Princess Pearl."

A roar of approval could be heard in the background.

"Good afternoon Princess, how are you today?"

"Very well thank you ... and you?"

Dizzy didn't expect the question to be thrown back at her and fumbled a little as she replied "Oh ... er ... fine thank you."

She got straight to the point: "We've heard rumours that you're thinking of opening a dialogue with the humans."

"Not exactly, although we will do that one day. At the present they are not fully aware of what they are doing to the planet. When they become aware we may guide them. The decision has not yet been made."

"Why don't we just talk to them?"

"It isn't quite that simple; I think the shock alone of finding out you are not the only smart thing on the planet, when for thousands of years you thought you were, could be psychologically very damaging for them."

"But how can you guide them if you aren't going to talk to them?"

"I have never said that we would not talk to them, in fact we will. However, it will not be a two-way conversation. They will not know who is speaking to them!"

"How will you do that?" asked Dizzy

"I cannot go into detail, it is too sensitive and as I said, it may not happen for quite some time."

"Why do you feel the need to help these humans?"

"We have been monitoring them for a considerable length of time. In the past we thought we might have to completely write them off and let nature take its course. They were far too aggressive towards the planet and the environment. However, over the last twenty years or so we have noticed a slight change in attitude and we now believe they are worth helping.

Their change in attitude has come very late and even now they are still not fully aware that they are endangering the planet. Once they realise what they are doing they may not be capable of reversing the situation themselves, or they may not have enough time. They may need our help and they may need it quickly!"

"Do you ..." Dizzy was just about to ask the next question when she was interrupted by the Princess.

"No, let me finish ... we will only help them if they themselves are serious about changing their ways."

"Sorry your highness," said Dizzy, apologising for not waiting for the complete answer. The Princess just nodded her head and smiled.

"The T&TWU (the Thunderstorm and Twister Workers Union) tell us that a change of rules is in the pipeline on thunderstorm and twister size."

"It is something we are considering, but as you can imagine, this will affect thousands of individuals so it is not a move we can make in isolation."

"We've heard that the T&TWU are in a spin about the proposed changes."

"Yes, we would expect the changes to be rather unpopular among our most aggressive subjects." There was a distinctive 'so who cares?' tone as she replied to the last question.

"Is that enough now, Dizzy? I need to go, I have lots to do." The Princess was just about to rise when Dizzy came in with another question.

"Sorry ma'am, just one last question."

"Yes?"

"Another rumour persists that the humans are

experimenting with cloud formation and destruction, is this true?"

The Princess was struck silent. She couldn't say what she was thinking, which was: How did that get out? But nor could she think of a reply fast enough to make the conversation run smoothly. She thought only members of the royal family, her own family, and the entourage knew about this. Ha, yes! She knew what to say:

"Yes, Dizzy. We have heard these rumours and have investigated them. We found that the cloud the humans talk about is contained within a chamber and cannot be released. There is no real danger that suddenly we will have lots of artificial clouds in our midst.

"As for destroying clouds, well, we have found out that the humans have played with the idea of doing this but have not carried the research on, so one should not be too concerned with this notion. Now I really must go."

"Thank you for letting us discuss these matters with you, Your Highness."

"You're welcome my child."

And with that she was gone.

"How does she do that?" thought Dizzy.

- Chapter Two -

The Inspectors

As soon as Hammerhead had passed over the storm track, the Inspectors moved in to judge his effectiveness. Each individual had his or her job to do:

"Look Spiral, you can't put number seven down as partly demolished, there's nothing left"

"Ah! To be sure, there's at least three pieces of wood on that foundation, Atmos."

"Look, I know it's a bit vague where it says bare foundation versus partly demolished, but that's ridiculous. There's nothing there that resembles a house."

"No Atmos, there are some pieces of wood left on that foundation, so it's only partly demolished."

"OK! How do you know that wood is not from another house?"

"Oh! I never thought of that, Atmos!"

"Ha! You see. If those three pieces of wood were from a different house then it would prove that for this particular house you'd have to record bare foundation!"

"That's very true, Atmos." Spiral was suddenly very uncertain as to what to record. "I'll just put it in both categories!"

"No! Look, Spiral, you can't do that. The records would then show too much damage because you'd be doubling up every time you were unsure."

"Oh dear, what can I do, Atmos?"

"Well remember, for partly demolished, you have to be able to see something that looks at least a bit like a house, and for bare foundations, you mustn't be able to see any structure there at all. If you can't see any structure, then, even if there are bits and pieces on the actual foundation, you should class it as bare foundation."

"Well that's a bit clearer now, Atmos, thank you!"

Atmos was the inspection cloud's adjudicator, the one who decided right from wrong, just like a referee. He could be called over by any one of the inspection team at any moment to decide on issues that were in any way vague, and believe me there were always plenty of them.

Not just any inspector could become an adjudicator. In Atmos' case he had earned that privilege by clearing up issues on the inspection sheet that had been there for many years. Because he'd been found to be very logical in his approach to classifications he had been promoted to assistant adjudicator some twenty years ago. Over the last five years he had been studying projectile mathematics and had become somewhat of an expert on the subject. He was also very well respected for his specialist knowledge on projectile fragmentation, you know, the study of how things break up when they hit hard objects. His increase in stature among the inspection hierarchy was recognised last year by his promotion to adjudicator. Many think that he will become inspection team controller once the present post-holder retires.

Atmos, satisfied that Spiral was once more back on track, moved on, looking over the shoulders of individual Inspectors to see if they were completing their assessments correctly.

Inspectors always travel around in what can only be described as formation. Human scientists have a name for these inspection teams. They call them Mammatus Clouds.

A full inspection team generally consists of between 300 and 500 individuals. There is no point in having less than 200 individuals since there are at least 180 items on even the smallest of inspection checklists and you need adjudicators and controllers on top of that. Anyway, the inspection team would not get registered without at least having that sort of number. However, having more in the team is the key to a successful operation because having more means you can get the job done quickly and much more accurately. In the end this is what an inspection team is judged on: accuracy and speed.

Atmos' inspection team is judged to be one of the best in the business and luckily for Hammerhead they had been in the vicinity when he had decided to go for his first Supercell generation. To get such a prestigious inspection team to judge your first outing was a bit of a coup and could only enhance Hammerhead's long-term reputation.

Now humans find the Mammatus cloud formation a little scary in appearance. In the past humans thought this formation was responsible for the creation of tornados. This is not the case. No! Inspectors do exactly what they're supposed to do and only that – they inspect things. As for generating tornados: you will notice if you look carefully that they only appear after a storm has visited, not before. Lets face it, there's no use doing an inspection until the storm has passed, is there?

There are hundreds of groups of Inspectors. Accuracy is their byword and reputation is all. If they were to gain a reputation for inaccuracy they would find little employment and so they become very honest brokers and very precise individuals.

There are only two cases where it is compulsory for inspection teams to attend. Their number one priority is to inspect the aftermath of any first time thunderstorm to ensure that the individual does not 'play' with the powers they have received. The only other 'must attend' in the world of inspection is when a team is given responsibility for overseeing the twister games.

All other duties are optional. A large number of storms, especially the larger ones, request the inspectors' presence at various times of the year to measure their success rate. These inspections can be very important in ensuring the storm head gains a reputation for being reliable in terms of strength and work ethic. Their presence, however, is not guaranteed and some impressive events sometimes can go completely unrecorded.

The inspection checklist always reads like a disaster menu, a gruesome one at that – I've included a small sample of what the checklist looks like below, so you can get a feel for what they do:

Animals – Cows – Moved
Animals – Cows – Killed
Houses – Partly Demolished
Houses – Demolished
Houses – Bare Foundation
Mobile Homes – Lifted Off Foundations
Mobile Homes – Demolished
Projectiles – Small – Generated
Projectiles – Small – Embedded In Structures
Projectiles – Medium – Generated
Projectiles – Medium – Embedded In Structures
Projectiles – Large – Cars
Projectiles – Large – Boxcars
Roofs – Damaged
Roofs – Removed
Street Signs – Bent
Street Signs – Broken

Tarmac – Removal of Road Surface Coating
Trees – Leaves Stripped
Trees – Broken Branches
Trees – Uprooted
Trees – Removal of Bark on Trunk
Walls – Part Demolished
Walls – Demolished

The above items are listed in alphabetical order but the inspection team does not hold to any particular order.

When it comes to the final marking of the event, the highest points are given to items that have the greatest effect on humans or animals.

It is considered that death has the greatest effect on humans or animals because deaths tend to affect not just the local population but the wider population also. The inspection team does not differentiate between animal deaths and human deaths; they are all animals to Cloudkind.

The thing considered to have the next greatest effect on humans or animals is the loss of a home, stable or enclosure. From houses to mobile homes to a fenced off field, the effect is the same; and so the list goes on detailing how many points are awarded for each of the items on the list.

The low hum from the inspection team consisted of hundreds of voices whispering numbers and discussing with each other, in a quiet manner, whether or not an item should be included on their particular list.

From the ground the whole scene looked most peculiar with the individual clouds looking down at different areas of the storm track, jostling among each other for the best viewing position, and talking to each other about various aspects of the damage they were seeing.

When Atmos spoke this time, it was to the whole team: "Remember everyone, make sure you don't count items twice. If you feel that an item may belong in another inspector's category, talk to him and make your decision together. Remember I'm here if you can't quite decide which category to use."

Priyana had been part of the inspection team for a long time, well over three hundred years, yet there was always something new cropping up. She was glad Atmos was around. 'He thinks more clearly than most of us', she thought. The particular item she'd found this time was giving her some concern:

"Is it a projectile or did that cow sail that boat?"

She was looking down on an extraordinary scene. A cow had just removed itself from the pilot's seat of a boat. When she first arrived overhead, it was sitting behind the wheel of the boat looking like it had just sailed it out of the lake and onto dry land. Its front hooves were in the air as if it had been holding the steering wheel.

"Do cows normally sail boats?" she pondered. She'd never seen one do that before but she wasn't at all sure. It was time to involve Atmos, so she called him over.

"Atmos, do cows pilot boats?"

"Priyana, what has that to do with your inspection duties?"

"Well I've just seen a cow get out of the pilot's seat of a boat, after sailing it onto dry land."

"The cow was alive then?"

"Yes."

"Well, I suppose it may be possible?" Atmos raised his voice so that the whole team could hear, "Has anyone ever seen a cow sail a boat before?"

The consensus was 'no', but one reply made everyone

think. "I've seen them swim a few times. I suppose if a cow can swim, it might get interested in boating."

Atmos thought there was nothing at all wrong with that reasoning.

"You see, I don't know whether to put it down as a projectile or ignore it?" said Priyana.

"You think that the cow was lifted into the boat?"

"I don't know."

"Well let's analyse the situation Priyana. Firstly, I have never seen a boat sailing on land, so I would say that the boat has been moved on to dry land by the winds of the storm. Do you agree?"

"Yes," said Priyana, very sensible she thought.

Atmos continued: "... and if the boat has been moved by the storm, so has the cow, whether it was sailing it or not. Do you agree?"

"Yes," said Priyana, with an admiring smile for Atmos' clear thinking.

"So both of them must have been projectiles at one time or another."

"Atmos, you're a marvel!"

"Let's keep going, Priyana. Look at the end of the cow's front legs. They're not hands, are they?"

Atmos paused and waited for the realisation that would surely come to Priyana. Unless he had overestimated her intellect.

"Ha! The cow couldn't have sailed the boat! It wouldn't have been able to grip the wheel with legs like that!"

"Well done, Priyana. Even though both the boat and the cow were moved by the winds of the storm, I definitely wouldn't give that storm any points for that. Now you see if you can work out why!" Again, Atmos waited for Priyana's intellect to click in.

"... I suppose it could have been arranged like that just

as a joke! ... certainly the chances of a cow being accidentally blown into the pilot's seat of a boat, well! That's got to be very slim ... so, if the cow had been placed there then maybe the boat was placed also. If they were both *placed* they can't be called projectiles, so we can't give any points."

"Well done Priyana!"

Atmos walked away, quite pleased that he had helped Priyana to reason it through.

Priyana just looked at Atmos and sighed.

Probably the only inspection team member that Atmos didn't want to hear from was Serio. Serio wasn't like the rest of the inspection team. He looked for order in the midst of disorder.

You see, the inspection team's most important job is to ensure that humans don't realise that clouds possess the ability to think. As far as clouds are concerned, having humans know they are intelligent would be a disaster of immense proportions. So Serio was there just to look out for such things.

"Atmos!" Serio called.

Atmos responded immediately, rushing over to Serio's side.

"You've found something?"

"A signature."

Only an extremely naive cloud would have left a signature. It's a rare event (although statistics show there has been a marked increase over the last few years). Nobody knows why.

"Where is it?"

"There, in the park, between those two fallen trees."

As Atmos' gaze fell upon the offending structure, he realised what he was looking at was a large 'H' . There was a timber yard off to the side of the park and some of these timbers had been used to construct the 'H'. They had been sent vertically into the ground in such a way, that looking from above, you could immediately recognise the letter.

"You'd better send Gusto in to knock them over, on the double!"

Gusto was the fixer for the inspection team. Every team had one. If you can imagine having all the individual Windlets of a two hundred strong inspection team organised together, well it provides a very powerful tool when disorder, not order, needs to be re-instated.

"Yes, I'll get on to it." Said Serio.

"I'm going to have to have a long talk with Hammerhead about this." Atmos muttered as he moved away.

Once the inspection team have done their work the controller constructs the summary. Atmos' controller was Stats: "Are we past the affected area yet, Atmos?"

"I'm getting no more reports of further damage Sir, but I have to report that Serio found a signature."

"How obvious was it?" asked Stats.

"Very obvious, we had Gusto cure the problem straight away."

"What's your conclusion, Atmos? Do we need to ban Hammerhead from storm activity altogether?"

"I can't be sure. I think that's a decision we have to leave until we see his reaction to our discovery."

"Then line them up, Atmos. Let's construct the summary."

"Very well." Atmos called the team to order and the count began."

The inspection team now filed in one by one, and in no particular order, in front of the controller:

"Diametric – Trees – Uprooted – Five."

"ZigZag – Animals – Horses – Dead – One."

"Squall – Trees – Broken Branches – Thirty Eight."

"Cosmic – Large Projectiles – Cars – None." The clear tone of disappointment could be heard in his voice.

"Smog – Humans – Dead – One."

"Spiral – Houses – Partly Demolished – Fourteen."

... And so it continued until all the inspection team had reported everything back to the controller.

As the inspection team filed past the controller, passing on their particular piece of data, the controller memorised everything they told him. Clouds don't go in for paperwork, so pen and paper are out. They do go in for memory training and to pass the controller examinations you need to be able to demonstrate your ability to retain vast quantities of data.

The adjudicator also has to memorise the reports, not only as part of his training, but also so that if a thunderhead wants a detailed summary, he can be given one.

There are times when a thunderhead may question the accuracy of the report. If this happens, the adjudicator will discuss the reports findings with him. In the end though, the adjudicator decides whether or not to amend the report and his decision is final.

Once all the data has been passed over to the controller, he can then calculate the exact number of points that can be given to the storm and thus what classification the storm has.

The long line came to an end.

"That's it, Sir. No more inspection reports."

"Thanks, Atmos. I'll just calculate the storm's effectiveness rating and pass it on to Hammerhead and the records department. Well done, and in quick time, Atmos."

"Well, the storm was just a little smaller than usual, so I suppose we were bound to finish a little early."

At the same time that the controller started his calculations, Atmos started his own. He did this as a matter of course, to ensure that if he ever got the chance of being a controller, he'd be up to the mark. He was proud of the fact that for the last thirty-six calculations his answer had been exactly the same as his boss, although *his* calculations always seemed to take a little longer.

Hammerhead had just finished the interview with Cloud TV when the controller came to report to him.

"I have your effectiveness summary, Sir."

"Speak out, Stats, speak out!"

Stats was of the old school; he thought a report like this was a very personal thing. Hammerhead, on the other hand, didn't care in the least who would hear the contents. In fact Stats could have shouted out loud from the cloud tops to the rest of Cloudkind and he wouldn't have minded.

"The classification is Supercell Thunderstorm With Twister – Grade Two."

Hammerhead was a little disappointed with the grade, as he'd been hoping for a grade one. "Why 'Grade Two', Stats?"

"Well to be honest Sir, you would only have made Grade Three if it hadn't been for the utter destruction around the two deaths."

"Oh! I see." Hammerhead was even more surprised and disappointed at that remark.

"Sounds like I need to improve. Can I have a full summary?"

"Yes, that is possible, Sir. We have the time at present. It's not my job to give out summary details; I'll send Atmos to you. He wanted to speak with you anyway, but you'll need to see him immediately!"

"I understand," said Hammerhead.

Atmos came out with the full listing still in his head

and he and Hammerhead went through the list in detail. Atmos gave advice where he felt compelled to do so:

"You see here, with the cow and the boat, you actually missed out on thirty 'projectile points' there!"

"I thought it was quite funny having the cow sit in the boat," said Hammerhead.

"Yes, but you can hardly call it a projectile, if you're 'placing' the objects in various situations. That's a common occurrence with beginners like you. You want a bit of fun so you 'arrange' items. In the long term that sort of behaviour will reduce your score and your standing. You must treat your work more seriously." The last sentence from Atmos came across quite sternly.

"See! Look at the foundations of those two houses, they are nearly clear. All you had to do was take one more wall out and you'd have got triple the number of points.

And look at those planks in the road. Again, if you could have embedded one or two of those in that telegraph pole, only inches away, your score would have increased dramatically.

And see those..." Hammerhead stopped Atmos

"OK, Atmos I get the point!" Hammerhead felt sufficiently chastised. "I'll do a more professional job next time," he said.

"I'm afraid there may not be a next time."

Atmos' words cut through the air like a knife. Suddenly Hammerhead was deeply concerned. The inspection team had the power to stop Hammerhead from ever being a storm again. Hammerhead didn't like that idea at all.

"Why?" Hammerhead said meekly.

"You left a signature," Atmos said sternly.

There was silence. Atmos continued:

"Do you realise how grave a matter that is?"

Hammerhead clearly hadn't realised at the time, but he

certainly did now. Before Hammerhead could reply, Atmos added: "You must know the rules for storm generation?"

"Yes" Hammerhead replied

"What do they say about signatures?"

"We must never use them."

"So why did you use one?"

"I didn't think it would be noticed."

"But we always notice them," said Atmos

"I'm sorry, Atmos, it won't happen again, I promise," said Hammerhead.

Atmos weighed the facts: did he believe Hammerhead's promise never to repeat a signature? Was he really to be trusted? Atmos had made his mind up ...

"If you had denied knowing the existence of the signature, you would now be banned from any activity to do with storm generation for the rest of your existence. If you had taken this matter flippantly, then you would also be banned. As it is, I believe you when you say you're sorry.

You will find that your next few forays into storm creation will be monitored very closely. Do not make the same mistake again!"

With that, Atmos departed.

- Chapter Three -

Fluff And Cindy
(28 Years Later)

"Aren't you coming, *man*?" came a voice from one of the clouds in the group passing just over Fluff's head.

Fluff had been relaxing in the sun over a small stretch of water, probably going no faster than two or three miles an hour, when he was overtaken by this disorderly group of Fluffies. They were all going roughly in the same direction as Fluff, but just a few miles an hour faster and a little higher. The Fluffy that had asked the question had a very strong Jamaican accent: "C'mon, *man*, come to the *festival!*"

"Now that's an accent I don't recognise. Where are you from?"

"All around the world, *man*, but I was born in Jamaica."

"What do you mean all around the world?" said Fluff

"I've done it, *man!*"

"What, you've travelled all around the world?"

"Yeah, *man.*"

Fluff was totally knocked out by that answer, "Now that's what I call impressive. How long did it take? Did you see lots of interesting places? Were you in any danger? How did you cross the Great Salt Seas?"

"Hold on there, slow down!" said the Jamaican "One question at a time, *man.*" The Jamaican was quietly pleased that someone was interested in his journey. He paused for a moment.

"Look, I can't stay long. Lets see: it took me a couple of years and yeah, I did see lots of interesting places. I don't remember being in any danger because I deliberately avoided it; for example, I just went north to skirt round the desert areas. As for the Great Salt Seas, they're just like big lakes and I crossed them just like I crossed the land."

"But didn't you get pestered by the sea-sirens?" asked Fluff.

"No, they only seemed to bother the larger clouds."

"Tell me about the sights you saw."

"Would take too long!" The Jamaican started to drift away again. "I'll tell you one thing though. The humans have built a Great Wall that divides the world in two ... "

The little Fluffy white clouds that humans see during a normal day are precisely the ones that humans tend to ignore the most. Yet, strangely enough, Fluffies are the one type of cloud that actually like human contact; in fact, a large number of them study humans.

Fluffies range drastically in intelligence – some are as thick as two short rainstorms, while others have brilliant minds. Every Fluffy can change shape and you can generally tell how bright a Fluffy is by the number of shape changes he or she makes during the year. The really bright Fluffies have a tendency to show off when it comes to shape, although there has never been a reported sighting of an equilateral triangle yet.

There is a rumour, however, that if a Fluffy ever became intelligent enough to create an equilateral triangle they would immediately be co-opted into the royal circle. In fact, because of that rumour, there are plenty of Fluffies trying to do exactly that.

A lot of Fluffies like to be known by the name of their favourite shape and so you can get an idea of their intellect from the name they choose. To protect names there is a register and in order to be named after a shape, the cloud must demonstrate their ability to form that shape. And even if they can take the shape, it's not guaranteed they can have the name. It all depends on whether someone else wanted that name first. For example: if a cloud was called Starship, a popular name some years ago, there couldn't be another Starship. So you'd have to choose variations, like Starship-1 or Staarship say.

Temperament is as varied in Fluffies as it is in humans. Some clouds, it must be said, are permanently sad, while others are renowned for their happy demeanour. It's funny how humans sometimes stumble on to facts such as this. We all know that humans are aware of 'Cloud Nine', one of our ever happy Fluffies, but just how you humans got to know the name is a complete mystery. I know that this may sound obvious, but sad clouds tend to generate more rainfall and also tend to be greyish in appearance compared with happy Fluffies.

Fluffy younglets are placed in nursery during the day and you'll find that under these clouds, which can get quite large, you'll get a fine drizzle, especially if they cry – although they may drizzle anyway just because they're so young.

Our Fluff was a very unassuming sort of cloud but he was streetwise and he knew what the Jamaican meant by festival. You see, most clouds avoid storms if they get the chance. However, there are Fluffies who do the exact opposite and treat joining a storm as a game. The Jamaican was obviously one of these. They don't mind 'losing their minds', as they put it, in order to be with the 'in cloud'.

Fluff shouted after him: "Who's doing the gig?"

"Jake, *man*, he's going for the wall cloud, a couple of twisters, buckets of hail, the whole scene, *man*. His updrafts and downdrafts will be tremendous. Come for the ride, *man*, it'll be incredible."

Fluff again ignored the invite. "Where's the venue?"

"The whole scene kicks off in the next valley, *man*. Are you coming?"

"Sounds cool, where's the drift?" Said Fluff.

"South *man*, we're all going south"

"Can't join you! I'm moving in the opposite direction. Got to see some friends up north."

Another cloud chirped in: "You're going to miss the show *man*, it'll be spectacular!"

Fluff just smiled but didn't reply; in his head he heard himself saying: *You're* the one that's going to miss the show – you'll be out of your mind in more ways than you think.

He knew it was no use trying to persuade the group to stay away. He'd tried to do it before with other clouds and it had only caused a rumpus. In the end, if you're convinced you want to try being part of a storm cloud, you're going to do it no matter what anyone else says.

Fluff settled back again to enjoy his view over the lake but another of the passing clouds, more of a hippie type this time, shouted down at him "Come to the gathering, *man*."

That was it. He'd had enough! There was no way he could just relax now; it was time to move on. He shouted for Cindy.

Cindy was Fluff's Windlet.

Now as I have already mentioned, wind is made up of millions of little entities called Windlets. I know you may find this hard to believe but every single one of these Windlets has a name; just like every single human has a name.

You humans actually know the names of some of these Windlets, although how you found out these names I'll never know. For example: the humans who live in Northern California, know a Windlet called 'Santa Anna'; In South Africa they know a Windlet called 'The Doctor'; In Central Sudan there's a Windlet called Haboob; In the Gulf of Lions in the Mediterranean Sea most humans know a Windlet called the Mistral. Need I go on?

Windlets communicate in two distinct ways. One way is to talk to each other but this method is very slow. This is a problem because, as you can imagine, they don't tend to stay in contact with each other for long periods of time. So Mother Nature has given them the additional ability to communicate by touch. This method allows large amounts of information to be transferred very quickly.

When Windlets talk to each other, humans can hear them. But humans can't understand 'wind speak' just like they can't understand 'whale speak', so they tend to ignore the Windlets' conversations. 'Wind speak' is easily heard: you just have to stand on any street corner where the Windlet from one street meets the Windlet from another street and you'll hear it. In fact, I bet you already have.

I know for a fact that 'whale speak' is studied by humans, yet only a few people ever come into contact with whales. On the other hand, all humans come into contact with the wind, yet 'wind speak' is not studied. Mmm!

When Windlets communicate by touch, it is instinctive and cannot be controlled by either party. A rapid exchange of information takes place. You see, they may not touch each other again for years, so this early exchange of information has become vitally important to them and to the survival of their species.

These instinctive exchanges of information are all encompassing and very accurate but that's one of the main problems with Windlets. They can't keep secrets from each other even if they wanted to, unless they can avoid touching each other.

Another rather obvious observation, but one that should be noted here, is that Windlets, although they can see what you and I can see, they can't see each other. In other words, just as you can't see Windlets, they can't see their fellow Windlets either, in spite of being Windlets themselves.

Most clouds pair for life with their Windlet. This relationship is not like a boy/girl thing; it's more like a person/pet thing. It doesn't always work but Cindy, Fluff's Windlet, has been with Fluff ever since he was born.

You might imagine that a Fluffy called Fluff would be a bit short of brainpower but in Fluff's case that wasn't quite the whole story. Fluff could change shape just like any cloud but he never felt the shapes he changed into were any better than his original shape, which was, well … Fluffy! So Fluff was as good a name as any and he liked it! Fluff was the first cloud that wanted to be called Fluff; goodness knows why no one else chose it initially. Anyway, if you wanted to be called Fluff these days, you'd have to settle for Fluff-101, Fluff-102, etc., there are so many clouds now wanting to be called Fluff.

If there's one thing that Fluffies like to do, more than any other cloud type, it's watch humans. It's a hobby with nearly all Fluffies. You see, Fluffies are always low enough to see clearly what's going on at ground level. They also drift over the human population at quite slow speeds, so it's easy to notice what they're up to. What is more to the point is that Fluffies think that humans are quite cute.

Fluff himself had been known to stay over neighbourhoods for as long as five days, getting to know what the humans were doing on his patch. Of course, he couldn't do such a thing without his Windlet 'Cindy' keeping him stationary or guiding him back again and again to the same place.

There is a limit to how long Fluffies can stay stationary though: the problem is weight. If they stop for too long they lose weight and evaporate; then eventually 'pop' and there's nothing left. Equally, if they move too fast they become aggressive and start to absorb other clouds. Eventually they become large enough to produce rain and even a storm cloud.

The same afternoon that he'd had the 'run in' with the Jamaicans, Fluff meandered down one of the main streets leading into Pensacola. He was in his usual 'go slow' mode and not thinking at all about the route he was taking. He'd stumbled upon this human by a shed in his garden with a rather tall tank with lots of wires and pipes coming out of the top. Fluff was already thinking of sticking around for a while to see what the human was up to, when a smaller human, probably a younglet, Fluff thought, came running out of the house.

"Are you *still* fiddling with that cloud chamber, Dad?"

"For some reason I just can't get it to make the cloud, Emma."

Fluff was taken aback by this revelation. Trying to make a cloud? How dare he? We don't try to make humans!

The younglet looked up at Fluff, "there's a cloud, Dad, just pull that one out of the sky."

At this Fluff became very nervous. 'Can he do that?' Fluff asked himself.

"Don't be silly, Emma. You know I can't do that, making a cloud in this chamber seems to be difficult enough"

'Thank goodness,' Fluff thought.

"Just joking, Dad. Anyway, why do you want to make a cloud? They aren't useful are they, and they only stop the sun from shining and make it rain all the time."

Fluff was deeply hurt by the remarks from the human

younglet.

"And where does the rain for the crops come from then? Clouds are useful; but in the future they may be even more useful."

Now that's more like it! Fluff thought.

"How's that, Dad?"

"Well you said it yourself, Em." Emma looked puzzled, but her dad carried on, "you said they stop the sun from shining."

"Yes, Dad! But to me that's definitely a *bad* thing not having the sun shining."

"You may not think like that one day, Emma."

"How can the sun not shining be a good thing?"

"Because if we're going to stop global warming, we need to find ways of stopping the sunlight from reaching the surface of the earth. Clouds can do this by reflecting the sunlight back into space before it can heat up the earth."

"Wow, that's a good idea, Dad!" Emma exclaimed.

"Well, that's the problem; it might be good but it's just an idea at present."

Fluff's head was spinning. It's a clone war; he's going to make clones of us all!

"Your Mom told me you wanted to come flying with us tomorrow."

By now Fluff was riveted to the spot.

"Can I, Dad? Can I?" Emma pleaded.

"Well just this once, Emma, but you'll have to help me carry the seed pods."

"Seed pods, what are we growing?" asked Emma, trying to pretend she didn't know what they were.

Jack smiled, "Very funny Em. But the formula in these cloud seeding pods is key. We need to force the cloud to produce rain early so we can disperse it quickly."

"Hang on, Dad! You just said you wanted to create clouds. Now you're saying you're going to break them up. That doesn't exactly fit together."

"Well that's true, it does sound a bit silly doesn't it? But you see, there are good and bad clouds. The good ones we'd like to grow, the bad ones we'd like to shrink."

"You make them sound like they're alive, Dad."

"Well, we all know they're not ..." Fluff was reassured by that remark. "... But in a way, you can think of them as though they were alive: they grow, they die, they're sometimes placid, sometimes angry."

"I suppose," said Emma.

A shout came from inside: "Dinner, you two!"

"So you're coming then?" said Jack.

"Oh! OK, Dad, I'll carry the seedpods!" said Emma, trying to sound resentful, but with a touch of glee in her eyes.

"Right, young lady, that's a deal then, let's go and have some dinner."

The two went inside.

Fluff decided there and then that he'd better be at the airport tomorrow when these humans took off. He wondered what the big human meant by seedpods; he was determined to find out and to discover what else they might be up to.

"Cindy!" Fluff shouted.

Cindy was a little ahead of Fluff, so knew nothing of what had just happened. Fluff was sure that once Cindy knew of the problem, the whole of Windkind would know of it. So he decided not to share what he'd heard, at least not just yet.

Cindy returned his call: "Fluff?"

"I want to stay here for a while."

"Why?"

"Oh! Just curious," Fluff succeeded in looking nonchalant.

"Where abouts?" asked Cindy.

"Put me about halfway between here and the airport, it's only a couple of miles away."

"OK, but you know there's a storm due in tomorrow just to the north of the airport."

"Yes, I know," said Fluff, "I was invited to join it by a cloud from Jamaica, wherever that is? You'll just have to make sure we keep south of the airport when the storm hits, we don't want to be pulled in."

"OK!"

Fluff figured they could always retreat a little in the morning if the situation changed, but there' was no denying that it was a bit of a risk.

Mary, Jack's wife, was already feeding baby Sarah by the time Jack and Emma sat down for their meal.

"Emma's agreed to help me with the seed pods tomorrow, Mom, so I've told her she can come on the flight with me."

Emma looked at Mom, hoping for a favourable reaction to the news. Mary smiled back at her, then looked at Jack, "Just a routine flight then?" Mary asked inquisitively.

"Yes, nothing special," said Jack, "The model suggests there may be a thunderstorm developing over the bay area. It's just a matter of checking it out. If it does develop, we'll seed it; take measurements, then return to base and see how the model did versus what actually happened. Nothing difficult or dangerous on the trip, dear."

Mary turned her attention to Emma, "Very well, but only if you do your homework tonight."

"Oh! *Mom!*" But even though Emma protested, she knew

this was the best possible outcome. She'd already nearly finished the homework anyway, so when dinner was over she ran to her room to complete the task. Of course, she had to talk to Scott on Facebook first.

"Scott, going up with my dad on one of the planes tomorrow – he's cloud seeding."

"Awesome, M. What's cloud seeding?"

"Cloud seeding is a way of making it rain – *you should know that!* If you can make it rain early then you reduce the effect of the storm. It sort of stops the build up of the storm in its tracks."

"You listen far too much to your dad."

"It's my future. – Anyway, got to go. I have to finish my homework or I can't fly tomorrow. I'll Skype you – after the event."

Scott was the son of Gerald Dayton, one of her Dad's old friends. They'd spent all of their childhood together when their dads were working on the same project at MIT. Emma was always the smart one though. The one who knew what she wanted to do when she grew up, which was to be a meteorologist. It was sort of being famous and being scientific at the same time. She thought that was a really cool combination. When their dads went their separate ways about eighteen months ago they had kept in touch. They were very close and Emma still missed Scott. They still chatted to each other every night on Facebook and used Skype to talk to each other face to face nearly as often. They got together as and when time allowed. Scott's Mom was still a very close friend of *her* mom's, although her dad didn't seem to contact Scott's dad as much as he used to.

The morning started well. In fact, you wouldn't have

guessed that there was a storm due at all. The sun was shining and there was hardly a cloud in the sky. Mind you, had you been a cloud you'd have known why there were hardly any in the sky, that morning. They had all scampered away because they were frightened of being dragged into the storm.

Fluff had changed his shape to ensure that the human younglet wouldn't recognise him. He found it peculiar to think that big humans would never even give it a thought, that a cloud might be watching them. But their younglets, well, they were nowhere near as stupid.

He wondered if it was because younglets looked up at the sky more often than the older humans, who quite frankly took clouds for granted.

Fluff could see the human and his younglet loading their pickup truck with silver cigar-shaped pods. As they climbed into the front of the truck, another human came out from the house holding a much smaller younglet in her arms and waved her hand. The first human and his younglet both waved back, got in the truck and drove off.

Following them along the road to the airport was easy; Cindy had just set enough breeze in motion so that Fluff could traverse the ground at a reasonable speed. Cindy was waiting at the airport for him to arrive.

"*Dad*, you said we were going out this morning to calm a storm down."

"I did, Em?" Jack said, wondering where the conversation was going.

"Why? It's only a *small* storm! It might create a bit of thunder and lightning but it won't do any harm."

"Well you have a point, Em, but our main aim is to calm down bigger storms. We're just starting small."

"Why bother? Why don't you just let nature take its course?"

"A long time ago, when I was a child, my Dad, your Grandpa, took me on a trip down south and showed me lots of ships that had been wrecked by storms. You have to remember, Emma, for every ship that gets wrecked, lots of people lose their lives. This is a good reason for trying to control the strength of storms."

Emma didn't react, so Jack carried on.

"Have you ever wondered where your Grandpa is Em? I mean, you see your Grandma nearly every week. Wouldn't it be nice if you could see both of them every week?"

"Grandpa's dead," Emma was looking at her shoes and not at her Dad.

"Do you know how he died?"

"Well, no."

"Well, *he* died in a storm. That storm had generated a tornado and he just didn't hear it coming. From that day forward I promised that I would work hard to reduce the dangers from bad weather, and that's exactly what I'm doing, young lady."

Emma changed the subject quite naturally; she looked up at the Fluffy white cloud that seemed to be keeping up with their truck and said: "Dad, that cloud's following us."

"Don't be silly, things in the air always look like they're following you, it's just an optical illusion."

Emma said, "Yes, Dad," but muttered quietly and out of earshot, "but this one's actually following us."

The journey to the airport was quite short and it was obvious to Fluff that some prior arrangements had been made since there were two airplanes, with engines running, waiting on the tarmac for them.

The writing on the side of both airplanes read "United States –Weather Research Institute."

He watched as the silver cigars from the back of the

truck were loaded into the two airplanes. Jack and Emma climbed into the leading aircraft. Once the doors had closed on the two aircraft they taxied around to the extreme end of the runway, readying themselves for take off.

"Pensacola Tower, this is Aero-One, we are ready for departure – do you read?"

"Pensacola Tower to Aero-One: You are cleared for take off, runway 2, wind is 350° 25 gusting 40; good luck!"

Sam Parks, or Uncle Sam as the other Weather Research Institute (WRI) pilots liked to call him, was piloting Aero-One this day. Sam looked like the body builder type, although he wasn't a fan of the gym. He was naturally heavy set with freckles and light brown hair. An 'All American' hero type, a veteran of the Iraq conflict and as good a pilot as you could get outside the military machine.

"Are you both strapped in, Jack?"

"Yes Sam, all clear."

Sam pushed the throttles forward and Aero-One accelerated to take-off speed. The plane started to climb into the air; the turbulence was severe. Jack could see that Emma was surprised at the rocky nature of the climb out and she looked a little nervous.

"Not quite as smooth as the rides on the passenger planes we've been on, Em!"

"Definitely not!" Emma was gripping her seat.

Jack added: "No need to worry, this plane can take a lot more of a pounding than this."

As they came out the turbulence, Sam called Aero-Two: "Aero-One to Aero-Two: Freddie, watch yourself on take off, it's a bit bumpy on the climb out. You'll be OK after two thousand feet, over."

"Roger that, Uncle Sam" said Freddie, in his best English accent. "Pensacola Tower, this is Aero-Two, we are ready for departure."

"Aero-Two is cleared for take off, runway 2, wind is 340° 30 gusting 45 – We've had reports that the weather's moving in, good luck!"

Freddie was the 'typical' English man through and through. He was slim with a thin moustache, greying and slightly balding. He wasn't the type to believe in luck. He was probably the best pilot in the fleet and a little bad weather wasn't going to spoil this jaunt.

"Roger Flight," and with that, Aero-Two took to the skies.

As both planes flew towards the storm, Aero-Two called in "Does Jack say we are to seed old chap?"

Sam looked over at Jack. Jack shouted so that both pilots could hear, "Yes, we'll get good data from this one."

"Did you get that Freddie?" Sam had to be sure that Freddie had heard.

"Roger, Sam."

"We'd better gain some altitude before we enter it, Freddie."

And with that the two planes climbed; they were probably at ten thousand feet before they entered the storm.

Jack had loaded the seedpods into the firing mechanism, ready for launch.

Fluff was so intent on watching the airplanes being loaded with their cargo that he hadn't noticed the sky over the airport had started to go dark.

Cindy had tried to warn Fluff that the storm was coming but he wasn't listening and no matter how hard she tried she couldn't make him hear her. If she didn't retreat to a safe distance this minute, she would be a 'goner' too. Her only option was to sit the storm out, from a safe distance, and watch what happened. Hopefully Fluff would be OK.

By the time the planes entered the storm it was too late for Fluff, he was only a few minutes from being absorbed by the storm cloud and he still didn't realise what was happening. In fact the first time he knew of any danger was when he felt himself being dragged into the storm.

As he got nearer to the storm cloud itself, he could hear the commotion of all the clouds that had already been absorbed. The sound was deafening but still he couldn't tell what any individual was saying.

His head was spinning now and his thoughts were getting lost among the thoughts of the hundreds of individuals that made up the storm cloud. He had a sense that there were Jamaicans within the throng. He was trying to remember where he was and why he was there, but the memory wouldn't come back to him.

Fluff could hear a noise above him; he glanced up and thought he saw what appeared to be two birds … no! They were aircraft flying above him, dropping something towards him. Cigar shaped things that split open, revealing lots and lots of little shiny objects that glinted in the sun.

Sun! He thought, how can I see the sun? … Yes, he hadn't imagined it. The storm cloud was breaking up and dispersing. Suddenly he remembered where he was and why he had come here. His brain was beginning to clear. Yes! It was the cigar shaped objects that the humans had loaded into the airplanes. They were the same objects that had dissipated the storm and freed him. Now all the individuals that were engulfed in the maelstrom could go back to what they were doing before being picked up by the storm. In fact, he had just realised that he could now hear all the individuals all talking at the same time, the Jamaicans among them.

Then another realisation came upon him; it was the humans that had saved him! It was the humans he had to thank for stopping him being absorbed by the storm.

"Fluff, Fluff!" came a voice from far away, he turned. It was Cindy, "Fluff, what happened?"

"I got too close to the storm, it pulled me in."

"I know *that*! I saw it happen but what happened to the storm?"

"I think the humans stopped it. I think they know how to break storms up."

Oh No! Fluff thought. How careless of me, Cindy will tell everyone of this now.

The storm experience had shaken him a little and as a result of the storm, both he and Cindy were now miles away from the airport. Fluff quickly regained his composure and with the recovery of his shape, he decided that they should get back to the airport as quickly as possible. "We need to keep a watch on these two humans, Cindy, I think they're dangerous to Cloudkind."

Cindy wasn't arguing; she'd just witnessed some remarkable events and was in no mood to fall out with Fluff. These humans can kill off a storm cloud, she thought. No one has ever done that before. Now Fluff was telling her that he saw them try to clone a cloud; these guys are a serious threat, she thought, and someone had better keep an eye on them.

Obviously for now it would have to be Cindy and Fluff.

"Wow, Dad! That was brilliant! The way you beat off that storm."

"We didn't 'beat it', we just calmed it down a little."

"I prefer Emma's interpretation," said Sam.

"Yes, I thought you might." Jack smiled.

As Sam flew the plane back to the airport Jack took the

opportunity to talk to Emma: "We are not warriors, Em. We are scientists. There's a heck of a difference. Today's exercise, for example, can you tell me what we did?"

"Well," Emma said excitedly, "we not only stopped the storm getting bigger, we actually shrunk it!"

"Is that all?" said Jack.

Emma thought for a moment "Well ... er! Yes."

"No, Emma. What we actually did was measure the reduction in intensity of the storm, for a given dose of seed material, at a given height."

"But how did you do that?"

"Well, we know how many seed pods we deployed and the altitude we were at when we made the drop. At the same time, Bill, back at base, will have measured the decrease in intensity of the storm."

"So what are you doing with all this information you're gathering? You must have been up in these airplanes hundreds of times, Dad."

"We use it to compare our mathematical models of the climate, in this case storm modification, with what actually happens in real life. The more measurements we can make the more accurate we can make our models. It's like trying to draw a graph only knowing a few points. With only a few points the graph is a bit of a guess, but if you have hundreds of points, the graph becomes more certain. I won't be happy until we have thousands of points."

Just as Jack finished his explanation, the wheels of the aircraft touched down.

"Back home," said Sam.

The human and his younglet were just disembarking from the plane as Fluff and Cindy returned to the airport. The larger human shouted to the pilots "See you when the next storm hits, lads. I'm hoping to have a better recipe for the seedpods by then and we'll give it a try."

"OK! See you, Jack," said Sam. Both pilots waved goodbye.

"Jack!" Fluff turned to Cindy, "His name is Jack!"

"But I thought the younglet called him Dad?" said Cindy.

"Oh yes," said Fluff, "... er, that's puzzling, oh well! We know the younglet's name."

"What's that?" said Cindy.

"Young lady" said Fluff.

"Oh yes!"

- Chapter Four -

The Calm Before The Storm

Emma was on Skype, talking to Scott.

"Wow! You should have been there, Scott. We climbed above the clouds and started seeding and the storm took hardly any time at all to break up."

Scott was frustrated that he hadn't been there. "Knowing you, I suppose you enjoyed the science more than the ride?"

"Well a bit of both, I did enjoy the ride though."

"Tell your dad I'm free to have a ride anytime he wants to take me."

"Scott, these are not just joy rides!"

"OK, don't start stressing," said Scott.

Jack Winter was standing against the main garden fence, pipe in hand and looking very serious. The pipe had the effect of making him look old for his age. He liked that; he felt others took him more seriously because of it. If truth were known however, people took him seriously because he knew what he was talking about, being America's foremost expert on the weather and global warming. It was definitely not because he smoked a pipe.

Mary was holding baby Sarah and her milk bottle as she came out from the house. She hadn't started feeding her yet.

"It's a beautiful night, Jack. The moon is shining and there's hardly a cloud in the sky," she said as she looked up at the small Fluffy cloud that was hanging just to the side of their house. The only one she could see for miles.

Mary knew what Jack would be thinking about. In fact, there was no doubt about it. Controlling violent weather had always been an obsession with him, ever since she knew him. She knew why this was the case. In their first year together his mother had told her how his father had died. At that time she hadn't realised how much it had affected him.

But it *was* an obsession, and at times it completely took over their lives. In the end she'd come to accept it and now she didn't mind. She was happy to share him with his obsession; she loved him and he loved her, that's all that mattered and he gave the kids and her plenty of quality time, when he could.

"How did your experiment go today? Emma thought it went well, she couldn't stop talking about how you beat the thunderstorm into submission."

"Our daughter would have enjoyed today no matter what the outcome. It fits in with her idea of the future and becoming a weather presenter. She especially likes the idea of reporting from an airplane.

"It was a bumpy ride up there today, so that would have made it even more exciting for her."

Mary could tell it was the proud father speaking because of the wry smile.

"Yes Mary, the experiment went well but it was only a small event. Global warming means that the storms are going to intensify over the next decade and after today's experiment, it does look like we should be able to control the violent nature of the storms, even if we can't actually stop them in their tracks."

Jack had walked over to Mary and placed his arm around her; they were both looking at their baby.

"They look very close," said Cindy.

"Yes they do," said Fluff, who was looking as melancholy as Jack Winter was looking serious.

"Have *you* anyone that's close?" Cindy said, sensing the sadness in Fluff's reply.

"Well ... er! ... No. Well I mean, there is someone that I would like to be close to but she's far too important to even notice me."

"Who's that Fluff?" said a surprised Cindy.

"The Princess Pearl."

"You've seen her?" Cindy said incredulously.

"Yes, she's very beautiful."

"You're aiming a little too high there, Fluff."

"I know," replied Fluff, "do you remember the day of storms, when we were very young? We got split up, in the morning, avoiding them all."

"Yes, when I found you, you were upset and crying."

"You didn't find me, Cindy."

"Of course I did."

"No Cindy, it was the Princess Pearl who rescued me." Fluff reminisced, "I'd spent all day avoiding the storms. I'd never seen so many and each time I felt the tug from one of them, it scared me, and I felt plenty of tugs that day. I was very young, I'd lost my best pal – you Cindy – and I'd lost my way. For all I knew at the time, I might never have seen you again."

Fluff was remembering how scared he really was that day. "I was so frightened I started to shed water, then there was this voice.

The voice said 'Fluff'. It was a gentle voice and at first I didn't know where it was coming from."

"Fluff, what is wrong? It's not often I sense a cloud that is so scared, whatever is the matter?"

"I've been running from these storms so as not to get absorbed, but now I've lost my way, and my Windlet has disappeared."

"Cindy is not far away," said the voice.

"How do you know her name?" asked Fluff.

"Never mind that, do you want me to take you to her?"

"Yes, where are you?" I replied.

"I am above you, Fluff, high in the sky. Why, of course I can take you to her. The storms have all gone now and there is nothing to be afraid of, just follow me and I'll lead you back to Cindy."

I looked up and there I saw the most beautiful cloud I had ever seen.

"Who are you? Where do you come from?" I asked.

"Well, Fluff, I am the Princess Pearl. I come from the frozen north. I have the ability to sense when my subjects are in distress, so having sensed your distress I thought I might come and help you."

"You're very kind."

"Not at all, maybe one day you'll help me?"

"I don't think so Princess."

"You never know, Fluff. Anyway, if you find yourself in this sort of situation again, just shout my name. But only if you are in danger," and with that she was gone.

"I was just about to say "But where's Cindy?" when you turned up shouting my name. I've never seen her since that day."

"And anyway," Fluff said indignantly, "I wasn't upset and crying the way you think. I was so pleased to see you that I was crying tears of joy!"

"Yes, I remember now! That's why Sparkle came," said Cindy.

"Well, well!" said Fluff, "I'd forgotten about Sparkle!"

"*Oh yes*! It was the first time you or I had seen a

rainbow. I mean, we'd heard about them, but we'd never seen one before."

It's important to understand that rainbows come from another dimension and they only appear if a cloud is crying because it's happy. Sad clouds don't attract rainbows.

Cindy started recalling what had happened: "Yes, I remember, I asked him his name............."

"Sparkle," the rainbow replied. "It's so good to meet a happy cloud again, are you its Windlet?"

"Yes, your happy cloud's over there, he's called Fluff."

"Hello Fluff," said the rainbow, "It's nice to meet you, what makes you so happy on this beautiful day?"

"The storms have all gone and I've just found my Windlet, so I'm very happy. It's certainly a pleasure to meet you. I've always wanted to meet a rainbow."

Sparkle started reminiscing: "Well it's quite a while since I've been here ... quite a while! I remember the last time ... yes, it was evening, there were some young clouds playing a game on a mountain top. You see, I can tell when a cloud is young – it's less craggy at the edges.

Now what were they doing? ... Ha! I remember, their Windlets had spun them into little disks and they were trying to be the first cloud on top of the summit.

Anyway, to cut a long story short, they ended up with five young clouds on top of each other in a stack, all going round and round and getting giddier and giddier. I think they called the game spinning plates. I ..."

Cindy interrupted Sparkle's musing, letting Fluff know the rainbow's name. "This is Sparkle," she said. "He's just appeared."

Fluff had saved up one particular question for the first time he ever met a rainbow. He never thought for one minute that it would be his rainbow, a rainbow he would create by crying joyful tears.

"Where do you come from, Sparkle?"

"Well Fluff, I can't really answer that question, you see I don't know.

The feeling you call joy that makes you cry with happiness is a smell where I come from, and when I smell it, I just follow the scent and it brings me to your world. It's such a joy coming here, it's such a fantastic sight and so different from my world."

"What's your world like then?" asked Fluff.

"I don't think I'll have enough time to explain, I can't stop long!"

"Give it a try," said Fluff.

"I'll tell you as much as I can, in the time I've got.

My world doesn't have any solid ground like your world does and it always feels strange when I touch the ground of your world.

Where I come from, I'm a complete circle and my world is full of bright colours. In fact, one of the really nice things about visiting you is that I can bring a bit of brightness to your rather dull world.

Where I come from...." Sparkle began to fade in and out "..and the stars..." Cindy remembered Sparkle fading slowly away...

"Boy, was that a day to remember!" said Cindy.

Meanwhile, Fluff and Cindy continued to watch the Winters.

Baby Sarah had decided enough was enough. She would never get fed if she stayed quiet and still in her Mother's arms. Her bottom lip started to quiver.

"Uh Oh!" said Jack.

Then Sarah started to cry.

"I think you'd better give her that bottle, Mary."

Mary shook a little bit of milk from the baby's bottle onto the back of her hand. "Well, it's cool enough now," and she put it in Sarah's mouth. The noise stopped instantly.

Jack's voice dropped in tone. "It's for her and all her friends, Mary, that the human race needs to get its act together and quickly. The time for talking about global warming is over, it's now time for action. In 1994 the 'Larson A' ice shelf broke up and in an instant we lost 965 square miles of ice – the shelf used to be 50ft high, it was massive. It took only three days to disintegrate. Now 1994's a long time ago and the melting has been relentless ever since. In 2002 'Larson B' ice shelf broke up and so it carries on. West Antarctica with 630,000 miles of grounded ice, up to 2 miles thick, is melting faster than ever before. If that goes, we've estimated it will add 16ft, that's nearly five metres, to the average level of the sea all around the earth. You can see these figures start to add up. There are a lot of scientists out there, and you can include me on the list, that think we just may be in big trouble."

Mary looked up at Jack.

Jack continued: "When I first heard about global warming I was at university and none of us were sure it was real. There were great debates about whether it was just the natural cycle. It was only as we started getting hard evidence from Ice-Cores, about the relationship between CO_2 and temperature, that we realised we had a significant problem. The trouble is that most of us have now known about this for tens of years, and yet hardly anything has been done to combat the problem." Mary could sense the frustration in Jack's voice. "We are literally running out of time!"

"Has anyone any idea what may happen, Jack?"

"We have ideas because we have models of what may happen, but to be honest, Mary, the models are our guide *and* our problem. We can't get them accurate enough, quickly enough. As time goes on we'll have stronger and stronger models but time's running out. The problem is that there are so many variables to consider. It's mind blowing."

"What do you mean?"

"Well let's take one or two variables, as examples: first let's take the principal of Albedo."

"What's that?"

"Well, pale colours reflect sunlight more than dark colours. The pale colour is said to have a high Albedo and dark colours have a low Albedo. We know that the world is cooler with lots of ice because the ice is cooler than the ocean. Well, let's imagine for a moment the ice to be the same temperature as the ocean. In that case the world would still be cooler because all the white of the ice would reflect the sunlight back into space, whereas a dark ocean would absorb it and become warmer.

"Now there are lots of these variables that have to be included in modelling. So let's take a second one: let's consider airplane contrails, the thin white trails left behind by jet aircraft, as they fly through the upper atmosphere. You've probably noticed that these thin white lines spread out over time. The more of these there are, the less sunlight gets to the earth. After 9/11 all aircraft were grounded and thus, in the following days, there were no contrails and guess what!"

"What?"

"The temperature shot up. The evaporation rate shot up. You see, the less sunlight that gets to the earth, the lower the evaporation rate, yet another variable. *All* these things complicate the model and there are thousands of other complications. Some of which we don't even know yet!

"Recent data suggests melting of the ice is happening much faster than the current models predict, so there must be a lot we haven't put in our models yet.

"Things are so complicated; for example, the global average temperature rise over the last century was around 1.8° but as an example of how complex things are, the average temperature rise in South East Greenland, in the last twenty years alone, was 5.4°.

"Now Greenland contains about eight percent of the world's ice. There are seven hundred thousand square miles of fresh water up there and if that went into the sea, the sea would rise by twenty-three feet, just over seven metres, all over the earth. We'd lose this house. Millions, not hundreds, nor thousands, but millions of people would be in the same boat."

Jack just realised what he'd said, "Excuse the pun!"

"Just to complicate matters, all that melt-water is fresh water and so, as that mixes in the oceans, the salinity of the sea will decrease. None of us knows for sure what effect this will have but there is a theory, which most of us believe to be fairly accurate, that predicts the ocean currents may stop circulating. This is because cold salty seawater is heavy. As the current moves north and cools down, the surface water sinks, taking oxygen with it, to the bottom of the sea. As it sinks it displaces the water below, which moves back south, thus aiding the circulation of the ocean currents. If this sea water is less saline then maybe the water doesn't sink; if the water doesn't sink, the current *will* switch off."

"And?" Mary asked.

"Well, if the ocean currents don't flow, we have a totally different world than we have now and none of us know what would happen then – including me."

Mary was so wrapped up in the conversation with Jack that she hadn't noticed that Sarah's bottle had been slowly slipping away from her mouth. Sarah was having none of that and started wailing again at the top of her voice.

"Oh, dear, dear, what have we done?" Mary said to Sarah in her high-pitched, baby-talk voice. She slipped the bottle back into Sarah's mouth and the baby returned to chomping on it. Mary returned to the conversation.

"You must have some idea of what may happen if the ocean currents cease?"

Jack started to pace up and down as he spoke.

"No, we can say that the poles will get much colder and, I suppose, the equator much hotter. We could probably say that, just like in a fish tank, if you stop oxygenating the water, then if the fresh oxygenated surface water never gets to the bottom of the sea, then the bottom of the ocean will become more and more stagnant and poisonous. We know that in the past the closing down of the ocean currents nearly killed the earth; it nearly turned into a giant snowball. But the conditions then were different than the conditions now. No! No one knows what may really happen if the currents switch off."

"But if you think about it ..." Mary was looking into the distance as she started to speak. She looked like she had just realised the consequences of what Jack was saying. She repeated her own words as if she'd just thought through what she was about to say: "If you think about it, it doesn't matter how far you look into the future since a rise of just twenty feet would devastate our world. Would a simple thing, say like electricity supplies, be safe?"

"It's the same old story, dear, no one has ever given a thought as to what the consequences would be if the sea rose so rapidly." Jack, however, did give it a thought: "I would imagine that a lot of power generation is done on the plains. If they flooded, then the answer is no, it wouldn't be safe."

"What about the cities?"

"Most of them are on the coasts. They'd be taken out well before it got to a twenty foot rise. You know a third of the world's population lives near the coast?"

"Oh! Good grief, I've just realised! Most of the food industry is on the plains. There would be hardly any place left to grow food."

"So we're looking at starvation too?" Jack pondered.

Mary fell silent and looked lovingly at baby Sarah; Jack walked back over to give the baby a kiss. Sarah's eyes followed Daddy but there was no way she was going to stop drinking from that bottle.

"Let's hope we crack some of the problems quickly, especially the models."

And with that, the two sat together watching the moon and the stars, and listening to Sarah Winter chomping away at her bottle.

"Well Cindy, they do look after their younglets."

"Yes Fluff, they do, don't they?"

"And those aircraft saved me today, Cindy."

"I know," said Cindy comfortingly.

Fluff couldn't stop thinking about the airplanes that had saved him from being absorbed by the thunderstorm that day.

Right from the very first airplane flights, clouds were a little nervous of humans and their flying machines.

At that time there was great debate, in the cloud community, about whether these machines might harm them in some way.

Up to then it had been mainly balloon flights and mountainsides where clouds had come in direct contact with humans. There were no reports of damage to any clouds because of such encounters, so the cloud community was hoping that the airplanes would be equally unthreatening.

In fact, at first, a large number of clouds were quite excited at seeing humans at their level. As flights increased in number, clouds realised that these flying machines were relatively harmless contraptions.

I say, relatively harmless, since in fact, like all human activity, it carries a health warning in regard to waste gases and pollutants. But with the advent of aircraft, clouds got a much better view of what humans were really like. In fact, with the early aircraft you could actually touch and smell these humans and may I say some of the smells were not very pleasant!

As time moved on, this ability to touch the humans disappeared, only returning lately as sky diving and hang gliding have become popular. I think overall, with the big aircraft, clouds are quite happy because these planes climb and fall relatively slowly. But with the development of the jet fighter things are very different. These fighter jets can really mess up a cloud. They churn the middle of the cloud, making the cloud feel sick and nauseous. There's no permanent damage but that's not the point; there's the inconvenience of having to re-arrange oneself; and feeling sick is not a pleasant experience, even for clouds!

Funny thing this interaction between humans and clouds, Fluff thought.

- Chapter Five -

Hammerhead Finds Out

"Look Hammerhead, I heard it direct from Spike: humans can make clouds; did you hear me ... *make* clouds! And what's more frightening, they can destroy them too!"

Hammerhead was struggling to believe Cutter, his Windlet, although Cutter *was* normally spot on with his information.

He had heard a rumour about the destruction of Jake's Mob at some airport near Tallahassee by a human called Winter – Jack Winter – but he was sure it was just a rumour.

Hammerhead was currently getting on with making mischief in the Mid West. He had already spun up Clyde to a category three tornado, just to the east. For some reason however, Clyde couldn't keep the rotation going long enough to do any real damage. Oh yes, they'd took out a few farm-houses and raised a few cattle (literally) but it wasn't what Hammerhead, or for that matter, what Clyde had wanted.

It was obviously Cutter's fault and not Hammerhead's, who could never blame himself for such a poor show.

Cutter's news, however, that there were humans tinkering with the weather down in Pensacola, was definitely worth investigating. They weren't that far away. With that thought, Hammerhead told Cutter to move south.

"The telephone's ringing!" shouted Mary.

"I'll get it," said Jack, as he wandered over to pick up the phone.

"Jack, it's Bill. There's a thunderstorm just north of us and it looks like it's heading our way. Is it worth taking the planes up and testing the new formula?" Bill was one of Jack's colleagues at the WRI. He'd been hired to look after and improve their computer models but just staying at a desk and programming was a little too tame for him at times.

"I haven't got enough of the new mixture ready yet, Bill. Certainly not for three plane loads. We could use the old formula left over from last week's encounter; the more data we collect on dispersal, the better! Are the planes ready to go?"

"Yes, they finished major checks on all three airframes at the back end of last week. If we're going up today, I'll get the pre-flight checks under way, so they'll be ready for take-off by the time you get here."

"OK, what's the estimated time of departure?"

"Well, I'd estimated that we'd need to be in the air by around one O'clock this afternoon and the computer model agrees."

"Then let's do it! I'll get the pods in the truck. I should be with you within the hour."

Jack put the phone down, shouted to Mary, "Got to go!" and headed outside to the truck.

Mary intercepted him, "What's up?"

"Just another thunderstorm heading our way. We're going to get up there and seed it, I won't be gone long."

"So what about a kiss then?" Mary said, with a twinkle in her eye.

Jack gave her a kiss that lingered a little.

Emma squirmed "Behave you two!"

Mary smiled and went back to feeding the baby, "You be careful now!"

"Can I come, Dad?" Emma said, excited at the thought of yet another plane ride so soon after the first.

"No way – not this time partner, you look after baby Sarah and your Mom."

"Oh, *Dad!*"

At that, Jack left the house and loaded the standard pods onto the truck. Normally that would have been it but there was something, maybe instinct, telling him to load a couple of the experimental pods into the truck as well.

By the time Jack set off for the airport, the wind had picked up considerably. Jack wondered whether they had left it a little too late.

As Jack pulled up alongside Aero-One, the skies were turning black. Bill and Mike were standing aside their airplanes.

Jack jumped out of the truck and shouted to the ground crew "Ok, Guys, let's load the pods. Put the same number in each airplane." His voice was only just audible over the wind noise. He lifted the two experimental pods and tucked them under his arms.

Bill and Mike were much closer to Jack.

"The storm's coming in faster than we predicted," said Bill. "I've held the pre-flight briefing, Jack. Sam's flying Aero-One, he knows the details, so I've told him to fill you in on the way up."

"Thanks, Bill" said Jack.

Bill was looking at the two experimental pods that Jack was holding.

"They're filled with the new formula, Bill. I thought that if we had a chance we'd try them."

The wind blew Mike's hat off.

"I think we'd better get in the air, Bill," said Jack, and with that, he took the two experimental pods into Aero-One.

He didn't load the experimental pods into the deploy mechanisms but for some reason he was re-assured by the fact that he'd brought them along. He strapped them down and tapped them several times, just like you would an old friend. "Just in case, boys, just in case," he muttered to himself.

As Aero-One taxied down the runway, Sam covered what had happened in the pre-flight briefing: "Jack! The basic flight plan is to climb to ten thousand feet but keeping around three miles apart. Once we've entered the storm, Aero-Two and Aero-Three will wait for our signal to deploy the pods."

Just as Sam rolled to the take off position, Bill's voice crackled over the coms link: "Sorry about the estimate Jack, the storm came in a little faster than the computer predicted."

Bill was on board Aero-Two, following directly behind Aero-One.

"That's the trouble with the computer, Bill, our models are not quite up to scratch yet – we're not very good at modelling real life events, in real time"

By the time Jack had loaded the pods into Aero-One's delivery system, they were entering the thunderstorm.

The coms crackled into life. "Boy, this is a biggie cobber!" said Joey in Aero-Three.

Joey was the latest member of the WRI flight team. A well built, sunburnt Australian blonde who could easily be mistaken for a wrestler, he'd spent a little time away from flying because of his rather dubious activities in South America. However, the confined quarters he'd found himself in, during a short period of imprisonment, seemed to have left a legacy: a zest for freedom and going straight. Jack had taken a big chance in hiring him but both Sam and Charlie had taken to him straight away. That was good enough for Jack.

"Spot on, Joey, I think this is probably the most dynamic event I've witnessed," replied Freddie in Aero-Two.

Sam joined in, "It's a wild one alright!"

By now all three planes had reached ten thousand feet and were well inside the storm cloud.

Jack's voice came on the coms. "OK lads! Deploy the contents, on my mark. Five ... four... three... two... Mark!"

All three planes started to disperse the pod contents.

Hammerhead had seen the planes take off but thought nothing of them, simply because airplanes had never troubled him before, and he saw no reason why they should now. He did think it unusual for them to climb so rapidly; he'd never seen that before and he'd never before seen what looked like ice particles falling out of a plane. At first, Hammerhead was too intent on destroying property and producing mayhem at the airport to realise that there was something wrong. It was his hold on the minor members of the thunderstorm team that he noticed first – he was losing his grip on them. Slowly but surely they were splintering away from him.

A thunderstorm is like a pyramid: take away the support structure underneath and the whole thing collapses. That's exactly what was happening.

"Cutter, change your direction," said Hammerhead in a terse voice.

Cutter did so immediately.

"Clyde, it's spin up time; avoid those ice particles coming down from above and try to get those hangars on the left."

"Right Boss!" said Clyde.

In the meantime, while the others were doing his bidding, Hammerhead threw his own ice particles at Aero-Three.

Cutter's change of direction ensured that most of the falling chaff was avoided. Hammerhead's masterstroke, throwing ice particles at Aero-Three, led to the sudden ice build up on the leading edge of Aero-Three's wings, which plunged the plane into free fall.

As the ice started to have an effect on Aero-Three, the altitude alert system sprang into life. Meanwhile, the instrumentation on the other planes was showing Aero-Three's altitude dropping like a stone.

"You're too low, Aero-Three, repeat Too Low – gain some height." Charlie's voice rang in Joey's ears.

"I know, Charlie, the wings have iced up. I'm trying to remove it now!"

"Joey, it's not just the floor coming up at you, you need to watch the twister to your left," added Sam.

"Good Grief!" Joey exclaimed and as he loosened the ice from his wings he pushed his throttle forward to climb away from the danger. It didn't work.

"I think I'm caught in a downdraft."

Charlie came on the coms link: "Joey – dive through it – you've just got enough altitude, don't fight it, dive through it."

Joey stopped trying to climb and headed for the deck. He hoped to Goodness Charlie had got it right.

At about six hundred feet from the ground, Joey could feel that the controls were beginning to respond; at four hundred feet he was in control; at two hundred feet he was levelling out and at one hundred feet he started to climb again. He could hear the strain on the airframe, which was making the most unusual noises.

Through all this, Hammerhead was examining the planes that were trying to kill him. He could feel the seed pod launch system – this was something new, something he had not felt before. "Cutter, try to rip one of those round tubes off the plane that's climbing through us."

"OK, Boss!" Cutter lowered the pressure outside the launch tubes to such an extent that the launch tube and a small part of the fuselage came away.

Again Hammerhead felt the chunk of metal and now its form and function were becoming clear.

"Clyde, have you spun up enough yet?"

"Yes, Boss. I'm just about to touch down, just north of the hangars. I'll be on them in no time at all."

Aero-One had been above all this mayhem as it unfolded. Jack had placed the experimental seedpods in the launch tubes, just in case, and was pondering what to do when the coms again crackled into life. "Flight Control to all inbound traffic – there is a Category Three tornado heading directly for the air strip and the hangars – avoid this airspace, I repeat avoid this airspace."

That was it. No time to worry; if the new mix was going to have any effect at all, it had to be tried now.

"Charlie, get as close to the hangars as you can, without going too near that twister – let me know when you're in position."

Charlie was there in less than a minute.

"Ready when you are, Jack."

Jack launched the canisters.

The change to Hammerhead's group happened in an instant. The tornado didn't even make ground contact. It was immediate annihilation. The new mix had also fallen onto a good portion of the storm cloud, instantly removing support for the storm. As the mix did its work, one by one the captured Fluffies were freed, leaving an awful lot of clouds wondering where the heck they were and wandering off in all directions, chattering among themselves.

Hammerhead tried to regroup the troops but it was impossible, there was hardly anyone left. He couldn't raise Clyde at all. It was all too obvious that Clyde must have been destroyed!

Slowly but surely it was dawning on Hammerhead that this particular battle was lost. He knew it would take some time for him to regroup his forces, but regroup he would. The defeat had hurt his pride and revenge was now uppermost in his mind. He'd already decided he'd be back with a new team, a team much bigger and better than the one he'd just lost. "Jack Winter and all his family WILL DIE!" Hammerhead shouted as he and Cutter limped away from the airport.

By the time Aero-One and Aero-Two came in to land, the skies were almost clear. Yet there was no sense of elation from the team. The reason was obvious. There had been no contact with Aero-Three since its plummet to earth and everyone was worried for the safety of the crew.

Aero-One and Aero-Two had been on the tarmac for a full ten minutes when the silence was abruptly broken: "Aero-Three to control tower, Repeat Aero-Three to control tower, do you read me?"

Everyone on the tarmac and in the control tower screamed with delight!

As the noise decreased, the controller responded: "We read you loud and clear Aero-Three, are you alright?"

"Not sure, Cobber! Have indication that the undercarriage has not deployed. I'm going to fly directly over you. Could you look to see if you can spot a problem?"

"Will do, Aero-Three."

Joey flew Aero-Three over the control tower.

The controller was looking through binoculars at the underside of Joe's plane. "It appears to be just the port wheel that's not fully down. The front wheel and the starboard wheel look like they're fully deployed."

"OK!" said Joe, "I'm coming in on the next pass."

"Roger that!" The controller hit the emergency button. Immediately the sirens sounded around the airport. The fire trucks and ambulance set off to their emergency stations.

By now Jack had reached the tower. He'd seen the fly-past and the starboard wheel. He knew the landing would be tricky.

"Can I speak with him?" said Jack to the controller.

"Be my guest!"

"Joey!" Jack's voice crackled in Joey's ears "You make a safe landing, you hear. I need to know how that pod launcher got ripped off!"

"Piece of cake, Jack," Joey replied.

The airstrip had been cleared of everything but the emergency landing team. All other aircraft had been told to stand off until Aero-Three was safely down. On his final approach, Joey dumped his remaining fuel, deciding to make the landing on fumes – it was the safest way. He knew he couldn't go around again. He also knew that there wouldn't be a problem until the plane was actually on the ground and so the approach was very much as normal. Once on the ground he knew what he had to do. It was quite simple: hold the portside off the tarmac for as long as possible. Then, once the plane had slowed down, as late as possible, let the port wing down.

As the port wing touched the tarmac there was lots of noise and sparks flying all over, but the plane came to rest, straight as a die, in the middle of the runway.

There was instant clapping in the control tower and from the crew of the other two aircraft. The emergency team sped to the plane and covered it in fire resistant foam, just in case.

By the time Joey and Mike had cleared the aircraft, Jack was alongside in his flatbed. He jumped out and shook Joey's hand and smiled "I knew I'd picked the right man for the job."

"I think I may enjoy my time here after all," Joey smiled, "You OK, Mike?"

"A bit shaken, Jack, but better now we're back on solid ground."

As the three climbed into the flatbed, Jack asked Joey what had happened but Mike chipped in: "There was an almighty gust and ripping noise under one of the deploy chute mechanisms. I think we lost it!"

Jack looked at Joey.

"Well Jack, after the jolt that Mike's talking about, we just suddenly iced up. I can't understand where that came from. I didn't think we were that far up."

"You weren't, Joey, you weren't!"

As soon as Fluff and Cindy had heard that Hammerhead was coming down from the north, they'd both agreed that watching what was to happen, from afar, was the safest bet. So as events unfolded, they had a ringside seat.

They saw Hammerhead come in and the airplanes take off. They saw the seeding taking place, and what looked like an attempt by Hammerhead to down the plane. They even saw Clyde's demise. They'd both cheered as all the individual Fluffies were freed from Hammerhead's grasp. They had also sensed Hammerhead's anger as his main mass dispersed.

After these events, Cindy was in touch with most of the surrounding Windlets, who were busy telling her of Hammerhead's murderous promise to wipe out Jack Winter's family. She passed this on to Fluff.

"It's against Cloudkind's code of conduct to seek

revenge," said Fluff. "What were his exact words, Cindy?"

"Jack Winter and all his family WILL DIE!" Cindy repeated exactly what she'd been told.

"Then we have to report this situation. Besides, there's only one thing that's much bigger and better than Hammerhead and that's a hurricane."

"No! You don't think? ..."

But before Cindy could finish her sentence, Fluff carried on:

"There's no way that the humans will survive the power of a combined attack from a stronger Hammerhead, a hurricane and probably more twisters."

"What can we do?" said Cindy, not expecting a reply.

"We'll report the problem to the Princess Pearl and see if she's willing to help the humans."

"Fluff! You don't know where she is! You don't know whether she can help them, and what's more you don't know whether she would want to help them!"

"You saw it for yourself, Cindy. Look at all the Fluffies the humans just freed! They're not doing harm to us and I don't think the Princess would let Hammerhead do harm to them."

"But where is she?"

"I'm not sure, but I have an idea. Cindy, let's go north." And with that, Cindy and Fluff set off towards the northern lands, leaving Hammerhead brooding and gathering his thoughts, still in their patch of the sky.

- Chapter Six -

Fluff And Cindy Go North

I've always found that one of the great things about travelling very long distances is the dramatic change in scenery one encounters. Sometimes Mother Earth can be breathtaking in her diversity. Whether moving among lush, green forests, or dry deserts, from the vast plains to the high mountains, the changes are always wonderful to behold.

Now I'm not talking small distances here, a hundred miles that way or a hundred miles the other. No! We're talking a thousand miles in one direction, maybe even more. This is exactly what Fluff and Cindy were experiencing as they moved ever further away from the area they called home ...

It was early morning on the fifth day when Fluff and Cindy encountered their first desert, and I mean their first desert! Neither Fluff nor Cindy had *ever* experienced this type of environment before.

Fluff knew there was something different on the horizon since he had felt the dryness in the air many miles back. But as they approached the desert margin, he knew, through pure instinct, that this was not a good place for a cloud to be.

The sand dunes and the dry rocky outcrops stretched further than a cloud could see and Fluff was feeling very nervous at the thought of having to cross such a hostile place.

"I'm not sure crossing this land is a good idea, Cindy!" Fluff spoke nervously.

Cindy had already picked up some useful information on how far the desert stretched and the best times of day for crossing it. She'd done this from occasionally touching passing Windlets that were heading in the opposite direction. "It's not too far to cross, Fluff, but you wouldn't want to dawdle. I suggest I send you off at speed and I'll catch up with you later in the day."

"You're sure it's possible Cindy?"

"Yes, I wouldn't put you at risk now, would I?" she said reassuringly, "and it's the right time of day. If we send you at speed now you'll be through it before noon."

"OK, let's do it!"

Cindy sent him off at a pace.

Making a cloud accelerate from a reasonably slow speed to a very fast one isn't quite as easy as it sounds. For one thing, clouds are not solid objects, so just pushing hard doesn't work. That would just make a large hole in the cloud and even then it would hardly move. By pushing hard through it you would just create vortices within the cloud. This would tend to make it spin rather than go in the direction intended.

Suddenly putting a lot of energy into the motion of a cloud can only be done in one way. Cindy would have to race in front of Fluff, accelerating all the time. Once at a reasonable speed she would effectively sling shot him in the direction of travel. This results in an enormous transfer of kinetic energy from the Windlet to the cloud. The cloud is propelled forward at an increased velocity but the Windlet is left behind, drained of a great deal of the energy it once had.

Cindy had estimated that, at the speed she could travel, she wouldn't emerge from the desert until early morning the next day. So once Fluff was up to speed, Cindy wasted no time and immediately renewed her journey.

It was a few hours later; the sun was baking hot now, which seemed to slow her down even more. She had the feeling she was being followed. It was as if there was another Windlet close by that didn't want to announce its presence.

The floor of the desert had changed colour a few miles back. Cindy had just accepted the change without questioning it, until she glanced down. She was surprised to see what could only be described as rock carvings covering the desert floor for mile after mile. She decided to have a closer look.

"You like them?"

The voice made Cindy jump! ... She wasn't expecting a voice from anywhere, even though she had sensed the presence of a Windlet nearby, "Who's that?"

"It's me, Scraper!" said the Windlet, as if she should know his name.

"And who are you?"

"I'm the one that carved these rocks!" Scraper said proudly, "It's my work."

Just like humans, clouds and Windlets can have hobbies. And just like humans some let their hobbies take over their lives. It looked like Scraper was such a Windlet.

"How did you get into this?" said Cindy.

"I was just passing this large overhang one day when I noticed that every time I went past, a little bit of dust came off. Well, it intrigued me, you know. So I circled back around and tried it again. Wow! It came off again, so I tried the other side of the rock and the same thing happened. Well, I was hooked"

"So how long have you been doing this?"

"Oh! About three thousand years."

"Three thousand years?" Cindy was so surprised that she instinctively touched him lightly, to see if the Windlet was telling the truth. He was.

Scraper could hear the surprise in her voice and knew why she'd touched him. Feeling slightly embarrassed, he said: "Well, I can't be really accurate because you tend to lose track of time out here – especially when you're all alone."

Cindy felt a little guilty for not believing him and a little bit sorry for him too, being that he *was* out here all alone. "Say, don't you miss having others around?"

"Well yes, it would be nice to have friends, other Windlets, I mean. I've never got attached to clouds, like I know most Windlets do. I live in a desert area you see and there aren't that many clouds around."

Scraper suddenly realised that Cindy was not with a cloud. "I see you're alone. Why don't you join me? You know, not many Windlets get the chance to have a real effect on the world. As you can see, I've had that chance. I *have* made a difference," Scraper had a distinct sense of pride in his voice.

"Well it's very beautiful, but I *do* have a cloud, he's just not here because I sent him ahead, to avoid the worst of the desert heat."

"Oh!" Scraper said sadly.

"I'm afraid I can't stay here to help you. Sorry. I can't even stay to look at everything you've done. I have to get to my cloud or he'll dry up." And with that, Cindy took off.

"Come back any time!" Scraper shouted.

"Bye ..." Cindy called; she wondered whether having an effect on the world was worth the time and effort if nobody ever saw your work.

As Cindy gained height she started feeling bad at leaving Scraper all alone, back there in the desert. He's probably been by himself for three thousand years, poor guy needs company. Maybe even a bit of care and attention, she thought. And with that she turned back.

"Scraper!" she called

Scraper wasn't far away; he flew back to her, calling to her excitedly, "Cindy! You've changed your mind."

Cindy could almost feel the delight in his voice.

"No, no, I haven't changed my mind, Scraper. I just thought maybe you might like to come with me? Have you ever thought of trying somewhere new?"

"This is all I know Cindy, I don't know anywhere else to try."

"Well it's a big world out there, Scraper. There'll be lots of places I'm sure."

Scraper was very unsure of what to do. "I don't know," he said.

Cindy was trying to think of an area that might interest Scraper; 'Ha, yes!' she thought.

"My cloud Fluff and I are going north towards the snow line. They say that being in dry snow is like being in a cold desert and even further north there are Ice Sheets and Glaciers. You could shape them. I would imagine snow and ice are a lot easier to shape than solid rock."

"That sounds exciting! But I don't know the way. Could I come with you and your cloud?"

Cindy suddenly realised there could be problems. She'd not discussed this with Fluff and what's more, she knew she and Fluff wouldn't be able to stay with Scraper; they were on a mission, not out for fun.

"Now I can't guarantee anything here, Scraper, but if

you come with me to the edge of the desert we'll meet up with Fluff and see if he'll let you travel with us until we get to the snow line."

"Thanks Cindy."

"There's one more thing, Scraper. Once we arrive at the snow line we can't go any further and you'll have to carry on going north by yourself; you'll be alone again."

"I'm used to being alone, Cindy, so don't worry about that. I'm not used to travelling and meeting other clouds and Windlets. If you could stay with me on the first part of the journey, I'll be fine after that."

"Well let's go and talk to Fluff then."

All the way to Fluff, Cindy was worried. Worried that Fluff might say 'no' to helping Scraper find a new life, leaving Scraper to return to his lonely place in the sun.

Cindy spotted Fluff a good twenty miles away on the northern horizon. He was easy to spot; there wasn't another cloud in the sky.

"Scraper. Stay here; I need to talk with Fluff first."

"OK!"

Cindy raced towards Fluff: "Fluff, you're looking a little thinner than when I last saw you."

"Cindy! Wow! It's great to hear your voice again!"

"It's wonderful to be back, Fluff. Hmm! I have a little surprise for you."

"What do you mean?"

"I found another Windlet in the desert, a very lonely Windlet. He needs help to find his way north to the snow line and I told him you'd let him come with us while we travelled north," Cindy sounded uncertain.

Fluff was unphased "So long as he doesn't slow us down Cindy, that's fine."

"Yippee!" Scraper shouted in delight.

"Scraper! I told you to wait over there."

Scraper calmed down.

"Come on, you two, we've a long way to go," Fluff hurried them.

Scraper rushed closer to Cindy and Fluff. He'd been let loose for the very first time.

As they travelled north, Cindy and Fluff maintained a steady speed and remained roughly at the same altitude. Scraper kept flying up and down, round and round, changing speed and pushing on things to see if they'd move.

At one point he dived down to push a small sailboat along. It was sailing in the middle of a lake, in a park in the middle of a city. His enthusiasm nearly capsized the boat. Then he dived through the trees to blow a number of papers off a park bench, where an unsuspecting human had settled to read.

"Oh, the joy of being a Windlet," Scraper cried.

On the very first day of their journey, Cindy had tried to calm him down, but it was no use. He was like a child in a candy store, wanting to try everything, all at the same time.

Cindy, Fluff and Scraper were moving over farmland when Scraper noticed three children running around in a field, playing with what looked like another Windlet.

"What's that down there, Cindy?" asked Scraper.

"It's a play twister, humans call them dust devils."

"What's it doing?"

"It's just playing with the human younglets, as you can see."

Scraper flew down to talk to the twister: "What's your name?"

"Kidslikeme," the twister replied.

"Well! I can see that, but what's your name?"

"That is my name! 'Kidslikeme' is my name!"

"Oh, I see. Are you a Windlet?"

"Yes, but a sort of special version."

"What do you mean?"

"Well I'm a play twister. I was a Windlet but I asked to be spun up so I could enjoy a few days playing with human younglets and the like. What's your name?"

"Scraper. What else do you play with?

"Oh, lots of things: animals, washing lines, windmills. Lots of things."

Cindy arrived to listen to the conversation. She couldn't trust a twister, even if it was only a play twister, with a Windlet as naive as Scraper, but she didn't let her presence be known.

"Sounds like fun, how do I become a play twister?" asked Scraper.

"That's easy. You ask a storm to spin you up."

"What's a storm?"

"Where have you been that you don't know such a thing?"

"I've been stuck in a desert for quite a long time."

"Ah! Where's your Fluffy?"

"I don't have one."

"Well, if you're not paired with a Fluffy, you're a perfect candidate for being spun up to be a twister."

"You haven't answered my question, what's a storm?"

"It's where a lot of Fluffies and their Windlets gather together to have some fun. All you have to do is join in, then ask the Fluffy in charge to spin you up to be a twister."

Cindy thought it was time to speak: "You haven't told him about the downside yet!"

Kidslikeme was surprised at the interruption "Who's that?" he asked.

"Just a friend of Scraper," Cindy replied.

What do you mean 'downside', Cindy?" asked Scraper.

"Once you're spun up to be a twister, Scraper, there's no

turning back; you can't become a Windlet again. Twister's lead very short lives. I think the oldest recorded twister was four years old; most of them only survive a few years and some only a few months."

"Wow! I don't think that's for me," said Scraper.

"Well, it's not for everyone," admitted Kidslikeme. "I lost 'Wheatear', my Fluffy, in the dry season over farmland like this. It was a very bad year, there was hardly a drop of water left in the air and he just evaporated and joined the great Cloud Computer in the sky. I tried to get him to move but he just wouldn't leave the area. He threatened to fall out with me forever if I moved him. I just watched him disappear and it was heartbreaking. I had no problem signing up to be a twister after that."

Cindy's tone changed, "I'm sorry to hear of your loss."

Cindy had a lot of sympathy for Kidslikeme; she'd often thought to herself that if she lost Fluff she wouldn't mind being a play twister for a while. It would be a good way to go.

Kidslikeme, Cindy and Scraper had forgotten about the children for the moment. That is until they threw grass into Kidslikeme's funnel, which immediately spiralled upwards.

"I think we'd better be going, Scraper," said Cindy.

"I think so too," he said. "Bye, Kidslikeme."

"Bye, you two."

And with that, they flew into the air to rejoin Fluff.

"And what did the twister have to say for himself?" said Fluff, as he felt the two Windlets return.

"Oh! Nothing much," replied Cindy.

Fluff, Cindy and Scraper had been travelling north for many days now and Cindy was beginning to feel a little chilly. Fluff was also feeling the cold and feeling a little stiff inside.

As for Scraper: well, even though he'd spent all of his life in a desert, to Fluff and Cindy's surprise, he didn't feel the cold at all. He was just as comfortable with the icy temperature of the north as he was with the heat of the desert.

"The stiffness might be ice particles," Cindy's voice was slightly shivery. "I don't think so Cindy, but I do think we should go no further. There's already snow on the ground just north of us and I don't think either of us should cross that line."

Fluff nudged Cindy and looked down at Scraper, who was chasing a flock of Canada Geese. "You need to talk to him, Cindy."

"Yes, I know. Scraper!" Cindy shouted for him to come back.

"Yes, Cindy?"

"Look, Scraper. As I told you before, we can't go any further north than the snow line and there it is right in front of us."

"Not only that, Scraper, we are on a mission here and it's important you're not involved." added Fluff.

"I understand," said Scraper, "It's because we Windlets are useless at keeping secrets, isn't it?"

"Yes," admitted Fluff.

"But it's been a pleasure having you with us," said Cindy.

"I'll second that, Scraper. Most entertaining."

"Thanks for your help and your companionship," said Scraper.

As he took off, he added, "If you ever come up north, look me up, you hear!"

Fluff shouted back, "No chance Scraper! It's far too cold even here, never mind further up north. You take care!"

"Bye, Scraper," called Cindy. She was sorry to see him go, but boy was she happy to see he was no longer stuck in that desert.

After Scraper had disappeared over the horizon, Cindy turned to Fluff.

"Do you think we'll be able to contact the Princess from here?"

"Hope so," said Fluff and he called her name.

He didn't expect an instant response, but by the next day, when she still hadn't arrived, it worried him slightly.

"Do you think we should move further north?" Cindy asked.

"No, I don't think we would survive up there."

Cindy was relieved at the reply.

After several more hours of waiting, she interrupted the silence: "What's that?"

"What's what?" said Fluff.

"There! On the horizon."

Fluff looked up to see something rather strange. It was a sort of white mist, approaching very quickly from the north. Fluff and Cindy thought it could possibly be a snowstorm; they'd witnessed a sandstorm in the desert and decided this was very similar in appearance, except that it was white. So obviously, snow.

Judging from the speed of approach, if it was a snowstorm it was being driven by a very strong and powerful Windlet. Cindy felt it would be sensible to shelter in the lea of a high cliff face, just to the west of their current position and so, while the storm raged, they hugged the steep slope of the cliff face to avoid being dragged along by the strong wind.

Without question, if they had been engulfed then by the time they were able to separate they would have found themselves a considerable distance south and having to re-trace their steps.

As the snowstorm passed them, the ferocity of the wind became clear. The snow was being driven so hard it didn't actually look like it was falling at all.

Cindy was rather glad, although surprised, that the new Windlet hadn't touched her. She didn't want to be dragged south, but on the other hand her natural curiosity had been awakened and she was desperate to know why the Windlet was in such a hurry. She decided talking was probably the best solution. "OK!" she said, "Can you tell me why you're going so fast?"

"I like to create an effect you know. You don't have much effect if you're going too slow!" said the Windlet.

"What do you mean?" said Cindy.

"Well, I like to cover up the things that mankind makes with a good thick blanket of snow. It always looks so much cleaner, so much nicer, so much more natural somehow. I like to hide their silly, ugly structures. If I go slowly it doesn't get covered in quite the same way, does it? So I go fast."

"Why do you want to cover things up, anyway?" asked Cindy.

"Well, they think they're in charge of the planet, you know. They seem to want to take over every little bit of it. I get the impression they think they own it, so I like to give them a reminder now and again that they're not entirely in control."

The fast moving, fast talking Windlet paused for a second, as he remembered he should have introduced himself "Oh, sorry! My name's B.L. Izzard, by the way. Just call me BL. What's your name?"

"Cindy! So is it that you don't like mankind then, BL?"

"Does anybody like them? No, I haven't met many Windlets who like mankind." Then a thought struck him. "Why! do you?"

Cindy wasn't sure how to reply.

"I haven't made up my mind yet," she said.

"Well, there are plenty of examples of how bad they really are. It shouldn't take you long to consider the facts. Take a simple thing like the roads they make!"

"What do you mean?"

"Well, in order to make that road down there, the one that goes through the forest, see!" BL was looking towards the road in question. "They had to kill huge stretches of trees. So they chopped them down. By doing that, they removed the homes of all the animals that lived there. Even after doing all that, they hadn't finished reaping their destruction. They proceeded to kill the animals that lived in that area of the forest by driving over them, as the animals tried to cross their newly built highways. To cap it all they then decided to pollute the air and the waters surrounding their new road with the toxic fumes coming out the backside of their vehicles." BL paused. "Convinced yet?"

Cindy held firm, "No!"

"Well if that doesn't convince you, I don't know what will." BL was beginning to sound a little indignant. "Well, when I've finished doing my work, sometimes you can't even see the roads they've built," he said, with more than a little pride in his voice. "They have to come and dig their vehicles out of the snow. It certainly stops them travelling along the roads for a time, saving many animal lives. I find that very pleasing." If Windlets could smile, he was smiling. "Look! I can't stop. I've too much work to do. Nice talking to you."

As his voice trailed off in the distance, the storm died down and Fluff and Cindy returned east to the point where Fluff had called the Princess.

Cindy and Fluff thought there was a lot of anger in BL's soul and it wasn't something they could sign up to.

The Princess was hundreds of miles away when she first

heard Fluff's calls. Her hearing was attuned to certain words and frequencies, but even though she heard the call, she couldn't be absolutely sure who it was, or whether it was a distress call. She wouldn't know the answer until she was much closer; she immediately changed direction to head towards it.

When she was some fifty miles away she realised it was Fluff and also thought that it was probably a distress call: not just because of Fluff's tone, but also because a temperate climate Fluffy wouldn't be this far north without having something really important bothering him.

She watched him for a while before making contact. He was very cute. No doubt about it, he was the best looking cloud she'd ever seen.

He was obviously talking to his Windlet. Depending on how serious the issue might be, it might be necessary to separate the two, to prevent their conversation being broadcast to the rest of Windkind.

In the evening, just as the sun was going down, Fluff heard a faint whisper; one that he had only heard once before in his lifetime. The Princess!

"Princess?" he asked.

"Yes, Fluff, I'm here."

"I need to speak with you about an urgent matter."

"Fluff, it may be wise to ensure that no one knows of the things we talk about. You will have to send Cindy away. She cannot remain here."

Fluff looked at Cindy. Both Cindy and Fluff knew that Windlets couldn't keep secrets; this was the right thing to do. Cindy retreated to a distance where she couldn't overhear the conversation between the Princess and Fluff.

"Fluff, do you remember what I told you when we first met?"

"You said I could call you if there was danger," Fluff said

meekly, knowing that was not quite how it was phrased.

"I said not to contact me unless YOU were in danger." There was a long silent pause. "I see no danger to you, Fluff!"

"I'm not in danger, Princess, but..."

The Princess interrupted: "Then who is?"

"A family of humans."

"Why are you concerned about humans?"

"They're tinkering with the weather. I think for good reasons, but they don't realise the strength of the forces involved. They've completely underestimated the power of the wind and clouds and have angered some very powerful and dangerous enemies. One of which is organising their destruction."

"His name?"

"Hammerhead, but ..." Fluff continued: "We think he's going to enlist a hurricane and more twisters."

"That would be a truly dangerous combination. But how is it possible that a human family could cause such a powerful set of enemies to work together against them?"

"They think the humans are trying to kill them. The leader of the human family has a device that can calm storm forces down and disperse them as simple rain clouds." Not wanting to be in any way inaccurate, he added, "We have reason to believe he's also trying to make clouds."

Fluff knew that the last sentence wouldn't go down too well with the Princess.

"But that's far from destroying and killing," said the Princess.

Fluff was reluctant to say the next sentence but he had to be honest.

"He did kill... whether by accident or design... he killed a tornado called Clyde, one of Hammerhead's closest allies."

"Well, Fluff," said the Princess "this is a little more complicated than I thought. I need to consult with others.

I will be back later. Meanwhile, do not cross the snow line as it may harm you." With that, the Princess glimmered and shimmered and disappeared.

"Cindy!" Fluff shouted, "It's OK to return now."

After a few attempts by Fluff, Cindy finally heard him.

"I hope she's not long, Fluff, I'm freezing!" said Cindy as she returned to him.

Fluff didn't say anything. He just smiled. In fact, for the next few hours he was very quiet, because he had a lot to think about. He was not altogether sure he should be helping humans who were trying to make clouds and killing tornados.

The Princess flew over to her father's palace.

"Hello, my dear, I thought you had gone off to check the aurora?"

"Something more urgent has cropped up. 'Hammerhead', Father, look up a storm cloud by the name of 'Hammerhead'. What has he been doing lately?"

The King accessed the cloud computer to review Hammerhead's recent activity.

The Great Cloud Computer in the sky is not like your computers down on earth. It's composed of trillions and trillions of cloud filaments left over by the remnants of clouds that have gone before. Their intelligence isn't lost when they evaporate but becomes part of 'The Cloud' as it is known, a sort of distributed computing system that operates faster than any human built computer could ever do.

These filaments can't normally be seen by anyone outside the Cloud Kingdom. It must be said, though, that on occasion large amounts of filaments have been seen.

"He's been working in and around Pensacola airfield... oh,

that's interesting!"

"What is?"

"He was forcibly reduced in volume by an organisation known as the Weather Research Institute. They seeded his cloud base," said the King.

"Apparently Hammerhead is now on a vendetta against this Weather Research Institute and its founder," said the Princess.

"It won't be the founder dear, he's dead and long gone. It will be the current head. A man named Jack Winter. Vendetta, you say?"

"Yes, Father, and that's against our code!"

"Yes, it certainly is. Are you sure of your facts? How do you know this?"

"His Windlet overheard him swearing vengeance on Jack Winter, his family and everyone else associated with this Weather Research Institute."

"Well, we'll have to stop him!" said the King.

"It's more than just him, apparently. As we speak he's enlisting a hurricane and some twisters to help him with his vendetta."

"I'm thinking you know too much, dear. Where are you getting this information from?"

"Well, Father, a few years ago I was drifting over the earth when I saw a young Fluffy who was very upset. He had been separated from his Windlet... anyway, in short I helped him, and, well to be honest, I thought he was rather cute." She smiled at her Father. "*So*! I told him that if he was ever in any danger again, to contact me."

The King gave her a questioning glance: "And is he in danger?"

"Well no, but he thinks Jack Winter and his family are ..." She trailed off, searching around for something that would seem more important to the Cloud King than a bunch of humans. Ah! She continued: "… and he was desperate to report a breach of our code to you!" She wasn't sure that sounded convincing enough.

"There's no doubt about it. He has to be stopped," said the King. He gave the Princess a wry smile. "So what are you going to tell your *little friend* then, dear?"

"That we will stop them from carrying out their vendetta."

"Well, it may be more accurate and more prudent to say we are going to help Jack to stop them, rather than *we* are going to stop them!"

"Yes, Father, a much wiser message."

The Princess didn't want her Father to see she was really in a rush to tell Fluff, so she stood there for a second or two.

"Well, go on then, go and tell him!"

She hurried back to Fluff.

It was nearly a full day before the Princess returned. Cindy knew her place now and quietly flew away out of earshot.

The message the Princess returned with, certainly in the beginning, was not at all as clear as Fluff would have liked.

"Well Fluff, we have a lot to consider here. Let's take it a little bit at a time and see what you think. On the one hand, humans are doing many things that are bad for the world: we see ice caps melting, the sea rising, we see animals in distress – the polar bear for example. In fact, humans are slowly using up all the resources on the planet and a large number of them just don't care.

"On the other hand, humans have only just realised the damage they are causing and to be fair to them, now they have realised what they are doing, some of them are working towards putting things right. Jack Winter is one of these 'good' humans."

Fluff was stunned. How did she know his name? He had never mentioned it.

"Excuse me," Fluff said, "how do you know his name?"

"It's a little hard to explain, Fluff, you're a rather intelligent cloud. You must be aware of *our* cloud computer."

"Yes."

"Well, the humans have invented their own. It's not like the sort of cloud computer we know, but we can talk to their cloud, which told me Jack Winter's name. The humans do not know we can talk to their cloud and it is important that it remains that way. Their cloud is very young and nowhere near as intelligent as ours, but they are getting there, and in some areas they know more than we do. So they can be very helpful to us. We have studied the events leading up to Clyde's death and do not hold Jack Winter responsible. He was only defending his people at the airport and so the actions he took were actually forced upon him.

The cigar shaped pods you have seen are what the humans call seeding canisters. They hold materials which when deployed calm the atmosphere. This seeding does not destroy individuals within the storm, it simply frees them from the storm's grip: a result we find particularly pleasing. As for making clouds, well it's not that simple. What Jack Winter is trying to do is strengthen small clouds, so that they can reflect more sunlight back to the Sun and away from the Earth. If he succeeds this would keep the Earth cooler, and help to slow down global warming. So we believe what he's doing is for the benefit of us all, both Cloudkind and mankind. We will therefore help to defend him against Hammerhead and the others."

Fluff was ever so pleased at this news.

"But how can you help him?"

"We cannot tell you, Fluff, you would not understand."

Fluff was a little disappointed with that reply.

"Can Cindy and I help in any way?"

"Yes, there is one thing you can do that we cannot. You can warn us if there ever comes a time when there's immediate danger to Jack Winter's family – will you do that?"

"Yes, but why the family? What about Jack himself?"

"We'll be taking care of Jack, but we need *you* to take care of the family."

"Cindy and I will do this," said Fluff.

"I need to go now and prepare for the events that may follow. We are in your debt, Fluff. Thank you for letting us know what has been going on and the dangerous nature of the threat to come. We will meet again soon." And with that the Princess was gone.

'How does she do that?' thought Fluff as he called Cindy.

Cindy was well out of earshot this time and did not return for another hour.

"Has she gone?" asked Cindy.

"Yes, and we need to get back to our warmer climate."

'I should say!' thought Cindy.

And with that, the two of them set off for Florida.

As they headed back south, Fluff was feeling very pleased with himself. First and foremost he'd arranged some additional protection for the Winter family. Secondly, he felt justified in bringing it to the attention of the Princess. She had actually said she was in his debt! Wow! It *must* have been the right thing to do. But thirdly, and much more important to Fluff on a personal level, was the fact she had said they would meet again.

Fluff couldn't help thinking how little he knew of the world. Humans having their own type of cloud, wow!

The trip north had been a real education.

Fluff didn't want to fly over the desert again. He'd lost a fair amount of weight and at one point had nearly dried out completely. Going back through the desert would also mean Cindy having to blow against the prevailing Windlets. No! Crossing the desert again wasn't a good idea at all.

Cindy, on the other hand, was eager to show Fluff Scraper's handiwork.

"Look Fluff, we'll not do the whole desert trip, we'll just go in far enough to see one or two of Scraper's carvings. Then we'll come back out on the double and take the long way round."

"OK, how far in do we need to go?" asked Fluff.

"Not too far. You can almost see it from the edge of the desert."

They were nearly twenty miles into the desert before Fluff saw the first of Scraper's carvings.

"What do you think?" asked Cindy.

"It's unbelievable that a little Windlet could do all that."

"Well he did have three thousand years."

"That's how he did it! Wow! I thought it must have taken a long time." The words came from a voice behind Cindy and Fluff.

"Show yourself, Windlet," said Fluff.

The Windlet swept past them both and scraped the sides of one of the carvings with sufficient force that small rock particles fell from the surface.

"What was the name of this Windlet?" said the new voice.

"Scraper," said Cindy.

"Then I'll be 'Scraper the Second'; I've been wondering what to do with myself since I lost my Fluffy. I was thinking about spinning up but this is much more interesting."

"And longer lived." said Fluff.

"Quite so," said Scraper the Second

"Well, we must be on our way," said Cindy, "we only came out here to have a last look at what Scraper did."

"Bye then."

As Cindy and Fluff left the desert, Cindy remarked: "It's nice to know Scraper's work will be remembered and continued."

"I totally agree."

Fluff and Cindy knew that taking the route back over the prairies, rather than continuing through the desert, was a very long way round. However, it was a much more sensible route from Fluff's perspective. It would obviously take much longer, but return time wasn't really a problem. If Hammerhead was going to get help from a hurricane, that alone would take a month or more to organise, so they had plenty of time.

Fluff and Cindy were nearly half way home when again they noticed something strange below. There were some very strange shapes in the wheat fields, extremely complicated shapes. Fluff asked Cindy to take a closer look. As she came back up she told Fluff what they were: "The complicated lines are just wheat stalks lying down as if someone had just pushed them to the ground."

"They're crop circles," came a voice from out of nowhere. "I use them to solve complex equations for the Pearl Institute."

"Not another Windlet out of the blue! Show yourself," said Fluff.

And the Windlet obliged by creating a design in wheat, right before his eyes.

"What's your name?" asked Cindy.

"Equation," replied the Windlet.

"Oh! I like that name," said Fluff.

"Thanks."

"Have you done all this stuff?"

"Yes, all of it."

"But doesn't the farmer get a little cross with you?"

"Doesn't seem to. He does bring a lot of people here to see them but they don't understand what they mean."

"Why haven't the inspection teams stopped you?" asked Fluff.

"I have special dispensation from the Cloud Hierarchy for the work I do here."

"But I'd have thought the humans would suspect a high degree of intelligence behind such displays."

"Yes they do, but rumours were spread early on to deflect their suspicions."

"What do you mean?" asked Cindy.

"Well, we suggested these designs were extra-terrestrial and so most humans think space ships are at work here."

"Well that's just plain silly," said Fluff.

"Not to the humans, it isn't."

"And what do all these shapes mean?" asked Cindy.

"They're equations. Well, actually sometimes they're solutions to equations, rather than just the equations themselves."

"What's an equation?" asked Fluff.

"Oh, I see!" Equation rolled his eyes "Not the brightest Fluffy on the planet then."

"What do you mean?"

"Well, equations solve problems; if you've got a problem then I have an equation to help solve it."

"OK, then how do I stop getting fat?" asked Fluff.

Cindy just laughed.

"Your size will be fixed unless your vapour intake is greater than your evaporation rate – at which time you will get bigger. You will need to regulate your water vapour intake rate or ensure your evaporation rate matches your intake. You could try precipitation, this would ..."

Equation was almost immediately stopped by Fluff. "Look, just forget I asked; anyway, who is the Pearl Institute?"

"The Pearl Institute is not a *who*, it's a *them*, a collection of the Cloud Hierarchy that keeps an eye on all of us clouds to make sure we behave – they're a sort of weather control service."

"Come on Fluff, this is far too complicated for *me*." said Cindy.

"In a minute, Cindy." Fluff thought for a moment. "Can you control hurricanes?"

"No, I can't; I could help with the equations that might be needed to do that, but that's all."

"You're obviously a very intelligent Windlet," said Fluff.

Equation was beginning to warm to this cloud.

Fluff continued: "Couldn't you figure out how to slow down some of these hurricanes? They cause so much damage to us all, you know, not just humans."

"Fluff, you're a nice guy, but it would take more facilities than I have at my disposal to do what you ask."

Equation could tell that Fluff was despondent but there was little he could do to help.

"OK, Equation. It's been nice talking to you," Fluff nodded in Cindy's direction. "I'd better go."

"No problem. Sorry I can't help. All the best though."
"All the best to you too," said Fluff.

Fluff and Cindy carried on moving south.

- Chapter Seven -

Hammerhead and Jack Make Plans

Hammerhead was seething with hate. How could a mere human reduce him, the great and renowned Hammerhead, to a snivelling cold shower? His anger fuelled his growth as he purposefully absorbed smaller and weaker clouds once more.

What a fool he'd been to doubt Cutter; Cutter had never let him down in the past and hadn't this time. It was his overconfidence that had let him down, although he wasn't about to admit that to any passing cloud or Windlet. Cutter had specifically warned him of the power of the human called Jack and he had disregarded the warning, totally underestimating Jack's capabilities. He should have known better.

He had now seen a demonstration of the human's power and it was awesome. He had touched the instruments of his own destruction, so he knew what had done the deed. But in the long term the humans were at a disadvantage since they had no idea that the storm they had overcome was intelligent. He felt sure that, with this element of surprise, he could defeat this human once and for all. I'll bring those humans back down to earth with a bang, he thought.

How to muster the forces required was a problem. He wasn't strong enough at the moment to face another battle. He'd just lost Clyde, the best twister he'd ever had, and Cutter wasn't talking to him because he'd warned him of the danger and had just been ignored. All in all, not a good starting point for a war.

Getting twisters wasn't going to be a big problem. For a start, they're always ready to be spun up for a decent run against humans, and secondly, contracting them for the job at this particular moment was going to be a flight through the park. This was because the annual Twister Games were due to start in a couple of weeks' time and he'd seen the latest ads on Cloud TV. There was a group of twisters called the Tornados Four that interested him greatly. No, the real problem was getting in touch with a Hurricane about to run in from the Atlantic; because Hammerhead knew that's what it would take to overcome these humans.

Hammerhead was deep in thought: I'm going to need overwhelming storm power. This human is going to come out fighting, I need to ensure that we can absorb his attacks and still fight back. Besides, the storm surge from the hurricane will give us an added advantage in helping to destroy his research facilities – the ones in those hangars close to the airport. Even more satisfying would be the destruction of Jack Winter's house and family. Hammerhead cheered up visibly with that thought. It should be a good show.

The order in which to do all this was obvious. The first priority was to contact the Hurricane because it would take about a month for the hurricane to cross the Atlantic. Hammerhead didn't want to wait more than a month for the next attack. He felt the venom might dissipate if a long period of time elapsed and he wanted to savour his revenge. The only way to do this was by using the electric pulse and the only way to use the electric pulse was to build up to storm force again.

*

Human knowledge of the electric pulse (humans call it lightning) is, in general, very poor. For example, most humans think that lightning never strikes twice in the same place. This is incorrect. Most humans also think that lightning always finds the easiest path to ground. This is also incorrect. In truth, most of the time, lightning doesn't go to ground; it goes up or towards another cloud.

The generation of the electric pulse within a storm cloud is much more complex than the human species understands. Lightning bolts that hit the earth are simply misfires or charge balancing pulses so that the head of the cloud can direct the important bolts of lightning upwards, towards space.

Now why would he want to do this? I hear you ask. Well, you need to think of this being like your long distance telephone calls. By doing this the storm head can send messages into the Great Conveyors and thus send messages all around the world. Using the same technique he can also receive messages from all around the world.

Humans call the Great Conveyors 'Jet Streams'. These winds are simply a direct result of a feud between two Windlets. A long time ago, you could say that the wind was, well, a little bit fiercer than it is today. At this time there were two brothers, very speedy guys, who were definitely the fastest winds on the planet. Now the faster a wind goes the crazier are their thoughts. It's just that the speed gets to them. It's intoxicating, a bit like when the head of the thundercloud grows in strength.

Anyway, not being satisfied with the label 'one of the fastest Windlets on the planet', both brothers wanted to be the fastest. So after much discussion and a heck of a lot of arguing, they decided to have a race. In order not to influence the outcome, they couldn't afford to get in each other's slipstream, so they decided to go opposite ways around the *earth. One would take the northern hemisphere, the other the southern hemisphere. And so the race began.*

The first few times around the earth they were neck and neck. There was no clear winner, so they increased their speed accordingly. After many, many circumnavigations of the planet they had changed. The speed had changed them so they didn't even know who they once were. Now, they carry on endlessly racing around the earth, still varying their path to try to be faster and faster than before.

Once Cloudkind had made the discovery that you could, by using the electric pulse, communicate with the Great Conveyors and send messages around the world, the Cloud Hierarchy asked for three volunteers to become additional conveyors. One around the North Pole, one around the Equator and a further one around the South Pole. Strangely enough, there was no shortage of volunteers. The three chosen were: Particle2, Quasar and Breezy3. I mention these names out of respect for the life they gave up for the service of Cloudkind.

Once these three additional conveyors were in position, the increase in the volume of message traffic was enormous. As a result, somewhere in the world, and I mean 'twenty-four, seven', you will always find lightning taking place.

To send the message to the hurricane, Hammerhead would have to grow himself to storm force proportions again, send the message by electric pulse to the Great Conveyor and hope at least one hurricane, at the African end of the Atlantic, would pick the message up.

He would then have to shrink back down again because there's no way a full-blooded thunderstorm would be allowed into the twister games.

Once he'd contacted a number of twisters at the games and the games were over, he could re-inflate to storm size and see if a hurricane had replied to his message and taken up the challenge.

The timing was just right to fit all that in within the next four to five weeks.

So Hammerhead proceeded with stage one of his plan: to grow into a storm large enough to generate enough electric pulse energy to send his message.

*

Jack was in the WRI hangars talking to Colonel Oliver Price of the 53rd Weather Reconnaissance Squadron (WRS). 'Ollie', as his friends liked to call him, was a tall, thickset man with brown hair and brown eyes, which seemed to match exactly the brown leather jacket he was wearing. The jacket sported a badge on the left side, at chest height with the words 'Hurricane Hunters' arched over the top and '53rd Weather Reconnaissance SQ' arched beneath a logo. The logo showed a hurricane shape in red, and above it an ascending blue airplane being chased by a yellow lightning bolt. Jack always thought this logo most appropriate.

The overall effect of Ollie in his brown leather jacket reminded Jack of the John Wayne movies he'd watched as a child.

"When are you up and running again, Ollie?"

"Well, we don't really close down, Jack, we just fly winter missions in other areas. We don't tend to worry about the Atlantic outside the hurricane season. This year we'll be operational a little earlier than usual. That's because we need to test your kit, prior to the start of the season, on June 1st.

"So you'll be fit to deploy seeding pods, if required, right from the start of this season?"

"Yep! Certainly will, we have your system fitted on all ten WC-130J's."

"Stop talking letters to me Ollie, do you mean the Hercules?"

"Sure do! The finest hurricane hunters there are."

"*Yeah* – have you enough fully loaded seed pods?"

"Yep! Enough for about four drops."

"Is the 53rd still flying out of Keesler Air Force Base during the hurricane season?"

"Yep, we've been moved around a little in the past but I think we'll be at Keesler for a while, from now on."

Hurried footsteps could be heard in the corridor. Bill appeared at the doorway: "Come and look at the Doppler radar, Jack. I think that thunder storm we tackled earlier is rebuilding."

Bill was the youngster of the WRI team, fresh out of college and eager to learn. His enthusiasm for the job was unsurpassed within the team.

Jack and Ollie accompanied Bill to the radar screen.

"Well, I'll be..." said Jack, "there must be more energy in the atmosphere than I thought."

"Should we go after it?" asked Bill.

"I can't," said Jack. "I have an Admiral coming to talk to me in about half an hour and a Three Star General an hour after that; do you want to tackle it yourself Bill?"

"Can do!" Bill was quite excited at the prospect of being in charge for a change.

"Bill, take Sam in Aero-One, he has more experience than the other two. I don't think you'll need more than one plane. The storm hasn't had time to fully develop yet."

"OK! Jack, see you later," and with that Bill left the room.

"Well I'd better shoot as well, Jack. You really should

have some decent aircraft, you know, not those silly little run-arounds."

"Couldn't afford your pilot's wages, Ollie, never mind the planes as well," Jack held his hand out for the handshake; Ollie duly responded.

"I'll see you again in a few months, Jack. Give my love to Mary and Emma; rumour has it you have another baby girl these days."

"Yes, Ollie, her name's Sarah, you'll have to come and see her next time you're in town."

"Will do," and with that the Colonel left the building.

Jack pressed the intercom. "Cynthia, has the Admiral arrived yet?"

"Not yet Sir!"

"Has Bill left?"

"He's airborne, Sir!"

"OK!" Pity, Jack thought, he would have gone with him if he had known the Admiral was going to be this late. He went over to see Lewis at the coms monitor.

"Has Bill called in yet Lewis?"

"No Sir, do you want me to contact him?"

"No, I'll talk to him later," Jack didn't want to have Bill think he was keeping an eye on him. He paced up and down. The intercom sounded:

"Admiral Parks is here now, Sir."

"Send him in, Cynthia, send him in!" Jack walked quickly back to his office.

The Admiral knocked on the door; Jack had just arrived there himself and was still standing.

"Admiral, come in, come in, have a seat."

Clean-shaven and tanned with dark hair, in full uniform and with all the gold braiding glistening, he looked the epitome of a naval officer.

They shook hands.

"Hello, Dr. Winter, pleased to meet you." He sat down, placed his briefcase on his knee, opened it and started to remove some documents.

"Well, what did the Navy think of my proposals, Admiral?"

"You have a large number of very high level friends, Dr Winter and so we took your proposals very seriously. So much so that we have a ship ready for your inspection, with the modifications you required, already in place."

"You're joking!" Jack couldn't believe his ears. To get a ship so quickly without having to argue his case for a good twelve months! He couldn't have been more pleased. "You can't be serious!" he exclaimed again.

"Well, to be truthful, Dr. Winter, the National Centre for Atmospheric Research in Boulder asked us for a very similar research ship nearly a year ago. So the news is even better than you think."

"What do you mean, Admiral?"

"We already have five ships down at the docks, fitted with Flettner Rotors."

Flettner Rotors were seen by most in the scientific community as a possible way to progress onto ships that would one day sail remotely.

"Wow, you're taking the threats seriously then?"

"Very much so. However, your research team is only allowed one of these vessels, Dr. Winter. The Boulder team are to have the other four."

"One will do just fine, Admiral. But what about the crew?"

"You have a crew, all five come with a crew but I must warn you, the ship is an old re-fit, it's not much to look at!"

The last sentence didn't even register with Jack. He

was too excited with the news.

"Can I take a team down to see her tomorrow?"

"Yes, the ship is the Lancelot. Her Captain is Brad Johnson; I'll contact him and tell him to expect you tomorrow morning. Say, around 09:00 hours?"

"Yes, tell him there'll be three of us, one of which will stay aboard."

"OK, Brad will discuss any further details with you tomorrow, I'm afraid you have to sign for her, Sir ... just here!"

Admiral Parks handed the document to Jack.

Jack signed the papers and the Admiral placed them in his brief case.

"Well, it's been a pleasure meeting you, Dr. Winter."

"And it's been a pleasure meeting you, Admiral. You have brought good news."

The Admiral shook Jack's hand and then left.

The moment the Admiral walked through the door, Jack remembered Bill.

Jack shouted through to Lewis: "Any news from Bill yet, Lewis?"

"Not yet, Sir!"

There had been no transmissions from Aero-One since they'd left for the growing storm, which was too much to bear.

"Raise him, Lewis," Jack said, as he walked into the coms room. Jack couldn't wait any longer and anyway he had an excuse to call him now.

"Base-Camp to Aero-One, Base-Camp to Aero-One, do you read?"

"Receiving you loud and clear, Lewis; what can we do you for?" replied Sam.

"Sam! Jack would like to speak with Bill."

Bill came on the coms, "Jack?"

"I've just had some good news, Bill. We've got a Flettner Ship."

"Wow, that's fantastic news."

Jack quickly switched the conversation.

"Have you reached the storm yet?"

"About forty minutes away."

Cynthia's voice interrupted: "General Grahams is here, Sir."

"Bill, I'll have to go, speak with you later."

"OK, Jack! Good news about the ship!"

Jack went back to his office.

"Send him in, Cynthia."

The Three Star General walked into Jack's office. His demeanour was much more officious than Ollie's or Admiral Parks'.

"Good afternoon, Sir," he said, removing his overcoat and cap.

"Good afternoon, General."

"I have orders to try to accommodate you, if it is at all possible to do so, but no one has informed me as to the nature of the task."

"That's because I haven't told anyone about it yet. Come with me General, I'd like to show you something."

They walked out of the office to the other side of the hangar and through a door into what looked like a large storeroom, its main contents being silver coloured, cigar shaped cylinders. Jack got hold of one of them.

Jack wasn't overly keen on being too official, especially when he was trying to create lasting partnerships between all the services and his Weather Research team, so he tried to introduce a friendlier approach during their conversation.

"This General.... by the way, my name's Jack, and yours?"

"Steve, Sir."

"Just call me Jack. Is it OK if I call you Steve?"

"No problem." Steve nodded questioningly towards the pod.

"Oh yes, this is a seed pod. We drop these cylinders into storm clouds to reduce the intensity of a storm."

"And you want me to fire them into the clouds!"

"Got it in one!"

"They're too flimsy, Jack. They would never survive the charge impact or the acceleration."

"No, I understand that but could the contents of this pod be loaded into a shell that would explode at a specific altitude, releasing what's inside?"

"Yes, we have a shell that would do the trick but they're expensive. Your current method is much more practical."

"Ha! Yes, I understand that but I'm *not* considering using this method as the prime delivery system. This would be ... let's say, an emergency back-up option."

"In that case the answer is a definite yes."

"Well, if such an emergency arose, what would you estimate your response time to be?"

"So long as we had the fill, we could turn around the shells in a few hours but that's assuming the emergency happened when our shell making facilities were operational. Transporting the shells and summoning the gunner crews to the appropriate firing positions would take additional time."

"It's obvious then that we need a reserve of shells ready to go. Could you arrange for some to be produced?"

"Yes! We would need to arrange test firings anyway. What sort of quantity are you talking about?" asked the General.

"Around forty, plus ten for test firing?"

"That sounds reasonable, Jack. Do you want me to

make the necessary arrangements?"

"I think it would be wise. Yes please."

General Grahams added: "Let's say an emergency arises. How would I know it was a significant event? One where you would need our *emergency* service."

"Good point, Steve." Jack thought for a moment.

"We'll use a set of code words, Steve, let's say '*Extreme Weather Event*'. That should do it!"

"Sounds sensible to me."

"I'll get Cynthia to organise getting the 'fill' down to your base over the next few weeks. Would you like a coffee?"

"No, I'm fine, duty calls." The General rose and started to put his coat on. As he grabbed his cap he added: "Are there any shelf life problems?"

"No, none at all."

"Right then, I'd better get on my way – I'll see myself out."

"It's been nice talking to you, Steve."

"Glad we can help."

"Make sure you give Cynthia your emergency telephone number before you leave."

"Will do!"

At that, the General left.

Jack went immediately into the coms room. "Raise Bill again, Lewis, please."

Lewis was already on to it: "Base-Camp to Aero-One, Base-Camp to Aero-One, do you read?"

"Receiving you loud and clear, Lewis; what can we do ya for, this time?" said Sam.

"Me again Sam," said Jack. "Have you reached the storm yet?"

"Just about to enter it. Bill says it's behaving in an odd manner."

"Put Bill on, Sam."

"Bill here, Jack"

"What do you mean, it's behaving in an odd manner, Bill?"

"Well, for the size of the storm there seems to be more than the usual amount of lightning." There was a crackle on the coms, "Entering storm now."

Hammerhead could feel the plane entering his space. He had sent his message early, so that he could accept more calmly what was going to happen to him. This time he wouldn't resist the seeding. He wouldn't resist it for two reasons: one was the fact that he now wanted to be much smaller in size for the twister games but the other more important reason was that he wanted to sense more clearly what happens when a cloud is seeded. It might help in the fight at a later date.

As for Aero-One and Bill, well they had a much smoother ride than normal through the storm cloud. The seeding went perfectly. The storm broke up as expected and the team flew back to base. Bill was thinking that he'd just witnessed a very unusual seeding experience, with far too much lightning and far too much calm, but he quickly forgot about the lightning. The Flettner Rotor ship was now uppermost in his mind. He'd heard about Flettner ships and seen photographs of them but he'd never seen one for real, so he was looking forward to the experience.

The next morning Jack and Bill, with Mike carrying his suitcase, went down to the harbour to see their new ship. There were five ships lined up on the quayside, all of which were looking a little worse for wear. The two Flettner Rotors on each ship made them look very odd.

The Captain of one of the ships was giving orders to several seamen as the three approached:

"Hello there, Dr Winter I presume?"

"Yes, and you are?"

"Brad Johnson, I was told to expect you."

The two of them shook hands.

"Hello Brad, which one's ours?"

The Captain pointed to the last ship in the line, which looked like it was the last one in every way possible. The name Lancelot was on the stern and sides of the vessel. The WRI Team were less than impressed.

"She's a bit of a rust bucket, Captain!"

Brad Johnson was a mountain of a man, with full moustache and beard. Through it all shone a red face that beamed confidence and joviality. He brushed the remark aside.

"She just hasn't been painted yet. We pulled her out of dry dock because the Admiral said that your report and the Boulder team's implied there was some urgency and with the hurricane season about to start, we thought we'd better start the sea-trials as soon as possible. We can always do a paint job during the breaks."

"Well I can't argue with that, Captain."

"So are you coming out to sea with us, Dr Winter?"

"Just call me Jack, Captain. The Doctor thing is only for people outside the team. No! I'm afraid me coming along isn't possible at present, I've got too much going on. But Dr Andrews..."

Dr Andrews interjected "Mike, to you Captain."

"Mike will be joining you until I can reorganise my schedule; I'll be keeping a close eye on how things are going though."

At that, the Captain smiled and gave the research team a detailed tour of their new acquisition.

Mike Andrews was one of Jack's trusted inner-circle. They

had met during Jack's time at college and both of them had shown an interest in studying violent weather events. At one time they had spent a whole summer storm chasing together. When Jack went off to study meteorology, Mike had gone off to study engineering. But even though they'd lost touch for some years, Jack never forgot their stormchasing adventures.

The year Jack was promoted to head honcho at the WRI, the chief engineer retired, so Jack got in touch with Mike to see if he would be interested in the job. Mike was so enthusiastic about joining the WRI team he was down the next day for the interview.

Just a few years ago Jack could have hired Mike over the phone but these days he had to follow the correct procedures and an 'interview' had to take place. Mike was going to get the job regardless and became the first person Jack hired.

So when it came to deciding on whether the Flettner Rotor ships would be up to the job or not, Mike was *the* man to do it as far as Jack was concerned.

As Jack and Bill were about to leave, Mike took Jack to one side and said in a quiet voice: "Look Jack, one ship isn't going to be enough if things get out of hand."

"Yes, I know. When the other team arrives, have a word with whoever's in charge. Try to get a co-ordinated approach. As a minimum, see if you can persuade him to stay within fifty miles of our vessel, especially during the early part of the hurricane season. Oh! And try not to have more than one ship in dock at any one time."

"Will do!" said Mike, relieved that he and Jack were in one mind regarding ship deployment.

Hammerhead's plans were also coming together quite nicely. He'd grown enough to send a general message, via the electric pulse, to any hurricane listening. He'd managed to shrink back to what can only be described as a small cloud, if not the smallest, and he'd experienced seeding again. It was now time to find a twister or two and he knew exactly where to go to do that.

What intrigued him about the recent Twister Games advertisement on Cloud TV was the name 'Tornados Four'. That name suggested there were four tornados used to working together. Now that would be something, wouldn't it!

It was time to get down to the games.

"Cutter!" Hammerhead shouted.

- Chapter Eight -

The Pearl Institute

"I'm worried about the data overflow," said Diamond.

"So the Northern Lights will be a bit brighter tonight, so what?" said Sapphire.

"Well, one day they might crack the code."

"No chance, they're not even looking."

Sapphire and Diamond, who were the Cloud Hierarchy's finest brains, had argued this point for decades. There was, and still is, no way on earth that humans could understand their algorithms, even if they intercepted their intranet signals from 'The Cloud'. As far as humans were concerned, the Northern Lights were just emanations from the sun, something to do with sunspot activity, and absolutely nothing to do with the Pearl Institute's Cloud Computer.

In reality, as all clouds know, the Northern Lights are just data overspill from the Great Cloud Computer. A lot of the equations being run are wave equations, so it's no coincidence that the curtain of light that descends as the aurora is very much wave like.

"Where are Sapphire and Diamond?" asked the King.

"They're tinkering. They're trying to reduce data spill," said the Princess.

"Why do they bother doing that? It does no harm."

"Sapphire is of the opinion that if she can reduce or even stop the data overflow, her results will be more accurate."

"There's absolutely no need. The accuracy is currently at a hundredth of a microsecond, when a tenth of a second would do; and distance is down to a tenth of a nanometre, when a centimetre would suffice."

"Well, they think they could make it run faster," added the Princess.

"There's no need to go faster, either. We can run the simulations two hundred and ..." he'd just realised he didn't know the exact figure ... "Just hang on." He accessed the computer: "286.7 times faster than real time; when just three or four times faster would be quite sufficient. Why do they persist in trying to improve these figures all the time?"

"Diamond also said that if he couldn't control this data overflow then one day it may be picked up by the humans."

This made the Pearl King laugh, "We are at thirty thousand feet, and no one can see us. They have satellite systems up there, looking down on the planet every second of every day and they still haven't found us. We have a host of inspectors down there, checking that no clues of our intelligence are left behind during storm events. No, we won't be found unless we want to be found."

"Well, it gives them something to do, Father!"

"I already have something for them to do, Dear. We are just about to start up our Cloud Computer's new interface so that we can talk to Mankind's Cloud Computer and they should be here."

"Do you want me to go and get them?"

"Would you, Dear?"

"Is it two way?" asked the Princess, changing the subject.

"Is what two ... oh, yes it is! But I've disabled the Human to Cloud Link, for the time being."

"When do we start talking?"

"Now that the humans are awake to global warming, they're trying to model the surface environment of the planet. We obviously have a little bit more experience a..."

"*Yes*! About twenty thousand years."

"Boasting does not become you, Dear! As I was saying, we have more experience than they do, so the intention is to give them our model."

"Have you decided how to do that?"

"I can only think of one way," said the King.

"Which is?"

"We'll pretend to be a scientific institution, maybe an educational establishment that's privately funded, with an uplink and we'll talk to them their way. Via the net, using emails."

"You'll have to be based in some remote place or they'll just want to come and see you. The day they do that, you'll be in big trouble."

"Well that's true."

"Iceland," said the Princess.

"Iceland?"

"That's remote!"

"Right, Iceland it is," said the King.

"So who are you going to send emails to?"

"Now that is a difficult one. First of all I thought to talk to an individual rather than an organisation; that way we would retain some deniability. You know, it's just one man's word that things aren't quite as they seem.

Contacting an organisation such as NASA would be a disaster because they would have the resources to investigate us thoroughly, which might expose the whole ruse.

Then I thought that the type of individual we'd need to talk to would have to be a very well respected scientist. The problem with that is if mankind respected his word then maybe they would believe him if he said that Cloudkind existed. This leaves only one option."

"And what is that, father?"

"It has to be a child!"

The Princess was shocked, "Surely not! A child would never be believed."

"See, you have just said to me the very same words that entered my head when I thought of the idea. A child would not be believed, that is precisely what we want.

You see, we only need the child to believe us and once she does then she will do what we need her to do. But if she is discovered and she tells the authorities that we exist, no one will believe *her*. Absolutely perfect!"

"Father, you've started calling this child 'she'. Have you someone in mind?"

"Yes, quite a coincidence really. Her name is Emma Winter, the daughter of Jack Winter, the eldest daughter of the family that Hammerfist vowed to destroy."

"Hammer*head*, Father. His name was Hammerhead," the Princess said in desperation, and then, "Why her?"

"I would have thought the choice was obvious. She has an extremely high IQ and she is computer literate. In fact, she's always on her computer day and night. If she's not talking to her friends then she's doing research to help her in her future career."

"Which is, father?"

"To be a meteorologist on TV, so ... she has a fundamental interest in the weather and a father that can influence the way that mankind tackles global warming. She is a perfect fit. Look, Jack Winter has a computer model. It's not as good as NASA's but it's not too primitive either. He runs his model on his home network, linked to his systems at work. Now guess who has access to that network?"

120

"Emma Winter?"

"Exactly. We feed Emma with the data to transform his model, she alters it and if she's found tampering with the model and tells them the truth she'll not be believed. As I said, 'Perfect!'

Not only that, but our modifications to his model will help him fight the out of control storm that's threatened him and his family. What was the name? Ah yes! Thunderhead."

"*Hammer*head, Father. His name is Hammerhead." The Princess continued: "Does Jack Winter have an uplink?"

"Yes, but it's better than that."

"What do you mean?"

"He's using their Cloud Computer to store the vast amounts of data his team collects," said the King.

"So we can feed information directly to him and check directly what he is doing with it, wonderful. It's a perfect match."

The King suddenly realised that the Princess hadn't gone to get his two chief scientists. "I thought you were going to get Sapphire and Diamond for me?"

"Oh yes! I'll go and get them."

The Princess went out to get her 'little gems' as she liked to call them. She found Sapphire and Diamond still arguing over the data spill.

"The King needs to speak with you both."

"Why? I can't get any sense out of her, so what hope does the King have?" said Diamond.

"You wouldn't know sense, even if you found it!" retorted Sapphire.

"Stop bickering, you two." said the Princess, who knew quite well that the arguments between the two were put on for show, rather than being heart felt. She led them back to the Palace.

The Princess returned with Diamond and Sapphire.

"When Fluff was here, he said that Jack Winter was killing and creating clouds. Now we both know that for 'killing' we can substitute 'seeding'. Jack Winter was not *killing* clouds; he was just reducing the energy within the storm, which actually doesn't kill anything. But what do *you* think Fluff meant when he said they were *creating* clouds, Father?"

"Well, it could mean several things. The first candidate is their so-called cloud chambers, where they try to simulate clouds, like Fluff, for research into the electric pulse and other phenomena. Their 'cloud chambers' as they call them, are very primitive and could not in reality create a real cloud. The second candidate has to be their new spray ships. To a Fluffy, what they're doing might look like they're making clouds rather than just thickening or growing them. The third candidate, and the one I consider to be the most likely, has got to be the human's term for their new way of computing. If a Fluffy heard the phrase 'Cloud Computing', then it might appear to him that the humans are making clouds for computational purposes." The King continued: "What other gems did Fluff impart?"

"Fluff said that the seeding killed Hammerhead's twister, Clyde."

"Yes, well the humans used the wrong name when they called them twisters. They should have called them 'bitter and twisted'. I'm sure he won't be missed!"

"Father!"

"I detest those things! I've never believed in killing animals. I think it should be part of our code that we should not kill animals. With the damage the humans do I can fully understand a cloud getting mad at a human but what harm does a horse or dog do to the planet? It's disgusting!"

The Princess fully agreed with what her father was saying, but she remained silent. The arguments for and against twisters were many but it was not for the Royal Family, especially the Princess, to take sides. She looked at her father and said, "I thought you wished to speak to Sapphire and Diamond, Father?"

"Oh yes!" The King turned to his chief scientists.

"It looks, to me as if we will have to start our dialogue with the human race a little earlier than we'd planned."

"Why?" asked Diamond.

"We have an incident brewing that, in effect, mirrors global warming. We all know that our population is predicted to increase and thus the weather is about to get considerably worse over the next ten years. As we have seen in the past, a significant population rise in Cloudkind tends to result in more aggressive behaviour from individuals that make up the population. You've seen the increased queues coming out of the Ethiopian Highlands; storms all wanting to be bigger and better than ever before. Hurricane control can hardly keep a cap on the rage that some of these thunderstorms feel. It never used to be like that. This increase in rage that they feel is entirely due to the increase in energy, which in turn, is entirely due to the higher temperatures. Even the sirens sound louder and they're much more energetic than they have been in the past.

It seems to me, now is the perfect time to try out our plan, since one of our number is out for vengeance."

"No!" said Sapphire in disbelief.

"Yes, we do vengeance now, and I'm convinced that this type of feeling within a cloud will become more and more common, as the earth becomes warmer. The humans would say, he is 'hot under the collar' and that's exactly what global warming is doing to our thunderstorms – making them feel hotter inside, which is showing in their more aggressive posturing."

"So what are we saying here -we need to teach this particular upstart a lesson?" asked Diamond.

"Yes, yes! I think that's exactly what we are saying. We need to help the humans, but at the same time we need to learn how to control our subjects' aggressive tendencies."

"Can we have a name?"

"Hammerhead" said the King.

"What have you discovered about his future plans, so far?"

"Just hearsay from a Fluffy: something along the lines that he's contacted a tornado or two and a hurricane, and is planning to bring all these assets together in one place. The intention is to wipe out someone called Jack Winter, his family, his friends, his co-workers and his place of work."

"Sounds to me like he's *really* annoyed!" said Diamond.

"You could say that," said the King.

Sapphire and Diamond consulted the Cloud Computer.

"Which of the Great Conveyors did he use?" asked Sapphire.

"It would have been Jeremiah. Hammerhead is based around Pensacola; that neighbourhood is under Jeremiah."

"Let's see. Yes! He has been in touch with two hurricanes, through Jeremiah."

"Two, you say?" asked the King.

"Yes, Bonnie and Colin, and from their communications it looks to me as if Bonnie and Colin intend to merge," said Sapphire.

"I agree. The humans think that's impossible, you

know," said Diamond.

"Why's that?" asked the King.

"A scientist called, Fujiwhara. He demonstrated how vortices behaved and how they merged. I'm not sure that he ever said they didn't merge but ever since his research was published humans have assumed they can't," said Diamond.

"So Sapphire... Diamond. What do you think of the plan?"

"It has merits ...," Diamond said, not expecting to be heard over Sapphire's retort. But Sapphire remained quiet and it wasn't like Sapphire to be quiet when she was asked for an opinion. In fact, Diamond usually struggled to get a word in. So everyone knew there was something wrong.

"What's troubling you?" asked Diamond.

"I'm very concerned that we'll make errors," said Sapphire. "Look, if we are going to get this right first time, then we need someone who knows their computer systems much better than we do. We use distributed computing up here, which is fundamentally different from what they do down there. We don't use circuit boards and displays. We use organic remnants. If we have to get involved at their level, we're going to make mistakes, big mistakes. And to put it bluntly, we really don't want any rogue thunderstorm winning the day, do we?"

"*Equation!*" they both said the name at the very same moment, which amplified its significance somewhat.

"Yes, Equation," Sapphire carried on, "He's the perfect choice. He understands both their computer systems and the fundamental differences in the way they think. He understands our systems completely. He wrote a large part of the code. With Equation on board, we should be able to avoid mistakes."

"It's settled then," said the King. "We start making

contact."

"Equation!" the Princess called.

Equation was busy checking an algorithm he'd just created. He was performing a test on the algorithm with his latest data set and things were looking good. He just couldn't be sure until he'd tried the last set of numbers.

From a 'casual observer's' viewpoint, however, the pattern in the wheat field was absolutely superb. It was obvious, from its sheer beauty, that the algorithm had to be correct. The trouble was, it was far too complex for a mere Princess to understand. "Go away, I'm busy."

"We need your help!"

Equation recognised the voice, he didn't need to look up to know it was the Princess; they had worked together many times in the past.

"Just a minute!" he said tersely. He was far too focused on his task to be disturbed by a mere Royal. He'd never been impressed with Royalty ... although he did like *them*, especially the Princess. In his opinion the Royals weren't very smart. In fact, not being interested at all in history, he could never understand why they were Royal in the first place. Anyway, why were Royalty *so* looked up to? They couldn't do simple math, which as far as he was concerned wasn't due to a basic lack of intellect. It was just their lack of interest in the subject that meant they were unable to focus on the subject properly.

He always thought that the main difference between intellectuals and non intellectuals was the first group's ability to focus: to concentrate on a task and see it through to the very end, without being distracted or going off at a tangent. When his computations were done, he would respond to her.

A few minutes later he glanced up. "What is it, Princess?"

126

he asked politely.

"Sapphire and Diamond need your assistance. They want to help the humans fight global warming. In their opinion, the only way of doing this is to give them a more accurate computer model – our model. They need you to interpret their equations, so that the humans can understand and use them."

Equation always thought that 'those two' as he referred to them, lay at the other extreme of the 'smart spectrum'. They were intellectual snobs. Intellectual know it alls. In his words: he couldn't stand the singularities. That was as near to swearing as one could get in his world.

"Is it not a little dangerous to be helping humans?" asked Equation.

"In a way, but we need to do this, because in helping them we are also helping ourselves."

"We don't need help; I've calculated that when global warming takes off, the clouds and their Windlets will benefit enormously. We will get stronger and become more abundant. We..."

"We've done the same calculations, Equation, and on the one hand you're right, we would come out of it better than the humans. But on the other hand, look more carefully at what those calculations really mean: there'll be much more sea than land, so it will be the sea-sirens that will be controlling us. We will be much less able to control ourselves. Our kind will become more violent. Even the most mild mannered of us will become more aggressive. Do you really want that?"

Equation knew what she was saying was right; he had looked into the consequences himself, and he didn't like what he had seen.

"Sapphire and Diamond are more than capable of doing

the job themselves."

"They don't agree with you. They say that they're used to their more sophisticated architecture. Which is a great deal more complex than the human's computer systems. As a consequence they would make fundamental mistakes. This would lead to the humans mistrusting us. We cannot afford for that to happen.

They say you have studied the humans computer systems and are familiar with their architecture. They know that you are the only entity in existence that can understand both parties, and interpret from one to the other. No one else could possibly fulfil this role as well as you." The Princess was hoping that her careful choice of words would find favour with Equation's ego.

"I have things I need to finish here!"

"This is *urgent*, Equation, *very* urgent." There was a new graveness in the Princess's voice.

"OK. I'll need approximately six hours, twenty minutes and 32 seconds, to finish my current task. You may access me after that amount of time has elapsed."

"I'll tell them you will help them and thank you, Equation, thank you very much!" added the Princess.

The following day Sapphire and Diamond called to see Equation.

"Hello Equation," said Sapphire.

"Hello Sapphire, how are we going to do this?"

"We have access to their computers and we could easily re-program their systems if we wished. The trouble is, doing it that way would be invasive and the humans wouldn't trust us afterwards; not only that, we think they would launch a full-scale investigation and we'd eventually be discovered. So we think they need to get hold of our model, somehow."

"What are you proposing to do?"

"Well, we're passing this by you to see if you think it'll work. When it comes to humans we value your opinion.

What we propose is to set up a 'virtual educational establishment'; we'll use the name 'Pearl Institute'. It's for anyone interested in learning about weather systems. We will be situated somewhere very remote so that contact with us is only via email and our internet site. Somehow we'll convince Dr Winter's daughter, Emma, to join – that shouldn't be difficult, as she's very interested in weather related phenomenon.

We'll teach her about modelling and give her our model to 'play' on. Somehow we'll persuade her to substitute it for her dad's. If at any time anyone else tries to get on the site it'll just look like it's gone down and is being repaired. The site will actually be for the exclusive use of Emma Winter although she won't know this.

What do you think?"

"It won't work."

"Why not? It sounds perfectly logical."

"It is perfectly logical, but there are flaws in the method. I think you need to use a simple model that will initially give the same results as her dad's. Then show her how to improve it. Then after the model has been improved run it against the old one, the one her dad's still using. Show her that the improvements work. That way she'll be able to improve her dad's model slowly and she'll take ownership of the changes. When she eventually shows her dad, she'll just talk about us like any other on-line learning experience.

Equally, her dad may just think she's a genius and not look any further than his daughter for the explanations he needs."

"OK, we'll play it your way, Equation. Will you help us?"

"Yes, but I don't understand how I fit in to this scheme

of yours."

"You've just given us a first class demonstration of how you fit in and why you are needed. You're the perfect intermediary. You know our systems well. You worked on some of the equations we actually use up here. But equally you know their systems and their architecture. You've studied them and probably more importantly you know their ways."

"Yes, I see what you're saying. OK! Let's decide what to give them first. It needs to be something minor in the beginning ..."

A few humans noticed that Equation's crop circles started to become a little more complex during the next few weeks.

- Chapter Nine -

Emma

"So how's handsome Scott today?" Emma was on Facebook.

"Missing my best friend. Nice to hear from you! How's it going Em? Why are you not on Skype?"

"I'm in the study hall, I don't think they would approve of me talking to you face to face at school. Anyway, using the keyboard is unobtrusive – what are *you* up to?"

"Just finished science – *boring*. About to go to the park, play ball with the guys. Did you ask your parents if I could come visit during the summer break? June 2nd is best for me."

"How can science be boring? Yes, they said yes, the guest room's all yours for two weeks beginning the 2nd. Mom said to remind you, though, that you might not get much sleep. Sarah's teething tends to wake her up during the night. Oh! And she also said there'll be no flirting with her eldest daughter while you're here."

"I knew flirting would be out, no problem. As for Sarah, I'd put up with anything to be with my best friend again, wind, rain, lack of food, no TV, no baseball ... well ... maybe not baseball."

"Fine, I knew I'd be second best to baseball!"

"Then the true nature of the world we live in has been revealed to you, wise one. Sorry, Em. Got to go, boys are here. I'll Skype you later!"

Emma returned to her homepage. She was just about to close her laptop down, and go to her next class, when she caught site of a headline in the news section. A headline that no one else could possibly have read, only she didn't know this.

The Pearl Institute, an educational establishment set up by specialists in weather related sciences to train students in the subject, has today predicted that Bonnie and Colin are going to turn into very powerful Hurricanes and, despite the National Hurricane Centre's predictions that the two will go their separate ways, the Institute disagrees and predicts that they will remain on the same path.

It was just a headline but it got Emma's full attention. She logged on to Google and typed in the words: *Pearl Institute*. She was surprised at how many sites Google could find with *Pearl Institute* in their scripts. She didn't expect so many results:

Pearl Fashion Institute
Pearl Institute of Management & Information Technology
Pearl Academy of Fashion
Pearl Institute for Headache & Neurology
Pearl River Fisheries Research Institute
Pearl Harbour Archive
... and the list went on and on.

At last she found what she thought might be the site she was looking for:

Pearl Institute for Weather Research and Education

She clicked on the link and their home page came on the screen. It consisted of a small amount of text against a background picture of a hurricane. There was a small data capture form at the base of the page, and that was it. The text read:

> Based in Akureyri, Iceland, the Pearl Institute is an independent, non-governmental, non-political, non-sectarian, non-profit making organisation, dedicated to the education of students studying the world's weather.
>
> Our contributing scientists are scattered throughout the world. In fact, we have data logging facilities located in every country on earth, from sea level to the highest known mountaintops.
>
> Membership is free but is restricted to the scientific community of climate scientists and their students. If you are interested in becoming a member please fill in the form below.

The 'Form' asked for an email address, name, age and a brief description of any work undertaken in relation to climate science and a brief synopsis explaining why you would be interested in joining.

Emma didn't think for one minute she'd be allowed to join such a prestigious organisation, but she sure was going to give it a try. She duly completed the form and stressed that, being the daughter of the best environmental scientist in the world, she wanted one day to follow in her father's footsteps.

She waited for a few seconds, expecting to see the usual automated response but was surprised to be instantly signed up:

> The Pearl Institute has accepted you as a student. Your first training module will be emailed to you shortly. Please look in your email folder for the module and your first assignment.
>
> Welcome

She looked in her email folder and within a few seconds the email she was expecting arrived. This was exciting stuff for Emma. Her normal class schedule, which had History as this afternoon's subject, was completely forgotten. She opened the email. The message read:

Welcome aboard, Emma!

Please download the five attachments. The first one is simply the required reading list. This semester we are studying climate modelling. The course you have joined is quite intense and you are joining it part way through the term. The other students have nearly completed attachments one and two and so you need to be reading the literature in attachment one as soon as possible. Judging from your school results you should have no problem with the math, but if you do, or if you have any other questions relating to the course work, contact:

angela.lingstrom@thepearlinstitute.com

Enjoy your reading!

Emma could not believe her luck. Just a chance reading of a press article and she was studying the subject she wanted to base her whole future career on! I wonder how they knew about my school results? she thought – and immediately shrugged it off as a probable connection via a shared database between educational establishments.

She set to work downloading the rest of the attachments and during recess went to the school library to check out books detailed in the required reading list, a number of which she would have to pick up later in the week since the library did not have them in stock.

One of the main attachments was called clim_mod_2.3v6.exe. She was informed that this attachment should only be executed when connected to the Internet as it uses the database stored on the Institute's mainframe.

She was very impressed with how quickly she had been integrated into their 'mail out' system. On the same day she'd joined she had her first 'email alert'.

That was the name they gave to emails about data model improvements that were worth implementing straight away.

That evening she logged on to Skype, impatient to tell Scott what had happened: "I mean instant access, Scott. How much better can you get?"

"Well, your dad is one of the big guns in climate research. He'll have a lot of influence."

"As would yours, Scott. Why don't you join?"

"Me, come on Em. It's definitely not my thing. Are you sure you want me over on the 2nd if you're going to be studying this new stuff?"

"Absolutely! Unlike baseball, you come before my studies ... well, possibly...."

Scott smiled, "I think I need to see Mary-Jane again."

"No way! I'll contact you tomorrow, see you."

"See you, Em."

Mary-Jane Fenton was head honcho of the high school cheerleaders and never got on with Emma. Mary-Jane considered Emma a dork, a bookworm, always at her computer. Emma was a beautiful girl and an ideal candidate to actually be one of the cheerleaders, but she wouldn't join. She thought prancing around in a costume at the side of a baseball game was rather demeaning. No, she'd rather study and be a dork any day!

Mary-Jane, however, had tried everything to get her to join. Nothing could tempt her and in the end she gave up, but this made her dislike Emma even more intensely.

The problem was made worse when all the cheerleaders took to Scott, who was the hunk of the moment. But Scott only had eyes for Emma and this enraged the cheerleaders all the more.

Needless to say, when Scott left for Boulder the whole situation calmed down a little and Emma didn't want it to start all over again.

The following few days saw Emma become more and more engrossed in her new project. She suddenly had no interest in what was happening at school. She'd decided concentration on her new subject was much more important than keeping in touch with her school subjects. Besides, she had already prepared herself for her finals so she was well ahead of the crowd when it came to her normal studies.

When she'd complained to her Mom that she wasn't feeling up to school, Mom had no hesitation in taking her out.

"A week at home will do you no harm," Mom had said.

Most of the time she stayed in her room studying the math or reading the suggested texts. On occasion Mom would disturb her. She would ask her to entertain Sarah for a short time while she did some chore or other. This wasn't a problem, since it helped her sort things out in her head. Sarah's vocabulary was improving too. If you could understand 'Sarah Speak' you would be impressed that she knew the words 'third integral' ... "da da da, urd ingril, gaga..."

Emma was learning the mathematics behind the principles of climate change at a phenomenal rate. It was better than school. Every time she had a problem understanding what was in front of her she had instant help from Angela Lingstrom. It was like having your own genius on tap: anytime, day or night, a response would arrive within two or three minutes of asking for help.

It was now the second week of her skipping school. She had never done this before, so faking illness did not come naturally. It was made even worse because she could see her mother was starting to get concerned. But it had to be done, this was a perfect time to learn the weather prediction algorithms since the hurricane season was about to start and her knowledge would be tested to the hilt during what was predicted to be a busier than normal hurricane season. Besides, she only had to fake the illness for a few more days. Finals were next week and there was no way she would be missing them.

"How's Emma?" Jack asked as he walked through the front door.

"She's feeling a little better. She says she'll probably be OK for next week. I checked with school and they know of nothing-untoward going on there. The principal says she's a star pupil."

"Of course. What's the doc say?"

"He can't find anything wrong with her either. He suggests it may be fatigue. He says if she's doing OK at school then don't worry, let her have her freedom for a while. It will do her good."

"I think we go with the doctor's theory. I don't think there's much wrong with her."

"Do you think we should cancel, Scott? He's due here on the 2nd."

"Gee, I'd forgotten all about Scott coming. Of course, he's here for two weeks isn't he?" said Jack.

"Should we cancel him?"

"Definitely not, I think Scott will be good for her. He won't want to be stuck in for two weeks. Which will mean she'll get some fresh air and be pulled away from her computer for a while. No! It'll be good for her, let him come."

*

By the time Scott arrived Emma had recovered enough to take her finals. Not only that, but she now fully understood why her dad's model was inaccurate and she was just beginning to understand how to modify it to make it much more accurate.

"Good to see you again, Scott," said Mary

"And you, Mrs Winter."

Emma ran up and gave him a hug.

"So this is Sarah!"

Mary turned Sarah so she could see Scott.

"This is Scott, Sarah. He's staying with us for a few weeks." Sarah didn't react.

"Did you have a good flight, Scott?"

"We were delayed a little getting into Memphis, so the changeover was a bit hurried, but otherwise fine. My dad's given me some money to rent a car for the two weeks so you don't need to wait if you don't want to … "

"I'm just sticking around until I'm sure you two have transport, then Sarah and I will be off."

As soon as the car rental was completed, Emma's Mom was true to her word and left them alone at the airport.

Emma and Scott bought food at a local McDonald's drive-through and drove to one of their favourite picnic spots in the local park.

"How did finals go?"

"OK, no problems. It was a bit hard to concentrate on school stuff that week but it was OK."

"Were you really sick the weeks before?"

"No, faked it, couldn't tell you over the net though."

"I guessed as much. Why?"

"I needed time to study for the Pearl Institute."

"Did it do any good?"

"Brilliant! Best month of learning in my life."

"So what are you going to do with all this learning, Em?"

"You already know, Scott. I haven't changed, I'm going to be a meteorologist, obviously. Although I think I need some friendly advice."

"You won't take it."

"I might."

"Well go on then, what's your problem?"

"OK! From what I've learned, my dad's weather model is not accurate and it needs to be replaced before it gets him and the whole WRI team into serious trouble."

"That doesn't sound like a problem, just tell him."

"No! First of all he wouldn't take my word for it and secondly he'd find out why I skipped school."

"So, what's the alternative?"

"Secretly update it."

"Is that possible?"

"Yes, I know how to do it."

"That's fine if you're absolutely sure, and I mean *absolutely* sure that *your* solution is right. Otherwise you would be in big trouble."

"Yes, I know, and with such a complex system how can anyone be absolutely sure about anything?"

"Sounds to me like that's a good enough reason for leaving things alone."

"No! Because *I am* absolutely sure, that my model is better than dad's."

"Are you sure you won't be discovered?"

"It'll be a while before Dad realises. He has a scientist called Bill working on the model. He'll think that Bill is doing all the updates until one day he'll look into it and then ..."

"Something will hit the fan," Scott said.

"Exactly. But by then we'll know whether the equations hold up."

"Sounds like you've already made up your mind, Em."

"Yes, it does, doesn't it?"

That night Emma logged on to the Internet and started updating her dad's model.

- Chapter Ten -

The Twister Games

What is a twister? I hear you ask. Well, a twister is simply a Windlet that has been spun up. The significance here is that all Windlets know that once they have been spun up as a twister, there is no going back. If they slow down too much, they will die. So to volunteer for spinning up is to volunteer for a shorter but more active life. The one thing that makes a twister so dangerous is that he or she knows their life will be short.

Some Windlets that volunteer for spinning up have lost their Fluffy and are effectively souls with nothing left to lose. Others tend to come from the dark side of Windkind and are only too glad to sign up to be killer tornados.

There are a few things about twisters you should know. For one, the head of a thunderstorm would never attempt to spin up a Windlet into a twister unless the Windlet had volunteered. The simple reason for this is that you can't make a Windlet spin unless he wants to.

Not all twisters are full blown psychopaths, some are much more benign; these tend to end up as dust devils or waterspouts.

Interestingly enough, humans have a scale for tornados that apparently stops at 318 miles per hour. This speed generates an F5 tornado. At the end of this scale, humans say that it is just possible to get speeds of up to 379 miles per hour, an F6 tornado.

Humans say, however, that attaining an F6 tornado would be inconceivable. Cloudkind and Windkind aren't so sure. If global warming were to get out of hand, could these speeds be exceeded?

As a matter of interest, I've yet to meet a twister I dislike. They are real characters, even the dust devils, but even they can be fearsome if they so wish.

The twister games take place once a year, in a valley near the missile proving grounds in New Mexico. I can't say the exact location, it's just one of those secrets that has to remain 'clouded in mystery.' Anyway, this particular valley is deserted during test firings of missiles, and so the games are timed to coincide with these events.

Like all winds, twisters like to get together to have a little fun, but unlike other types of wind they are competitive and aggressive.

A long, long time ago one of the Royal Family decided the best way to contain this aggression while still letting them get together occasionally, was to hold a series of games. Thus the annual twister games were born.

The main event of the games is the thirty-mile race. The best eight from the 'Speed Over Ground' trials are chosen to compete in this race.

Over the years, the twister games have become much more than a get together. They determine where in the hierarchy each twister is placed.

There are three levels of twister, dependent on how fast and how accurate the twister is:

The **Play** twisters are generally too weak, too slow and too inaccurate to move to level two. A lot of these twisters end up as dust devils. Their test certificate states that they MUST remain small and harmless to humans.

The **Standard** twisters are larger but tend not to pose a danger to humans. They are much less aggressive than the 'Hardened' type. Their test certificate states that they are allowed to practise on objects and properties, but where *possible they must avoid human contact. Most waterspouts are of this type. Note that the certificate says* **where possible***; it is still rare for humans to get injured with this type of twister, but it is not impossible.*

The **Hardened** *twisters are completely different. They are aggressive and their license allows them to kill – they are the 007s of the twister world.*

When the licenses are issued at the end of the games they will last for one year only. Every twister must re-attend the twister games the following year to re-apply for the licence. Any twister found practising without a current, valid licence will become a 'wanted' twister and will be permanently spun down when caught, that is killed!

Like all games the world over, the twister games have rules – four to be precise. The four rules of the games are as follows:

1. *Rotation Speed – rotation speed must not exceed control velocity. There is no actual speed limit as such, since some twisters can go very fast without losing control, while others can lose control at very slow speeds. If a twister is deemed to lose control of his/her funnel at any time, it will be given a chance to reduce its speed and calm down. The speed at which the twister lost control will be recorded. If the twister exceeds this speed a second time, it will be disqualified from that particular event.*

2. *There is no speed limit over ground in any direction.*

3. *Height and girth are restricted only when the event is running in lanes, since lane markings must be adhered to. Thus any twister wider, or as wide as, the lane markers, risks disqualification. This is because they may interfere with the path of others. This type of disqualification applies only to that specific event.*

4. *Performance Enhancements. The use of performance enhancing materials or objects will lead to
instant disqualification **for the entire games**. The
culprit's licence will be revoked and they will spend
a year as a 'Play' Twister.*

*The inspectors will be responsible for all measurements
and their decision is final.*

Hammerhead timed his arrival at the games perfectly.
All the preliminary stages were over. So all the play and
standard twisters had already left the games. or become
part of the crowd. There were now only two events left:
the final of the darting competition and the great race. As
Hammerhead flew into the games the darting final was
just about to get under way.

He was pleasantly surprised to find that he'd missed all
the preliminaries. To be honest, he was not in the least bit
interested in the games at all; he was there for one reason
only. To find the most aggressive tornados he could find to
wipe Jack Winter, his family and all of his cohorts off the
face of Planet Earth.

As Hammerhead entered the arena he could sense the
heightened atmosphere. The inspectors hung menacingly
over the arena, like a slack ceiling over a tent. He recognised the inspection team, but he didn't think they would
recognise him with his much reduced size. The only other
way he could be recognised was if he accidentally touched
one of his captives. He couldn't imagine any of his previ-
ous captives being at all interested in the twister games.
He sat back and waited for the events to unfold.

The lanes were coloured and the contestants themselves
were also being coloured, with what looked like some sort
of gas. There were eight lanes:

Lane one gold
Lane 2 red
Lane 3 black
Lane 4 orange
Lane 5 silver
Lane 6 blue
Lane 7 yellow
Lane 8 green

Hammerhead found out later that white was not allowed because it was too close to the colour of the sand.

As the colours were applied, it introduced a certain carnival atmosphere to the event. Some of the crowd were in stitches, laughing at the reaction of the competitors to the coloured gas being applied to them.

Some competitors were just stood there taking their colour, some sneezing as a reaction to the chemical, some even squirming as if the chemical was making them itch. The colour remained on the contestant until the winner of the event was announced, at which time all the colours were instantly removed. How the organisers did this little bit of magic, Hammerhead had no idea.

There were no places to be had other than the winner's position. There wasn't a first, second or third place. If you came second you were out, just the same as if you came in last. Winners would go on to the next event; losers would either go home or join the watching crowd.

Because there were only eight colours, this only allowed eight competitors to compete at any one time, and boy did this make the heats drag on. For Hammerhead this would have been more than just boring; it would have been purgatory – a waste of his life! He was sure he'd have enjoyed watching the final of each game, but the heats? He'd rather watch water evaporate!

There has always been one main problem with the twister games: because all twisters are expected to take part, the standard of competitors coming into the games is very variable. Another problem is that the numbers participating are also very high. To take the low-grade entrants out, a few at a time, is, to say the least, boring. The day will have to come when they find a better solution to this early stage of the games.

One of the main worries for the organisers of the games is 'cloud control', that is ensuring that the onlookers don't get too close to each other, especially the cloud crowd. With twisters it's not a big problem because they just tend to spin off each other. With clouds they tend to merge without actually thinking much about it and within a very short time you can have a major thunderstorm on your hands. This obviously would disrupt the games in a big way. So, with a cloud crowd of this size, you can imagine what would happen if the crowd became one entity. It would be something like a nuclear explosion.

Because of this, part of the inspection team monitors the crowd just as intently as the competitors, ensuring that spaces are maintained between the onlookers.

Time for the darting final had arrived. The darting final was the culmination of stage three, game two of the games. The winner would be a strong twister that showed the most accuracy in the least possible time.

The darts were big. Each competitor had six, one metre lengths with a cross section 9cm by 6cm. So the competitors needed to be strong just to lift them.

The objective was to throw six darts through six hoops into the six capture tanks as quickly as possible. The hoops and capture tanks were arranged in a semi circle around the centre of the throw point. The throw point itself was at the end of a 200-yard running track. Each running track was positioned like a spoke on a wheel so that when the competitors were running they couldn't judge who was in the lead. To anyone observing from above, the whole arrangement looked like a set of eight spokes with a fan at the end of each spoke.

A large number of hay bales were placed between the crowd and the competitor's launch pads, in an attempt to catch any stray missiles.

Each competitor was to pick up as many darts at a time as they could. They would then hurl themselves down the 200-yard running track and throw their darts through the hoops. The capture tanks were designed to stop the darts from continuing on their way.

The winner was the twister who got more darts in his or her capture tanks faster than anyone else. In case of a draw, the power of the throw was measured. This was accomplished by measuring the distance each projectile travelled into the capture tank.

"This is the call for the final of the Darting Competition. Competitors to the track please!" came the announcement over the airwaves.

The finalists arranged themselves as their colours determined.

"Clouds and twisters I give you:

In lane one and sporting the colour gold ... Trench-Coat

In lane 2 and sporting the colour red... Sledgehammer

In lane 3 and sporting the colour black, one of the current members of the incredible Tornados Four... Notorious.

Hammerhead gave a little smile. Found one, he thought.

In lane 4 and displaying the colour orange... Pierce-Me.

From what Hammerhead could see, she was the only female in the final.

In lane 5 in the colour silver... Bounty-Hunter

In lane 6 and sporting the colour blue... Stickpin

In lane 7 in yellow it's Times-Up

In lane 8 and sporting the colour green is Your-Choice

There was a slight pause, then the announcer said: "Prepare to start!" Another pause, then: "Let the race commence."

And with that, there was an enormous thunderclap and the game was underway. Sledgehammer was the first to pick his darts up. He'd got all six darts nicely rotating around him as he raced down the track. Notorious was a close second, followed by Bounty-Hunter.

Trench-Coat and Times-Up failed to get all six darts at pick up, which would cost them in the end. Stickpin, Your-Choice and Pierce-Me were hardly in it at all.

Sledgehammer let his darts loose first, followed only microseconds later by Notorious. Notorious seemed to have launched them with a little bit more force, because by the time they passed the rings they were neck and neck. All twelve darts were on target. There was only one other twister in the race and that was Bounty-Hunter. Again, he was only microseconds behind Notorious when he let his darts go. But you could tell straight away that the darts weren't on a true enough path for them all to make it to the capture tanks. Four did go in, but two winged their way past the capture tanks and towards the haystacks near the crowd. One dart buried itself in the haystack while the other seemed to go straight through the stack without slowing down at all; going right through one of the twisters in the crowd.

The crowd suddenly hushed.

The twister with the dart in him just laughed: "Just fresh air fellas, nothing to worry about."

The whole crowd cheered.

Once all the competitors had finished the event there was a lull in the proceedings as the judges came to their conclusion.

The announcement came: "The inspectors deem the final to be a tie between Sledgehammer and Notorious."

The reception from the crowd was mixed, with some cheering and others jeering.

Both contestants bulked up and waved to the crowd.

"The inspectors are requesting the adjudicating team, please!"

Two twisters with measures and calculators entered the arena and paid considerable attention to all six of Sledgehammer's capture tanks. They took measurements and made calculations. Then they moved over to the tanks of Notorious. Again they took measurements and made calculations.

The results from the adjudicating team were then sent to the inspectors for final confirmation. The inspection team handed down the winner's name to the announcer.

"The winner of the final of this year's darting competition is: ..." There followed a long pause, for effect of course... "Notorious!"

The crowd went wild!

As the crowd settled down after the darting final, the announcement for the big race was made:

"The final event of the games will take place tomorrow. All of the final eight competitors and their entourage will restrict themselves to their base camps while the course is being laid out. May I remind you that the inspectors are watching and any infringement will mean disqualification."

Having heard the announcement, Hammerhead made his way from the arena to the main concourse and waited for Notorious to appear.

As Notorious made his way out of the arena, Hammerhead shouted: "Notorious of the Tornados Four!"

Notorious turned to face Hammerhead "That's me... who's calling my name?"

"I am Hammerhead," he said much more quietly, so as to ensure that only those in the immediate vicinity would hear. He certainly didn't want any of the inspection team to know he was present.

"I don't know that name, what do you want?"

"I have a contract for the Tornados Four!"

"To do what?"

"To destroy a human population centre."

Notorious smirked, "It's not possible to do that with a few twisters, no matter how good they may be." Notorious started to spin away.

"I have already contracted a hurricane!" Even though Hammerhead knew that this statement wasn't true, he was gambling that at least one of the hurricanes, on the other side of the great salt sea, would sign up for the event.

"Now that's what I call a show stopper," Notorious turned to face him again, "and why would you want to do this?"

"The target has a device that he uses to eliminate twisters and storm clouds. He is a particularly dangerous human."

Notorious was more and more intrigued by each new revelation. "Then why are you targeting the whole population if you only want one human?"

"Because he has a base there: airfields, laboratories, equipment, his home, his family and his work colleagues. Yes we need to destroy *him*, but we also need to destroy his materials and his progress so far."

Notorious was rather impressed by what he was hearing but couldn't reconcile all this aggression with the mild mannered, unassuming cloud he was conversing with.

150

"And what is your role in all of this?"

"I will be part of the attack team. I have only reduced my size to get through twister games security, so that I could talk to the leader of the Tornados Four. I am normally a Supercell thunderstorm."

"Well, I will go and tell the leader of the Tornados Four that I have just met a thunderstorm, that is going to attack a whole neighbourhood. One who has hired a hurricane and wishes to hire four twisters to help him with his work. Does that sound correct sir?"

"It does," replied Hammerhead.

"You are not leaving anything to chance my friend, are you?"

"Will you take the contract, Sir?"

"I will have to speak with the other three. Leave it with me. You understand that we must complete these games first, in order to keep our Hardened status?"

"I do."

"Then I'll be in touch after tomorrow's final race; enjoy the games, Hammerhead." And with that, Notorious departed.

Hammerhead snarled; he could not possibly enjoy such trivia. The frivolous nature of these games did not impress him one bit. He had more serious matters to attend to.

This wasn't going to be a comfortable night for Hammerhead. He was surrounded by clouds and twisters he didn't know, noises and smells he didn't like and contract decisions still not made.

As the sun set in the distance, the Inspectors were lit up from beneath with a red orange glow that made them even more ominous in appearance. Everyone settled down for the night.

Suddenly there was a series of flashes on the horizon. Several miles away, a distant rumbling followed.

"What's that?" Hammerhead asked his nearest neighbour.

"Just Missile Testing..." the voice dragged slightly at the end, leaving Hammerhead with the distinct impression that his neighbour didn't want disturbing again with silly questions.

"Goodnight all," Hammerhead said with a smile.

There were numerous grunts and moans but not a single 'goodnight' came back.

That night missile testing lasted well into the early hours, so dawn's arrival saw everyone bleary eyed and tired. The final race wasn't due to begin until 11:00 am so Hammerhead took the opportunity to look up the Tornados Four at their home base. He first approached Notorious who, for some reason, wouldn't look him in the eye. He could sense there was a problem.

"Have you mentioned the contract to the other three?"

"Go speak with The Commander," Notorious said as he pointed to the large twister across the boulder field, to his right.

Hammerhead wandered over. "Did Notorious inform you of the contract?"

"Yes he did." The pitch of the tornado's voice was low with a certain boom to it on the lower notes. "However, as his name implies, Notorious is notorious for exaggerating, so I would like you to tell me the contract details; speak clearly please!"

Hammerhead could feel a dark presence here, one even *he* didn't feel comfortable with. He repeated the contract details and added, "maybe Notorious wasn't exaggerating."

The Commander smiled. "When a twister dies, I feel it. You knew a twister named Clyde. Why do I feel that you had something to do with Clyde's death?"

Hammerhead was taken aback by these remarks. How the heck could he know about Clyde's death?

"Clyde was a member of my team when we first tackled Jack Winter; he was killed by the human during the battle."

"It is true that Clyde was attached to a Supercell named Hammerhead. How do I know you are this storm? You look nothing like you're supposed to."

"You only have to touch my Windlet to know the truth."

"You will allow this?"

"I will," said Hammerhead.

The two touched. Cutter could feel his mind being probed. He felt something more, something darker than a twister, and for the first time in his life he was scared.

They separated with a jolt.

"We will take the contract. We will see you after the final race." And with that, the commander called over the other three twisters and the four made their way to the games arena.

Cloud TV couldn't miss the final of the Twister Games. It was far too important to the majority of Cloudkind, especially the male of the species. At the same time, they didn't want to broadcast the whole of the Twister Games, since the majority of it was downright boring.

It was Cloud TV's Bruce Cloudcover who was commentating: "Welcome to the 433rd Annual Twister Cup. We have a star-studded cast with the hardest of the hard in the line up for today's final event of the games.

Amazingly, this year we have the complete set: yes, all of the Tornados Four members competing in this final event. That's one better than they've ever managed before.

I spoke earlier to The Commander about the difference this year."

The broadcast switched to the earlier interview, "Well, I think we're just that little bit stronger this year, It's probably down to global warming, but all four of us are feeling good for this event."

"You'll be competing against last year's winner Max-Spin-Speed. How does that feel?"

"Well, we know Max-Spin-Speed and he's a good competitor, but the race holds no fears for us."

"Well! Talk of the devil, here he is, Max-Spin-Speed!"

The camera turned from The Commander to Max-Spin-Speed.

"Hi there, Bruce!" said Max-Spin-Speed.

"Are you ready for the big event, Max?"

"Of course. It's a little worrying having all four of the Tornados guys in just this one event." He smiled and nodded his head towards The Commander. "But I've beaten them before in the past, so we'll see how things go."

"Are there any of the other competitors that you feel are particularly strong this year?"

"Well, Slip-Stream ran a good second place last outing, so I think he will be strong this year."

"Right, Max, it looks like they're getting ready for the line up." Bruce patted both competitors on their funnels. "Good Luck, both of you." He continued, "Now while the lads are colouring up for the race, let's look at this year's course.

Remember, this race is run for the title of supreme Champion, so no one should underestimate its difficulty. This is not for wimps!

They will be racing for thirty miles overall. Fifteen miles out and fifteen miles back. Besides the canyon turn in the middle of the race, there are six main sections."

Bruce walked over to the side of a large display of the course and pointed to the start:

"The Beginning Straight is around two miles long. This is the same two miles as used in the 'speed over ground trials'. It is absolutely dead straight!

Then we run into the Sand Dunes, around four miles long. This is where competitors will pick-up sand in their funnels. You have to be fit to carry the extra weight and still make progress here.

Coming out of the sand dunes we have the Hill Climb and then descent. This is only a short one and a half miles but it feels like your whole funnel is being squashed under pressure as the terrain rises."

Bruce continued: "Section four is the Town Simulator; this is approximately four miles long. This is intended to simulate a real life situation, *but* in this case they have to do the exact opposite of what their instincts tell them. You see, they have to avoid wrecking the town because any energy they use up in destroying property will slow them down.

Section five sees the tunnels being used for the first time. This is a series of three very short tunnels spread over one mile. Windkind thought that travelling through any kind of tunnel was impossible. That is until fifteen years ago, when the great 'Who-deemed-it' went through a very tall but very short tunnel in the Italian Alps. These tunnels were modelled on his experiences. It should be said that these tunnels are very narrow.

Section six is probably the most dangerous section of all: the Lake. The Lake is only a half-mile across but after all that energy-sapping running, it will be a real strength sapper.

It'll do that in two ways. First, it will fill their funnels with water, which believe me is heavy stuff. Then it will draw the heat energy out of the twister. By the time they leave the lake they'll be at a very low energy level indeed.

155

Then we have the Canyon Turn, some four miles long. This is the mid point of the race. At this point in the race speed is secondary. They have to regain some energy reserves over this stretch before they re-enter the lake. If they don't, it's quite possible they'll exhaust their energy reserves and die long before they reach the other side.

Once they're through the lake it's just a matter of repeating each section in reverse."

Hammerhead was arriving on the concourse as the final announcements were being made.

"This is the final call for the Big Race. Will the finalists make their way to the track please!"

Hammerhead took his place at once; he wasn't planning on missing this one. The rest of the games may have been boring but he had a feeling that this wasn't going to be. This time Hammerhead recognised Notorious in lane one and The Commander in lane five; he still didn't know who the rest of the finalists were but he had no doubt he was about to find the other two members of the Tornados Four.

The largest crowd ever seen at the games had assembled for this race. Everyone knew that the eight were 'Hardened' but this eight were the cream of the hardened, the elite.

The finalists arranged themselves as their colours determined and the voice of the announcer crackled into life.

"Clouds and twisters, I give you:

"In lane one and sporting the colour gold is Notorious, the first of the Tornados Four.

"In lane two, dusted in red is Disaster-Movie.

"In lane three and wearing the colour black is Crime-Scene, the second of the Tornados Four.

"In lane four and sporting the colour orange we have Lightning, the third member of the Tornados Four.

156

"In lane five and sporting silver we have The Commander, the fourth member and the leader of the Tornados Four.

"In lane six, dusted in blue, is Slipstream.

"In lane seven, in yellow is last year's winner, Max-Spin-Speed."

The crowd went wild!

"And last but not least in lane eight, sporting the colour green, we have Night-Rage."

Hammerhead was delighted that all of the Tornados Four were in the race.

In this race all the rules are dumped. That's why the crowd was so wound up. They knew they were about to see a real race, not a game.

The crowd volume increased considerably as the start of the race drew near. Everyone was shouting for his or her hero.

Because Cloud TV had agreed to show up, the organisers had decided to use their expertise for the race commentary. So the commentary the crowd heard would be heard simultaneously, by the TV audience.

The TV announcer said: "Prepare to start!" There was a pause as the contestants prepared themselves.

"Let the race commence."

The thunderclap sounded and the race got under way. Only one of the Tornados Four started well.

Cloud TV:

"It's funnel to funnel in this early stage between Lightning, of the Tornados Four, and last year's winner Max-Spin-Speed. This two-mile straight run is the only part of the race where the contestants stay in their lanes, so expect a bit of mayhem at the end of this stretch."

157

"They're coming up to the sand dunes now and... yes! As we predicted, they're bunching up."

Hammerhead mused that if he had a team of four twisters in this race, nothing would be left to chance and probably a little cheating would be called for... he wondered?

Bruce was pleased his prediction was accurate and continued: "While they're in the sand dunes their objective must be to keep the spin speed low, so they suck up less sand.

All the contestants are in the sand dunes now and all eight funnels have darkened. They'll be pulling masses of weight now and you can see that the stronger twisters in the rest of the pack are catching up to the front two.

Yes, its Slipstream and Night-Rage that are making the running now. Both Lightning and Max-Spin-Speed are losing ground fast. Wait, The Commander, the leader of the Tornados Four, is making headway here. Look at the power in that run! This gruelling surface must be taking its toll. Yes, The Commander is gaining on Slipstream-he's along side him now."

Just as they came alongside each other they touched, and both spun off.

"Oh! My rain cloud! They've touched. Slipstream's a goner and The Commander ... he's getting up. That twister has guts. He can't possibly win from that far back but it looks like he's going to try. Yes! He's keeping in the race and he's still in the running.

The front group are leaving the sand dunes now with Night-Rage as the leader. In second place is Disaster-Movie, followed closely by Lightning and Notorious. Crime-Scene is further back and well out of it are Max-Spin-Speed and The Commander.

They're just starting on the hill climb and the group at the front are looking really tired. It's a very small climb to the top of this hill but you can see the pain they're suffering after that gruelling trek through those sand dunes. We're on the downhill section now and Notorious has just passed Crime-Scene.

The front-runners are now in the town simulator. It looks like The Commander is out of it, he's slipped even further back during the hill climb."

All the twisters were relieved to get to the town simulator and even though the order had changed little, by this time Lightning, Notorious and Crime-Scene were all catching up to Disaster-Movie. In fact, by the time the tunnels were in view, Notorious had overtaken Disaster-Movie and was closing in on Night-Rage.

"As we expected the town simulator was a little on the easy side and there's been no change in the running order, but now the tunnels are coming up. There's not a lot of room in there so we're expecting a difficult stage here."

The tunnel section is just a series of three very short tunnels, however the width of the tunnels is very narrow so care will need to be taken if the contestants are to stay in the race.

"Lightning, Crime-Scene and Disaster-Movie are funnel to funnel, as they enter the first tunnel. Yes! All three have come out of the tunnel with no change in order. Now the second tunnel is looming."

As they entered the second tunnel they were out of sight of the crowd, the inspectors and the TV Crew; Lightning and Crime-Scene took the opportunity to squeeze Disaster-Movie out. Both Disaster-Movie and Crime-Scene tripped.

"Hang on! Something's happened in the second tunnel. I can see dust and debris coming out.

Night-Rage is OK, followed by Notorious. Now Lightning then … Max-Spin-Speed and The Commander. I can't see

Disaster-Movie or Crime-Scene anywhere. Hold it! I've just had a word from the track side. Both- yes, both- Disaster-Movie and Crime-Scene are out of the race!

The remaining runners are entering the lake stage; their funnels have turned white with the water. I'll bet that's cooling them down drastically."

The front-runners came out shivering and entered the canyon turn.

"Judgement is going to be key here. After the canyon they'll re-enter the water again and if they don't judge it right they'll die of exposure. They've got to heat up sufficiently to be able to maintain their rotation. If they re-enter the water too early they won't be able to come out on the other side.

All the front-runners have slowed down drastically ... Oh! My goodness! Max-Spin-Speed is going for it. He's taking a chance. Surely he's going to slow down a little? No! He's overtaken everyone. The crowd are going mad. He's done the turn and you can see he's slowed a little but will it be enough for him to regain his heat energy, so that he can get to the other side of the lake on the return journey?

I'm hearing that bets are being laid. He's re-entered the lake. It's looking good. He's reduced his spin speed so the water is climbing up his funnel more slowly. Now the water's reached the top of his funnel. The crowd are shouting 'run'. He has only about a hundred yards to go to the tunnels."

Suddenly you could hear a large sigh from the crowd and then a hush. Max-Spin-Speed was no more.

"He didn't make it, folks!

I'm looking back at the four remaining runners and I can see that The Commander has pulled back considerably. He's still in fourth but he's now back in contention.

160

I wonder if he'll have enough energy to make the return journey through the lake?

The remaining contestants have entered the water – their funnels are now white. Night-Rage and Notorious are very close together; they need to watch that spacing or they'll touch each other. The pack is getting tighter, they're bunching up again as they leave the water."

At this stage of the race the competitors were far too weakened and the tunnels far too tight for there to be any real competition going through them. So coming out of the tunnels saw no change in order. Both the town simulator and the hill climb saw no change in the running order either, except that Notorious was getting closer and closer to Night-Rage.

"These guys are tired. You can see it in the bottom of their funnels and there's not a sand grain between Night-Rage and Notorious – talking of which, the dunes are coming into view."

Suddenly Bruce's voice became more strident.

"They've touched! Night-Rage and Notorious have touched and spun off. Yes, both of them have spun head-long into the sand dunes. They're both out of it.

So it's a straight race now between Lightning and The Commander and the dunes favour the strong."

At the beginning of the dunes, Lightning was well in the lead but you could see the relentless progress that The Commander was making, mile on mile.

"We're still in the sand dunes and The Commander has taken the lead. This is an incredible race – no one could have predicted this fantastic comeback! They're just coming out of the dunes now and starting the run in. There's a slight stumble there by The Commander. Hold on a minute, Lightning hasn't given up the ghost yet and his name gives us a clue how quick he is over solid ground. They're funnel-to-funnel at the flag. It's going to be a photo finish!"

The crowd was hushed, waiting for the result for what seemed like an eternity.

The announcement came: "The winner of this year's Champions Medal is...." Again there was yet another pause for effect... "Lightning."

Again the crowd went wild.

The Commander was the first to congratulate Lightning, who bulked up and gestured to the crowd.

After what seemed an age the winning twister made his way to the podium.

Bruce Cloudcover was the master of ceremonies:

"Well folks, that was a fantastic race and here to receive his medal is Lightning!"

The crowd applauded and cheered

Lightning stepped up to receive his medal.

The medal was in the form of a twister, poised as if to start a race. The twister was coloured orange, the colour that Lightning had been during the race. You could see through the medal and it reacted to the touch as if it was alive, a mini twister.

Cloud TV:

"Well we're here with the supreme champion of this year's games ... Lightning."

The crowd again cheered.

"How does it feel to be supreme champion, Lightning?"

"It feels great. I didn't think I was going to win, especially with The Commander coming up alongside me."

"And what about that run by The Commander. Wasn't that just awesome!"

"Yes it was, I thought I'd lost him way back. It was a complete surprise to see him running alongside me in the final mile." He turned to look at The Commander, "It was

162

a brilliant comeback by the boss."

"Of course, it's another victory for the Tornados Four!"

"It certainly is."

"Well, all the best and we hope to see you at next year's games."

At that Lightning waved and left the podium with the crowd still cheering.

By any standard, the Tornados Four had had a good tournament. Lightning was holding the Championship Medal. Notorious was holding the Darts Shield. All four had made it to the final, which to be honest, was important if their plan for Lightning to win was going to succeed.

As they left with Hammerhead on their scurrilous quest The Commander said: "Now it is time to stop playing games. Hammerhead says we have a great foe to conquer, let us see to the task!"

- Chapter Eleven -

Hurricane Control

If you can imagine a thunderstorm to be a large brutish person, then a hurricane is like an angry mob, full of them. There are a number of factors that contribute to the making of hurricanes. Let's consider some.

Hurricanes are created when thunderstorms traverse large stretches of water. Why is that the case you may ask?

The Atlantic Ocean crossing from Africa to America is such a stretch. So the first important factor is this huge sea crossing. Now, even though the heads of thunderstorms are eager to participate in the generation of hurricanes, some have been waiting all their lives for this chance. They are naturally cautious about crossing large stretches of water. There isn't a problem if they can see the other side of the pond but when 'the other side of the pond' is thousands of miles away, it makes them rather nervous.

Now the reason for this nervousness is quite simple. To a thunderstorm, water is much more slippery than land. Thus when storms are over water they feel they have less control than when travelling over land. It's a bit like you moving from pavement to ice. You'd take a bit more care over the ice wouldn't you? Maybe before you took to the ice you'd want to slow down a little.

The trouble is, this reluctance to start the journey causes them to bunch up, just as they leave the African coastline, and this bunching up is one of the reasons hurricanes exist.

Another issue is that of the sea sirens. You don't believe me? Well look, a long time ago your ancestors believed in them. It's very unlikely that you, as a modern person, would believe in them but I assure you they do exist.

I know most of you will be thinking, 'what a load of nonsense!', but your scepticism just underlines how different your interaction with the sea is from that of your ancestors.

In their day, your ancestors were much more in touch with their world than you are with yours. When they went to sea in ships they actually went to sea. They could smell it, feel it, see it and hear it.

In these modern times I'm not convinced at all that you ever hear the sea when you're out on it. In fact, I'm not convinced many of you have actually been properly 'out to sea'.

Getting on crafts that just hug the shoreline or island hop, is not exactly the same thing as going out into mid ocean.

These days when you actually go to sea, you don't hear the sea, you hear the engines of the ship, or the noise of the disco coming from the belly of the ship. Even if you accidentally wandered onto the deck, maybe to get some fresh air, the noise of the engine would drown out any noise from the sea sirens.

If you then consider the detailed maps that exist of all the hazards that have been charted and modern navigational aids, GPS and the like, well it's now possible to hug the shoreline in complete safety. Your ancestors were frightened of being too close to the shoreline, because of the sirens.

You see, another one of the reasons you don't believe in the sirens anymore, and probably the main reason, is the fact that they have moved far away from mankind.

Old tales tell of sirens on the rocky seashore, enticing ships to certain doom. But the sirens gave that up long ago. As mechanised ships came into being and they could not be heard, they reduced in number. When modern technology, including GPS, came into general use, it became nigh impossible to wreck ships on rocks, so they abandoned the shoreline for the Deep Ocean and abandoned the direct attacks on mankind for the indirect attacks they could generate by interfering with Cloudkind.

So it's perfectly understandable that you have never heard them and you should consider yourselves fortunate that is the case.

But beware! There may come a time, one day in the future, when your engine breaks down. Maybe then you would be exposed to the true sounds of the sea and just maybe the terrifying wail of the sirens.

Your ancestors believed that these sirens were evil. That they used to sink boats and drown people. This fear of sirens is well founded because they hate mankind and the sole reason they interfere with Cloudkind is because they wish to harm humans.

Anyway, I digress. Thunderstorms … Ah yes!

As the thunderstorms bunch up off the coast of Africa, the sea sirens suddenly have a captive audience. When a sea siren starts to wail, the song (well, most people would call it an excruciating noise) has a way of getting to you that most other sounds don't. The noise is hypnotic and tends to confuse you, and then you start imagining things, strange things.

Well this is happening to every thunderstorm in close proximity to the siren, so they gather together in a tight bunch to combat the pain and to re-assure each other.

As they gather together they find that if they face each other they hear the sirens less and less, so they form a circle and together with their Windlets they make more and more noise of their own. Then they find that moving around in a circular motion reduces the noise further.

As the circle rotates they find that the faster they go, and the more noise their Windlet makes, the less of the siren song they hear, so they go faster and faster. Suddenly it works and the wailing is gone!

The problem is another metamorphosis has taken place. As they were going around in a circle and creating the noise to drown out the sea-sirens they were going faster and faster and what happens if winds go too fast? They find that they can't stop or pull apart; they are locked together in a spin. You see, they are over water. If they were on land, which is what they are used to, they could stop quite easily. But the surface of the water is quite slippery and they can't get enough purchase to stop rotating.

It doesn't even stop there because the sea-sirens are enjoying this. They know the faster the spin the more damage will occur when the hurricane hits land. They continue to spin what is initially just a collection of thunderstorms up and up and up until a hurricane is produced.

Eventually the spin is so great that the circle of thunderstorms becomes the eye wall of the hurricane.

I couldn't imagine even in my wildest dreams trying to control lots of groups of thunderstorms, twisters and hurricanes all at the same time. I couldn't imagine it but that's exactly what Hurricane Control do day after day, year after year.

Hurricane Control ensures that the hurricane season starts on time – on the 1st of June- and ends on time on the 30th of November. Lately the control team have been thinking of extending the season because there are so many groups of thunderstorms wishing to take part in the annual events.

This increase in the number of thunderstorms wishing to 'have a go' in a hurricane, has been put down to the fact that global warming has allowed hurricanes to spin up to gain faster and faster spin speeds. This means that the records set by the older generation are now up for grabs. The younger generation like the idea that they can go faster, and be more powerful than their parents ever could.

Don't get me wrong. Hurricane Control is not infallible and the odd thunderstorm group will escape their clutches and generate a hurricane out of season now and again. This is not unreasonable since you can imagine that waiting at the beginning of the season, when you're all revved up to go, is a bit soul destroying to some thunderstorms and the call of the sea-sirens doesn't put them off. So now and again a group will break free and take off too early.

In the same way, if you've been waiting your turn at the end of the season and some official says, "Well that's it for this year fellas, see you in six months," and you're all revved up ready to go, it becomes very difficult not to, and some groups just go for it.

The punishment for thunderstorm groups that break away in this manner is quite severe. Firstly, they are banned from ever participating in the hurricane events again – and that's for life, not just for a season or two. And secondly, the Hurricane Control team at the other end of the Atlantic ensure that they spin down more rapidly than they would normally do. This reduces their effectiveness and obviously their enjoyment of the event.

The first job of Hurricane Control is to ensure that each hurricane embarking on their mission has a name.

Long ago, the cloud based Hurricane Control team would give the name to the hurricane. This name would be completely different from the name the humans gave the same hurricane. In the end this resulted in far too much confusion because Hurricane Control not only monitored the hurricanes themselves, but they also gathered information from the humans, and having different names lead to all sorts of confusion and eventually some serious mistakes.

So it was decided that Hurricane Control would allow the humans to name the hurricanes. This was thought a good policy because when humans track hurricanes they track them for different reasons. This means they collect different information and Cloudkind found that when this information was combined with their own, a much more useful picture emerged. So by keeping the names the same, which they call 'synchronisation', the cloud team could get a much better picture of how their hurricanes behaved and how effective they were when they reached the land mass of the Americas.

So far this year they have only sent out one hurricane. The humans called it Alex. Bonnie and Colin will be the next two Hurricanes to go, but they haven't gone yet.

As they prepared to embark on their journey, both Bonnie and Colin had been seen sending and receiving messages via the Great Conveyor.

There was nothing unusual about this. Many thunderstorms received messages wishing them well just before they set out on their travels, so Hurricane Control did not in any way suspect there was something unusual going on. However, the Hurricane Control team had noticed that after receiving each message the two hurricanes had become closer and closer and this concerned them.

There is a simple rule that applies to all hurricanes, which is that they should stay well apart from each other during launch. Hurricane Control's view was that Bonnie and Colin were too close.

It was an important part of Hurricane Control's remit to

ensure that only a set number of thunderstorms gathered within each hurricane and that each hurricane was kept a reasonable distance from the next.

Hurricanes were allowed to generate more thunderstorms within themselves once they set out and they were allowed to bunch up or get closer together when they were further out to sea, but certainly not just as they launched. "Hurricane Colin, you are too close to Hurricane Bonnie, would you please back off?" came the command from Hurricane Control.

Anyone watching would have seen immediately there was a definite reluctance to widen the gap between the two. Hurricane Control also noticed this reluctance.

"I repeat: Hurricane Colin, you are far too close to Hurricane Bonnie, back off please!"

Hurricane Colin backed off a little.

"Last chance Hurricane Colin, you get pulled if I have to repeat myself one more time."

It was rather obvious he didn't want to get pulled so Colin backed off considerably.

Both were allowed to proceed through the start gate although everyone, including Hurricane Control, was convinced they would be closer to each other by the time they'd made it to the middle of the Atlantic.

Even though one tends to think of hurricanes starting their existence just out to sea, west of Africa, Hurricane Control is actually based over the Highlands of Ethiopia and although they have been doing the job for thousands of years, they are definitely not a competent bunch.

As I said earlier, keeping hurricanes the correct distance apart is their responsibility and an important one at that. The behaviour of Bonnie and Colin is a perfect example of their inability to make this happen. What does happen is that when two hurricanes wish to travel together they just bunch up once they're out at sea. Even though Hurricane Control has the power to change this behaviour they just accept it rather than trying to sort the problem out.

So Hurricane Control effectively let the thunderstorms do as they please and as you know thunderstorms are not exactly level headed. Everyone knows, although no one will admit it, that there is going to be an incident one day.

- Chapter Twelve -

The Planning Stage

"Hello, this is Gus Denning NBC with up and coming weather events on this beautiful bright and blue Monday morning. With not a cloud in the sky, NOAA's (**N**ational **O**ceanic and **A**tmospheric **A**dministration) Climate Prediction Centre projects a 75% probability of an above normal hurricane season this year. They've raised the total number of named storms and hurricanes that may form.

Underlining this news and following tropical storm Alex, which affected the Yucatan Peninsula earlier this month, there are two more tropical storms heading our way, both of which are predicted to gain hurricane status: Tropical Storm Bonnie and Tropical Storm Colin. Storm watchers say these two storms are unusually close together. They're not predicted to make landfall for at least another two weeks.

Meanwhile, closer to home..."

Jack turned the TV off. It was his habit in the morning to just watch snippets of the NBC News Desk. Their weather reports were always on the button and anyway, he liked the way Gus delivered it. The news that Bonnie and Colin were close together bothered him.

It was just after eight-thirty so most of the team would be up and running by now. There wasn't a peep from Emma or Scott and Mary had been up during the night with Sarah so they were both crashed out in Sarah's room.

He decided to quietly sneak out the front door and make his early morning calls from the car on his cell phone. Mike was first, since Jack was dying to know what he thought of the Flettner ship.

"How's it going, Mike?" asked Jack.

"Well the food's OK, but the bunk is a little cramped!" Mike sounded a little bleary-eyed.

"I was thinking more of the science, Mike, when I asked that question!"

Mike laughed, "OK, the food's nutritious, if slightly stodgy, and I would estimate I ate far too many calories. The bunk bed is approximately 25.4 centimetres too short for my height and ..."

"Mike!" Jack laughed.

"OK, Jack. The Boulder team had their initial planning meeting yesterday afternoon. We were invited to attend. I got the distinct impression they felt that we had robbed them of one of their ships; it didn't start well."

"Who's in charge of the Boulder Team?"

"Gerald Dayton. He seemed a little put out when he knew we were involved, especially us having one of the Flettner ships. Does the department have some history with this guy?"

"No, not the department, just me. It's a long story," Jack tried to wave it away.

"I'm going to need to know the history, Jack, if I'm to work with this guy."

"OK. First of all you need to understand that Gerald is a good guy at heart. Of all the people in the world, he probably knows as much about weather systems as I do. We were students together. When we left school we both went to MIT and worked together for many years. In fact, his son Scott is one of our Emma's best friends and he's staying in our guest room over the next few weeks. Anyway, to cut a long story short we went our separate ways and slowly but surely we both became experts in weather prediction.

He started at Boulder and worked his way up. I had various positions, one of which was with NASA. Working at NASA raised my profile somehow, TIME magazine discovered what I was doing there and ended up doing an article on me. The article heading was something like 'Is This The Man That Saves The Planet?' The article was about global warming. The real damage was done by one of the remarks in the article."

"What was that?"

"The reporter said I was the leading authority in the world on climate change."

"You are, aren't you?" said Mike.

"No, no! A nice compliment at the time but Gerald is equal to me, anytime. The trouble is he took offence and we haven't spoken since. Of all the people that could have run the Boulder Team, it had to be him – not good!"

"At least I now have some idea what the real problem is, Jack."

"So I assume you're not running together?"

"Dayton basically told us that we're welcome to join in with his research project. In doing so we must surrender the ship to his command. If we work independently on our own research project he wants the ships separated by hundreds of miles, so that we can't interfere with each other's outcomes."

Jack was extremely relieved to hear that there was an option to keep the ships together. "What did you say to him?"

"After our little conversation I knew you'd want to keep the ships together so I agreed to let our ship come under his command. I told him if we decided to go it alone in the future, we'd give him plenty of notice."

"Well done, Mike! Perfect. So what's next?"

"At the moment we're checking out the Flettner systems. The command ship is leading – that's the Julian

– and changing course at random. The other ships, including us, are just seeing if we can follow that lead. We aren't cloud thickening until the Flettner systems have been fully tested."

"So what's your call on that, Mike? Are the Flettner Rotors doing their job?"

"Well, if we're going to have the ships running autonomously then they're a good option. For the same reason, I think sails would be a bad option."

"What about stability?"

"Direction, speed and stability all seem fine, so far."

"Is there a planning meeting set up for when the Flettners have been tested?"

"Yes. On the Julian this Thursday at 09:00 hours, after we've docked."

"Ask Dayton if it would be alright if I attended and see if he would have any objections to extending the meeting to include the 53rd and the WRI flying teams."

"Will do, Jack! I'll get back to you!"

Jack was now restructuring the team in his mind. From now on he would need to treat Gerald Dayton as, effectively, the fleet commander. He was the scientist in charge of the Boulder vessels and currently he was also in charge of The Lancelot. He made a note in his diary. The next call was to Ollie:

"Colonel Price is in a meeting at present sir, would you like me to get him to call you when the meeting's over?" said a young lady on the other end of the line.

"Yes please."

"Who should I say has called?"

"Jack Winter – Weather Research Institute – Thank you!" Jack hung up. He was just about to call the hangars, when the phone rang.

"Hi, Jack ... get it!"

"I've heard the joke before, Ollie. What is it with this morning? Everyone's a comedian."

Ollie was laughing, "What's up?"

"I thought you were in a meeting and couldn't be disturbed?"

"If I'm busy with an important matter and don't want to be disturbed, we call it a meeting. In your case the important matter can wait; what's up?"

"You've heard they're predicting a difficult season?"

"Yes, but to be truthful, it's no surprise."

"I'm slightly worried about the closeness of Bonnie and Colin. Could you have an early look at them for me, Ollie?'

"You're a little bit premature there, Jack, but we'll have a look."

"Thanks. Are you routinely carrying the seed pods when you go on missions these days?"

"Yes, one batch anyway."

"Could you extend that to two or three? Do you have the room?"

"Yes, we have the room, Jack; are you getting nervous? Is there something I need to know?"

Jack's tone lightened, "No, it's just that the next two hurricanes are close together so I thought it might be wise to prepare for anything unusual that may happen."

"If you say it's worth doing, we'll do it. No problem!"

"Thanks Ollie, Oh! I have a meeting with the Boulder Team. They're running the Flettner Ship trials – it's on Thursday at 09:00 hours. Are you able to come if I can get you a seat at the table? Your experience with hurricanes may be rather valuable to them."

"Just hang on, Jack, I'll check my calendar." There was a faint rustling noise, "Yes, I'll pencil it in. Just let me know if there's a problem. Where is it to be held?"

"Just ask for the 'Julian', down at the docks."

"I'll be there unless you tell me otherwise, bye!"

Jack's last call was to his own team. He had considered getting General Grahams involved, but that was for emergency only and he didn't feel this was an emergency.

"Hi Bill! Anything unusual happening today?"

"Not really; there have been a few sightings of tornados down near the Whitesands area in New Mexico but other than that ..."

"How many of the new type of seed pods do we have?"

"Enough for one drop on each of the three planes."

"OK, I want you to load the planes with the normal pods and then ensure that each plane also has new pods in reserve."

"Will do, Jack!"

"I want you, Alexandria and the fly boys to pencil in a meeting to be held on Thursday 09:00 hours. It'll be held on the Julian down at the docks. All of you show up unless I cancel it meanwhile."

"OK Boss!"

"See you there!"

Tuesday arrived, and by late afternoon, having had no telephone call from Mike, Jack's patience snapped. "Cynthia, see if you can get Gerald Dayton on the phone for me. He's the commander of the Flettner Ships for the Boulder Team."

Jack wasn't looking forward to this particular conversation but he thought it would be better to have it now, rather than in the middle of some crisis that may or may not arise in the future. Anyway, as far as he was concerned, the animosity was entirely one way. It would be nice to hear from his old classmate again.

"I have Dr. Dayton on the telephone, Sir!"

"Patch him through, Cynthia," Jack heard the switch over. "Gerald, nice to speak with you again."

"Well, well! If it isn't the greatest weatherman on the planet! What can I do you for, Jack?" Dayton always liked to rearrange the order of words when using that particular sentence. It reflected his character well.

"I hear you're having a planning meeting Thursday morning. Do you mind if I bring my team and we interact a little?"

Gerald Dayton, the person, just wanted to say 'No!' Gerald Dayton, the scientist, was intrigued. "Any particular reason?"

"Well, we have a couple of hurricanes on the way so I was wondering whether it would be possible to expand the scope of your group to allow us to try to reduce the severity of the first hurricane."

"We think very much alike, Jack. But I thought it might be a good idea to leave the first hurricane alone, as a sort of datum point – maybe calibration would be a good word for it. Then attack the following storm. That way we would be better able to judge the effect we were having."

From that statement alone, Jack knew that Dayton had not experienced the tragedy that a hurricane can leave behind. To let even one through when it was possible to calm it was not what Jack Winter was about. This was going to be a difficult meeting, he thought. "So if we're in agreement that action is needed, what about the meeting?" said Jack.

"Yes come, but Jack! ...... "

"Yes?"

Dayton's voice dropped in pitch, "Remember who's in charge of the ships!"

"Absolutely Gerald, absolutely."

Gerald Dayton's voice lightened

"And how's my boy, is he behaving himself?"

"Of course, as one would expect."

"And Emma? I hear she hasn't been feeling too well lately."

"She's fine now Gerald, it was just a bug."

"And I hear you have another girl?"

"Sarah! Yes, she's doing fine too."

"Well, can't stop, see you Thursday."

"OK Gerald, nice talking to you."

Jack muttered to himself: "Well that went better than I thought it would," as he ended the call.

Thursday morning arrived with a little light rain. Jack had risen early because of the meeting. He had charts to check, data to assimilate, and he needed to be well prepared for the meeting. Mary and the kids weren't up yet, although he did hear a faint noise from Emma's room. On arriving downstairs he automatically switched on the NBC news desk, just in time for the seven o'clock weather outlook.

"Hello, this is Gus Denning NBC with the weather headlines."

Gus was standing in front of his weather chart; the chart showed a simulation of the two hurricanes currently approaching the eastern seaboard.

"Well, we've been watching these two storms coming in for several days now. They've both reached Category One status and although we can't be sure which track they'll take, Hurricane Bonnie is threatening to be a very big storm, with Hurricane Colin a very close second."

The graphic changed, with the names of the two hurricanes appearing and a large H visible over the northern portion of the eastern seaboard:

"At the moment there's a blocking high pressure system in the North Atlantic which, if it stays there, will prevent the hurricanes from moving north while they're out to sea. So the most likely track will be towards Florida. Landfall is expected in eight days ..."

Jack turned the TV off, made himself some breakfast, opened his laptop and checked his email. There were several that looked like they should be read, so he opened the ones he considered important:

Steve Grahams ... Hello Jack – just to let you know that the contents have arrived. We're going to do a few test firings today – will let you know how we get on.

Sarah Winter ... Gurgle, Gurgle, Chomp, Chomp.

He smiled. Mary had a good way of keeping him in touch with the family, he thought.

Mike Andrews ... Dayton has just told me you've been in touch – see you later today.

As Jack drove down to the docks, he was thinking about the data he had just obtained from Goddard; NASA's predictions were very close to home, *his* home!

When he arrived at the docks, a sailor who had been waiting for arrivals escorted him onto the Julian. The rest were already seated. As he walked into the room they all stood as if he was the Commander in Chief. He wasn't, and he could see in Gerald Dayton's face that he'd better reinforce that point straight away.

"Good morning, everyone. You all know Dr. Gerald Dayton, who is in charge of the Flettner fleet, but I'm sure, like me, you don't know all of the strangers in this room. So would everyone please introduce themselves, starting on my left here with Gerald."

"Dr Gerald Dayton – Chief Scientist – National Centre for Atmospheric Research (NCAR, Boulder) – on Julian."

"Duncan Demarko – Captain of the Julian."

"Hello there, Mike Andrews – Science Officer – Weather Research Institute (WRI) – Seconded to Lancelot"

"Brad Johnson – Captain of the Lancelot."

"Steven Ford – Science Officer – NCAR – seconded to Lucia."

"Adam Brubaker – Captain – Lucia."

"Chris Olsen – Captain of the Barnard."

"Robert Delseni – Science Officer NCAR – Seconded to Barnard."

"Joey Buffet – Pilot – WRI."

"Alexandria Silva – Science Officer – WRI."

Alexandria was the only female in the room. She was as experienced as the rest. In fact, before joining Jack Winter's team, she'd worked up in Boulder for a few years herself. She didn't know any of the Boulder crew although she had glimpsed Gerald Dayton once or twice while she was there.

"Don Hudson – Pilot – WRI."

"Bill Wolff – Science Officer – WRI."

"Sam Parks – Pilot WRI."

"Matt Dannheisser – Captain of the Stinger."

"Patrick O'Connor – Science Officer – NCAR – seconded to Stinger."

"Oliver Price – Colonel – 53rd Weather Reconnaissance Squadron."

"Jack Winter, Chief, WRI."

Jack continued: "This meeting was initially called by Gerald to plan the next phase for the testing of the Flettner ships. Gerald has also agreed to extend the meeting to discuss the upcoming hurricane season. So let's get down to business. Gerald, the ships ..."

"Thanks, Jack! It may well prove to be a very happy coincidence that the receipt of these five vessels has co-incided with the start of this year's hurricane season. We now know the Flettner Rotors are doing their job, so the next stage is to find out whether the cloud spraying pumps and hoses will do their work effectively and efficiently.

There are two hurricanes headed our way at this moment, both of which are approximately the same magnitude and both of which may well stay on the same course. I intend to let the first hurricane through without altering it and then attack the second one, once the first has passed. This will enable us to calibrate any results we obtain."

The statement caused some disquiet in the room.

Adam Brubaker, the Captain of the Lucia, was the first to speak up. "Don't you think it would be wise to tackle the first hurricane? If we have a chance to stop some of the destruction and death it might cause, shouldn't we be trying straight away?"

Jack was glad that others thought as he did.

"We have absolutely no way of knowing whether or not we will have an effect. In fact the only way of knowing is to calibrate what we do, and in the manner I suggest," added Gerald Dayton.

There was silence for a moment or two, then Alexandria spoke: "You know, if the press get hold of this and they found out you're letting a hurricane through when it's possible to reduce its ferocity, you may well be in serious trouble. Inaction can be a dangerous route to take."

"I understand and it's a risk I'm willing to take," said Dayton.

"What do you mean? It's a risk *you're* willing to take?" shouted Sam, "If you let the hurricane through, the statistics show us that someone will die! I'm guessing it won't be you."

"Right, that's enough," Jack stepped in. He had thought of this problem ever since the idea was put to him over the phone. There was no way that he wished to hold off and wait for the second hurricane to strike but equally he knew if he argued directly against Dayton's plan, then Dayton would dig his heels in and that would make things much worse.

He'd come up with a solution that would work only if his hunch was right, that the two hurricanes would be too close together to tackle the second one individually.

"I think that Gerald's idea is sound. It's just that the data suggests that the two hurricanes will get closer together or their paths will diverge. In either of these cases, waiting for the second hurricane is not an option. So I suggest that if they remain close or get even closer, or their paths start to diverge, we tackle the first hurricane.

If they look like moving further apart and stay on the same track we tackle the second hurricane, is that agreeable, Gerald?"

"Yes!"

"OK, whichever hurricane we are to tackle, then it's important that the Boulder Team understands that we have other resources this year that we're planning to use. It appears that both Gerald and I have been thinking along the same lines and while Gerald's team have been concentrating on the Flettner ships, the WRI have been looking into a more concerted, airborne attack. So we need to work out a combined plan of attack and that's the reason we're all assembled here today. To come up with a plan that may, just may, give us a realistic prospect of modifying one or both of these hurricanes."

"What's the level of modification you're looking for?" asked Gerald Dayton.

"Let's say from level four to a level two, or even one."

"How can we do that? This is a hurricane, not just a little thunderstorm, you know!" said Chris Olsen, captain of the Barnard.

"By combining forces," Jack replied. "Gerald, what's your plan?"

"OK, Jack, this is our suggestion for the ships. We send the five Flettners into an area north west of the hurricane and they strengthen the clouds, well ahead of the storm. If we succeed we should be able to cool the ocean by a few degrees, reducing the available energy intake of the storm"

"We're going to sail into a hurricane?" asked Captain Schwartz.

"No!" Jack said, "You're going to thicken the clouds, then back off. You should have plenty of time to get out of there. Then, as the Hurricane is affected by the cooler ocean, Ollie's team will move in and seed the eastern side of the hurricane, while our three planes will seed the western side of the storm."

"I assume we've got the western side of the hurricane because of our fuel restrictions," said Joey.

"Yes, Ollie's aircraft have a much bigger range than ours. We can't carry anywhere near enough fuel to tackle the eastern edge of the storm."

"You make it sound like a war, Jack!" said Ollie.

"Just a battle, Ollie, although I think the war may have begun."

"The combined attack actually sounds as if it might work," said Gerald.

"It's the best we've got," said Jack.

He continued: "So looking at the problem of the hurricanes, our first problem is Hurricane Bonnie and, I'm afraid to admit it, followed very quickly by her brother Colin.

We've passed all our current data through Columbia, NASA's super-computer at Goddard and using their finite volume general circulation model (fvGCM) we've been getting a forecast from them, at noon and midnight every day. They're currently forecasting Bonnie to be a Category Five hurricane, weakening to Category Four, just prior to landfall.

They expect the track to give landfall, for Bonnie, at Pensacola in seven days' time. Their model shows the two hurricanes taking different paths, Colin to head for the Yucatan.

Official forecasts coming from NOAA's National Hurricane Centre in Miami and the predictions coming out of Florida State University's Super Ensemble Model are much the same.

So we have a good idea of the track of these two storms, and if these predictions are correct, the Flettners will be attacking Bonnie, not Colin. The trouble is, my model, which I admit is unproven, suggests that the hurricanes will stay on the same track. So, just in case, I think we should have some sort of back up plan."

"What sort of back-up plan" asked Mike?

"Well, if they remain close it will be a refuelling problem, so that we can attack the second hurricane, just like we attacked the first. If they get further apart then we need to practise fast deployment, so that after the first hurricane has hit we can be ready to attack the second.

My problem is that all my instincts – and my model – tell me that these two hurricanes will track together and get closer together. Now, if I'm right, after the first encounter all planes will need to return immediately to base to refuel, re-stock with seedpods, and be ready to fly back out on a second mission. I'd also like to see the Flettner ships tackle both hurricanes but obviously the seas are going to be rather choppy even if the planes succeed."

"If that's necessary, Jack, it shouldn't present a problem," said Dayton.

Jack was pleased that Gerald Dayton was joining in the debate on the positive side. It looked like his resistance to tackling the first hurricane, rather than the second, was weakening. "Well, I wasn't sure if the Flettner Rotors made the vessels more unstable," said Jack.

"No, they're fine," said Dayton.

"What the heck is a Flettner Rotor?" said Ollie.

Everyone, except Ollie, laughed.

"You must have seen them when you came aboard, Ollie," said Jack.

"You mean the chimney stacks?"

Captain Shaw of the Julian smiled and replied, "Yes Ollie, but they're not chimney stacks. They're devices that are used instead of sails. There are two rotors on each ship, which work independently, for steering.

The rotors spin and create a force, ten times as strong as that of a sail but that's not their only advantage. They don't require a crew to put the sails up and down. So long term, we can use the ships without having a crew on board."

Jack resumed: "Well, back to the plans. First of all, has anyone got any other ideas?"

The question was met with silence

"In that case, do we all agree to go with this plan?"

There was a nodding of heads and general agreement all round.

187

Gerald Dayton had been mulling over the consequences of such action, on a system as large as a hurricane. He spoke:

"You do realise, if we're successful, there'll be a deluge of biblical proportions."

"Yes," Jack replied. "That's why we have to tackle the problem while the hurricanes are out at sea. If we fail and the slowdown occurs over land, then it'll be like a storm surge coming from the opposite direction."

The room fell silent.

"Right then, let's go with that. I'll leave it to Gerald and Mike to deal with the ships' timetables and Ollie and I will deal with the air assault. Right gentlemen, keep in touch."

As the room emptied and everyone went their separate ways, Jack cornered Bill Wolff, who he'd hired to look after the WRI's environment model.

"Bill, I just wanted to say, you're doing a marvellous job on our computer model. I've never known it to be so responsive and so accurate, well done!"

"Thanks Jack," Bill said, instinctively. Then a vague unease suddenly swept over him. Yes, he *had* been working hard on improving the model but he wasn't aware that any of the changes he'd made were of real significance. He had it in his head to re-assess the model if time allowed.

- Chapter Thirteen -

Signs Of Distress

Mom and Sarah were out shopping, Jack at work. Emma and Scott were chilling out on the Sofa in front of the TV. The NBC weather forecast was about to be broadcast. Landfall was expected in three days:

"Anticipating that hurricane Bonnie might hit the Florida Pan Handle this weekend the cities of Miami and Tampa have warned residents that they should be planning to evacuate their homes, and even leave the state, if the predicted path remains the same. The National Hurricane Centre has indicated that Bonnie would likely come ashore at Tallahassee. However, forecasters have stressed that the unpredictable nature of hurricanes means that she could come ashore anywhere between Miami and Pensacola. Worst of all, she could change course right at the last minute.

The Mayor of Tampa said, "We are on high alert and we're continuing to monitor the storm but, until we know where landfall will be, there's little we can do to prepare."

Scientists at the National Hurricane Centre have said that this is a particularly severe hurricane and that they're also concerned about Hurricane Colin, which is less than 150 miles south east and moving this way."

"Scott, I can't possibly miss this, this is once in a lifetime stuff. Let's stay and watch it go through."

"You're joking, Em. Your Mom and Dad aren't going to let us stay here, with a hurricane raging through the State."

"They won't know. We're due to leave for Boulder tomorrow. We just won't get on the plane. They'll think we've gone up there and when they leave for Grandma's we'll come back to the house."

"No way, they'll check up on us."

"By then it'll be too late, they won't be able to come and get us. Dad will be too busy and Mom won't leave Sarah, and she definitely won't come back into a raging hurricane while Sarah's with her."

"Well, I must admit it does sound kind of exciting. We'll be in big trouble."

"Yes, I know," Emma said with a rather cheeky look on her face.

Gerald and Mike were somewhat closer to the hurricane. They'd positioned the five ships south of the Florida Keys, so that they were spread, from east to west, across the Florida Straights and into the Gulf of Mexico. The ships were roughly forty miles apart. Yesterday the plans had finally firmed up and everyone agreed, including Gerald Dayton, that both hurricanes must be attacked. The two hurricanes were far too close together for an independent interception of just hurricane Colin.

The plan was to start the salt droplet spraying tomorrow, but Jack had said, "Well why not start spraying now? It won't be wasted and it'll all help to cool the system down."

They couldn't think of any reason why not, so they'd started spraying early that morning.

It was a spectacular, yet peculiar, sight. It actually looked like they were polluting the atmosphere, which I suppose technically they were, rather than trying to help stave off atmospheric problems.

Mike had reported in to Jack that they had started to generate the salt droplets and Jack had duly put this new information into his computer model. Jack was busy running the model on the WRI computer system, in the hangar near the airstrip.

The twenty-four hour news channel was on and Jonathan Francis was giving a rundown of the local political situation. He'd got a message in his earpiece that Miles Ingram had uncovered an interesting story and the breaking news was just coming in. He had instructions to interrupt his news report in favour of the breaking story.

"I'm sorry, we have to interrupt this broadcast. We're just receiving some interesting pictures from Miles Ingram, just off Key West."

The picture changed from the rock steady studio shot to what was obviously a hand held shot of Miles Ingram on a boat somewhere out at sea. You could tell it was rough out there from the lurching of the horizon in the background.

Miles was holding the side of the ship with one hand and a microphone with the other. He was struggling to stay upright.

"I'm sorry to interrupt, Jonathan, but I thought you might be interested in some footage I have. We're on a boat some fifty miles south of Key West and I'd like to show it to your viewers if I may."

"OK! Miles, go ahead."

The camera panned round to the right, away from Miles and onto what looked like another ship, with two large funnels, spraying what looked like water very high into the air. Miles' narration was describing the scene:

"You're looking at what seems to be a ship spraying sea water into the air. The seawater is coming from what appears to be two funnels on the ship's main deck. The name of the ship is 'The Barnard' and emblazoned on the side of the ship are the letters NCAR."

"Do you know what the ship is doing, Miles?" asked Jonathan.

"Well, NCAR are the initials of the National Centre for Atmospheric Research, which is in Boulder, Colorado. But we have no information as to what these ships might be doing out here. They're a very peculiar shape." Miles added, "We're trying to raise the Captain of the ship now..."

You could hear one of the technicians in the background talking over the radio and asking for the Captain of the Barnard. The technician turned and smiled at Miles and handed him the handset:

"Hang on, I think we have him... " said Miles.

With what can only be described as white noise in the background, the captain's voice could just be heard:

"This is Chris Olsen – Captain of the Barnard. What can I do for you?"

"Hello Captain, this is Miles Ingram of NBC. We were wondering what your vessel was doing out here?"

"Well, it's no secret, Miles. We're a research vessel looking into cloud modification strategies."

"What are you spraying into the air?"

"Just salt water, that's all."

"Why are you doing that?" asked Miles.

"Well, it's a little difficult to explain but at present we're just trying to grow the clouds above us, a little."

"But there's a hurricane coming!" There was a touch of incredulity in Miles' voice.

"Yes, I know."

"Well, surely that will provide you with sufficient cloud without having to grow your own?"

"Ha! I see what you're thinking. No! We're growing our clouds in front of the storm, so as to cool the ocean a little. This may reduce the destructive power of the hurricane."

"Will that work?"

"We have no idea. We've never done it before. That's why they call us a research ship."

Well said, thought Jack as he watched the broadcast. Interesting that they can find a ship so far out. What the heck were they doing out there anyway?

"I must now get back to my duties, Miles," said the Captain.

"Of course, Captain. Thanks for the information."

"You may be interested to know that there are four other ships along the Florida Straights, doing exactly the same as we are," said the captain.

Now that's what a twenty-four hour news channel was all about, thought Jonathan back in the studio. The cameras were not yet back on him so he shouted to his team to get on to NCAR in Boulder to find out more about these ships. He also asked the helicopter control team to get in touch with the helicopter news crew, to see if they could find any of the other four ships that had not yet been sighted.

He'd just got a press release from Boulder, as the cameras returned to him.

"Apparently those funnels that are spraying out the seawater are actually a new type of sail. They're called Flettner

Rotors and I'm told they're more powerful than a standard sail and … Ah! We have Nicole Steel on screen in our news 'copter. What can you tell us Nicole?"

The cameras again switched from the steady studio shots to hand held shots of Nicole's cameraman inside the helicopter.

"Well, we've just come south in the news 'copter and I can confirm there's more than one vessel spraying salt water into the air. From up here, it does look like they're being successful in generating some cloud."

The hand held camera was now hanging outside the helicopter and viewers could see the other ship spraying the air with seawater. Above the ship and directly in front of the helicopter was a growing bright white cloud.

The news 'copter footage faded out and the steady studio camera took over, with Jonathan saying:

"We have in the studio our resident hurricane watcher, Alex Crawford. So what's this all about, Alex?"

"Well, it looks like the Boulder team have finally persuaded the government to let them have funds for their experimental Flettner Rotor ships. Although I don't think any of us expected them to be used against hurricanes, just yet."

"So what *is* a Flettner Rotor ship, Alex?"

"First of all, this is a very old idea. The first Flettner ship I heard about was built around 1926, called the Buckau. So we're not talking new ideas here.

The way they're using the ship is new, though, and it's all to do with global warming.

What these ships are designed to do is increase the Albedo of the clouds – that's the brightness of the clouds – by spraying salt droplets into them. As the clouds get brighter they reflect more sunlight back into space, thus cooling the ocean."

"This sounds like science fiction."

"Well, you would need an awful lot of ships to have a global effect – in fact it was estimated you would need about fifteen hundred or so."

"Wow! That's an awful lot of ships."

"Yes, according to the NCAR press release, they currently only have four ships. Now we know there's another ship tagging along with that group. That's the Weather Research Institute's ship, making five in all."

"Hardly likely to have an impact then!"

"Well not globally, but it may help in the fight against just one hurricane..."

"OK, Alex, but spraying salt using Flettner Rotors – what's that all about?"

"That's not quite the way it is, Jonathan. The Flettner Rotors are just propulsion devices. It's just convenient to spray the salt through the centre of the rotors if you have them there.

No, the rotor choice is because, first of all, you wouldn't want to use powerful engines to power the ships. I mean, fifteen hundred powerful engines burning fossil fuel wouldn't exactly help with global warming, would it? It would defeat the whole aim of the project. So you're left with small engines or sail. Sails mean manpower, lots of it. The idea of the Flettner Rotor is that it can be used with zero manpower. OK, you'd have to work out how you would do this. But it's possible, using Flettner rotors, to have large numbers of unmanned ships spraying seawater, and using very little fuel."

"So what do you think their intention is with hurricane Bonnie, Alex?"

"Well, as you know, hurricanes need energy to feed on. So let's say they cool the ocean, along the track that the hurricane is going to travel on. Well that would sap some of the energy from the hurricane; certainly enough to stop it from growing and just maybe enough to reduce it from a Level Four, to a Level Three."

"And do you think this is their intention?"

"I think it must be."

The view went back to a head and shoulders of Jonathan.

"Now as you know, we've had a camera crew down in Biloxi, at the Keesler Air Force Base this week following the 53rd Airborne Weather Reconnaissance Unit, as they prepare to fly into, and I mean this literally, the hurricane season. They do this every year and for every hurricane.

Now we've just heard that Colonel Oliver Price is with our crew, with some updated information. "Good Afternoon, Colonel Price. What's the latest?"

"Yes, good afternoon, Jonathan. I've just been watching your report on the Flettner ships. I have a little bit more information for you."

"We're all ears, Colonel."

"Well, for the first time ever, the Weather Reconnaissance team is about to change their role from being passive observers, to active fighters. You know in the past, up until last year in fact, we have simply measured hurricane strength and collected data so that we could better predict the path of the hurricane.

Well, that's all about to change. This year, we're about to get involved with hurricane modification, not just observation."

"How will you achieve this, Colonel?"

"The Weather Research Institute has designed cloud

seeding materials which, when dropped from an aircraft, will reduce the ferocity of any storm they're dropped into. We've modified our aircraft so that we can drop these materials."

"I've heard of these things working on a thundercloud, but would they work on something as big as a hurricane?"

"It's just like the captain of the Barnard said. We don't know, it's never been tried before."

Alex came in:

"Colonel, we've just heard that there are five ships out there, preparing to tackle the hurricane. You have now just told us that you're about to become active and try to reduce the hurricane's effectiveness, by seeding it. Could you tell me: is there some sort of co-ordinated effort to tackle this hurricane and, if so, why this one?"

"Yes there is, Alex. But as the Captain of the Barnard said, 'it's just an experiment'. We haven't singled out this hurricane as something special, it just came along at the right time when we were all ready to go with our experiments."

"Then there's an obvious next question, Colonel."

"What's that, Alex?"

"Is there anyone else involved in this experiment?"

"Yes, NOAA is involved, the National Hurricane Centre and the Weather Research Institute." Ollie looked at his watch. "Anyway folks, I'd love to stay and chat but we're about to fly our first active mission – wish us luck."

"It sounds like you're going to war, Colonel."

Ollie just smiled at the camera and thought – Just a battle, as he remembered Jack's words, though the war may have started.

Jack wasn't at all concerned that the world now knew of

his experiments. In fact, he was enjoying watching the TV footage of the ships.

- Chapter Fourteen -

The News Conference

Ever since the Flettner ships had been spotted, Jack's phone lines had been inundated with calls, so much so that the team had started to get bogged down with answering the calls rather than doing any work.

Bill came into Jacks office, obviously stressed, and muttering to himself.

"Don't tell me! You've had a phone call," Jack smiled.

Bill didn't smile back. "Very funny."

Jack gave in. "OK! I'm convinced. We can't carry on like this; we'll never be able to work normally again. We need to issue a statement or something? Let everyone know what's going on."

"Yes!" Bill pleaded.

"OK! A News Conference," said Jack, "Let's call a News Conference. That way we can answer all their questions at once. We'll need to set it up quickly though, preferably tomorrow, so we can get it out of the way and get on with what we're supposed to be doing."

The two of them got to work, while Bill modified the website, notifying everyone who might read their Blog. He had Cynthia make strategic phone calls to the main TV channels, radio stations and newspapers. Meanwhile Jack called Ollie, who agreed to be on the panel in front of the press. Gerald Dayton was next.

"Cynthia, can you try getting hold of Gerald Dayton? He's on the Julian."

A few minutes later Cynthia phoned through to Jack's Office: "I have him on line one, Sir!"

Jack picked up the phone. "Gerald, we've been forced into having a press conference. Can you make it tomorrow at 1:00pm? We need you on the panel."

"A bit too 'short notice', Jack. I'd struggle getting off the ship that quickly. Anyway, the limelight's not for me, Jack. No! I'll give it a miss this time."

"You OK with us going ahead, anyway?"

"No problem, Jack. I'll be watching you on TV – and give Scott my love."

"Will do! Keep in touch!"

Jack replaced the receiver, "How we doing, Bill?" he shouted.

Bill's voice could be heard from the outer office, "I think we've contacted everyone who needs to know, Jack!"

The family were sitting around the dinner table as Jack came in.

"Sorry I'm late, we've just had to organise a press conference for tomorrow, took a bit longer than I thought."

"What's happened?" asked Mary.

"Nothing, it's just that with news coverage of the Flettner Fleet, our phones haven't stopped ringing all day. We need to put a stop to it so we can get some work done. We all thought with a news conference we could answer the questions all at the same time, and get the press out of our hair."

"Can we come and watch, Dad?" asked Emma.

"*Why?*"

"It sounds interesting!"

"Well, I suppose so – Oh! Your dad sends his love Scott."

"You've been talking to him?"

"Sure have. We're working together for a short time – in fact it's your dad that's in charge of the Flettners."

"Cool! I didn't know that."

"If you two are coming to the news conference I'll need you to stay at the back of the hall."

"No problem."

Both Emma and Scott were quite excited about the prospect.

The news conference had been booked for1:00pm. Ollie had decided to arrive at the Base a couple of hours before it was due to take place. The two hours before the conference would give him time to review, in more detail, Jack's plans, so that both of them would be 'singing from the same hymn-sheet' by the time the conference got under way. They both agreed that General Graham's seeding shells would not be brought up at this stage.

When Jack and Ollie turned up for the conference they were surprised to find a large crowd gathered outside the building. Even though the whole of Jack's team had spent the last few days on the telephone, fending off the press and others, he still didn't expect anywhere near this level of interest.

"I think we'll take the service entrance, Ollie," said Jack.

Jack obviously knew the centre well and led Ollie in via the rear entrance, through a maze of corridors, through the kitchen area and eventually into a room just off the main pressroom. A grey suited man, who obviously knew Jack, received them.

"Hello, Jack, you have another five minutes before it starts."

"Thanks, James."

Jack could hear the murmur of voices and the shuffling of chairs from the pressroom.

"Would you like a coffee before the start?" asked James.

"I'd rather have a bottle of water to take in with me," said Ollie.

"Same here, Ollie!" said Jack. "Make that two bottles, James."

"On the table!" James pointed to the table in the corner of the room that had numerous plates of assorted biscuits on it, together with glasses, cups and mugs. To the right there were bottles of orange juice and mineral water. Jack walked over to get two bottles.

"Are you organising the conference, James?" said Jack.

"Yes." James took out a small notepad. "I just need to note down some details ... Ollie is it?" He looked over to Ollie.

"Yes... Ha! Yes, Wing Commander Oliver Price – 53rd Weather Reconnaissance Squadron."

"That's all I need. The rest is up to you two. Looks like you've struck a nerve, Jack!"

"It does, doesn't it? I never expected this amount of press interest over a simple weather experiment."

James looked at his watch. "It's time, should we go in?" he asked.

"Yeah, let's get this thing over with. We've got work to do." And with that, the three men entered the pressroom.

Jack could feel the level of excitement in the room. Obviously the discovery of the Flettner Ships and their unusual shape had raised some interest in the press corps. As he and Ollie walked in, the noise in the room increased dramatically. Jack sat in front of the small collection of microphones, to the centre of the news desk. Ollie sat beside him. James had positioned himself off to one side of the desk.

Jack noticed that Emma and Scott were leaning against the wall at the back of the room – he gave them a smile.

James switched on the single desk microphone that was directly in front of him. "Good afternoon and welcome, ladies and gentlemen," he paused and waited until the hubbub in the room had abated a little. The noise subsided and he continued: "It's obvious that you have many questions to ask, but may I remind you that we can only answer one question at a time. So can we have order while the news conference is taking place?"

James again paused for a short time and then continued: "I would like to introduce the two gentleman in front of you. To your right is Jack Winter. Jack is the chief scientist at the 'United States Weather Research Institute' and is probably the one responsible for all this commotion." He smiled at Jack.

James continued: "On Jack's right, your left, is Wing Commander Oliver Price of the 53rd Weather Reconnaissance Squadron. You may have seen him on television recently." Again James paused for a few seconds. "Will you please remain silent while Jack Winter starts the proceedings. Jack!"

"Good afternoon everyone. Judging by the coverage I saw on the news yesterday, you're already fully aware that there's something new going on. My task, here today, is to inform you of just what is happening and allow you to ask questions, in order to clarify any points you don't understand."

"Let me make it very clear that *what is going on* is entirely experimental. So although we're attempting to reduce the ferocity of Hurricane Bonnie, we cannot guarantee success. In fact, the statistics make it likely that the experiment will fail.

OK! Just a little bit of science: hurricanes derive their power from warm moist air coming from the ocean. If you can stop this by supplying dry air, or you can cool the air, then the hurricane will lose its power. The weather modification experiment that is about to take place is on three fronts: first, we have already deployed over four hundred and fifty deep water pumps, just off the east coast of Cuba. These pumps will move cool water from deep in the ocean to the surface, thus reducing the surface temperature of the ocean in that locality."

This was complete news to Ollie, and to Gerald Dayton, who was watching the event on TV aboard the Julian. Boy, does he keep his cards close to his chest, Ollie thought.

"These pumps have been operational now for the last fifteen days and we expect them to cool the sea surface temperature by a couple of degrees centigrade by the time the hurricane passes over them. The only problem here is that, if the hurricane changes direction, then this effort will be wasted – although current predictions take it smack over the area of cooling.

"Second, further back from the pumps we have been using the Flettner ships, the ones you saw on the news yesterday, to throw salty water into the lower cloud base. These ships are being led by Dr. Gerald Dayton of NCAR, Boulder. The work these ships are doing will have the effect of making the clouds much brighter, reflecting sunlight away from the sea. Again we are expecting this to result in a drop in temperature of the sea surface.

"Third, we have a number of planes, including the WC-130Js from Wing Commander Oliver Price's Squadron," Jack nodded towards Ollie, "that are going to fly through the hurricane and drop seed pods that will hopefully widen the eye of the hurricane. This will reduce the wind speeds in the eye wall. Putting it succinctly, that, gentlemen, is all we are doing. James!"

"OK gentlemen, let's keep order so that we can all hear the questions and their answers. Raise your hand if you wish to ask a question." What looked like a hundred hands suddenly shot into the air.

Scott said to Emma, "Cool! What a reaction!"

James nodded towards one of the raised hands "Oh, yes ... start your question with who you are and who you represent, please. Thank you!" he nodded his head again towards the same raised hand.

"Stan Getz, CNN. One second of a typical hurricane's energy is equivalent to ten times, ten times! (Stan repeated the words to emphasise the sheer size of the problem) the total energy expended by the bomb dropped on Nagasaki. Imagine that energy every second; so what chance do you have of actually stopping any hurricane, never mind one as powerful as Bonnie?"

Jack replied, "What you're talking about Stan, is 'Landfall Energy'. The storm has been allowed to build, and build, out to sea and so it gets stronger and stronger. By the time it hits land it has become very powerful. At some point prior to this mega structure making landfall the storm system is transitioning from a collection of thunderstorms to the hurricane. So size isn't a factor that will stop the research or the solution. If we find out that we cannot tackle a hurricane over a particular size, and we may well do that, we can tackle them earlier when they're somewhat smaller. From a combative point of view, one beautiful fact about hurricanes, now we have satellite imaging, is that they can't sneak up on us. They build slowly and we've found that in general we're able to track this 'build-up' all the way back to the mountains of Ethiopia in Africa."

Stan Getz interrupted, "Professor, I'm aware of some of the theories you're trying to use here, but from what I know you would need thousands of deep water pumps, and at least five hundred Flettner ships before you could have a real and measurable effect on such a system."

Jack continued, "Look, there's no disputing that hurricanes are increasing, both in power, destructive potential and in frequency. Property damage caused by these hurricanes is in the hundreds of billions of dollars. Then there's the human cost – lives lost – we can't just ignore these facts, we have to look at ways of reducing their impact. We are not expecting that these small-scale experiments will completely cure the problem. This is research to find effective strategies for the future. It's no use investing millions until we know what is most effective," Jack looked at James.

James nodded to another raised hand: "Lorraine Croft, CBS. The Russians suggest that simply using a chemical film on the surface of the ocean would do the trick. Why haven't you included this in your arsenal?"

"In essence there's nothing wrong with that idea, in fact the Russians proved the idea to be useable. The trouble is that our team have a problem with any solution that would contribute to more and more pollution of the atmosphere or the seas. It was ruled out because of that, as was the Carbon Black idea for the same reason."

"Alan Smith, Fox News. There's a suggestion that you can steer hurricanes using microwaves or lasers. Are you using any such devices?"

"If I can steer the hurricane away from a population centre, and remember how big and how wide these events are, which other population centre would you like me to steer it towards?" Jack paused … there was no reply, so Jack continued, "We decided early on to concentrate on energy reduction, not direction modification. In the end this approach will save the most lives and reduce the billions we spend on repairing the damage wrought by these events. In answer to your original question though, Alan: my team are concentrating on what can be accomplished in the next twelve months and laser beams in airplanes, and microwave generation from space, are simply not in that category. It should be said, however, that these might well be being researched elsewhere."

"Sam Krischer, Miami Herald. Surely placing ships in the path of a hurricane is a rather dangerous move, is it not?"

"It's intended that the ships will do their work and then move away well before the more intense seas arrive," replied Jack.

Alan Smith from the Fox News desk butted back in, "I have a question I'd like to put to Wing Commander Price."

"Go ahead," said Jack, relieved to have a break from the questioning.

"As we know, these storms are incredibly violent, so how come you can fly into them without your airplane breaking up?"

"Believe me, the airplane wouldn't survive if we just flew head on into the hurricane. We don't do that. We note the wind direction and speed and use this information to plot a course. So even though we're heading into the eye of the hurricane we actually fly around it, gradually making our way to the eye and back out again."

As the questions continued to be answered, the number of raised hands in the press pack began to diminish. At which point James spoke up, "Right gentlemen, one final question, please!"

"Sarah Katlin, Tampa Tribune. I thought there was a moratorium on experiments to do with weather modification?"

"No, that's not true. It is true, however, that weather modification in warfare has been banned by the United Nations."

"Right gentlemen, if that's all? ..." asked James as he half rose from his chair.

No hands were raised.

He straightened up. "Thank you all for coming ..." he added, and with that James, Jack and Ollie headed for the exit.

"Do you want a lift back to the house you two?" Jack asked his daughter.

"No, Dad, Scott's in his car. We're off to the beach."

"Hey, Dr. Winter, that was cool," said Scott.

"Well it's your dad that's being the coolest at the moment, Scott. I wouldn't like to be out there in those seas."

"See you later, Dad."

"Have a good time, you two."

As, Emma and Scott left the conference room, Scott said, "Does the fact that my Dad is now talking directly to your dad every day alter the situation?" asked Scott.

"No way. Your dad's stuck on a ship in the Gulf of Mexico. He'll be far too busy avoiding the hurricane to even think about us."

Scott thought about it for a few seconds.

"You're right!"

"So are we still going for it tomorrow?" asked Emma

"Too right. I can't wait," replied Scott.

- Chapter Fifteen -

Hurricane Bonnie

"Are you sure you've packed everything, Emma?"

"Yes, Mom, stop worrying."

"What about your flight tickets, have you got them with you?"

Emma looked worried; she fumbled in her bag then slowly looked up and smiled at Mom. As she brought them out and waved them in front of Mary's nose, she said, "I must have forgotten them."

"Don't joke with me Emma."

The airport was much busier than normal. Emma assumed there must be a good number of these people just fleeing from the hurricane.

"Look, you need to get back to Sarah, Mom. Don't worry about us. We'll be fine."

Scott wasn't comfortable with this deception so he just stood there, smiling at Emma's Mom.

"We'll be fine Mrs Winter, I'll take care of her."

"OK! You mind you do now, Scott. I'm relying on you to keep her safe."

The words cut through him like a knife. He was sure his face must have been red with guilt. He was thinking there wasn't much chance of her being safe inside a Category Five hurricane.

Mary gave Emma a kiss and a squeeze and turned to walk away.

"See you in a couple of weeks, Mom."

"Bye, Mrs Winter."

As she left she turned and waved goodbye to her daughter and her daughter's friend.

The journey back from the airport was interesting. There was hardly any traffic travelling in her direction but very heavy traffic travelling north out of the area.

When she arrived home Jack was watching the news channel.

Even though Jack was concerned about the impending hurricanes, he wasn't more concerned than usual. He wasn't aware of any vendetta against him by the storms. For a start, he had no inkling whatsoever that a storm could be intelligent. He wasn't aware that, besides the two hurricanes that were bearing down on his location, a storm called Hammerhead and four twisters were also on their way to attack his home and the WRI facilities – in fact at the moment there was no sign of the latter. It was just one very dynamic storm after another – nothing unusual in that.

No, it was pure coincidence that he had brought all his forces together to attack Bonnie. What he was doing as a scientist was improving his data model, seeing if his equations would stack up, comparing them with the finite volume model at NASA.

So when his model started showing unusual trends, he wasn't sure whether it was the model that was the problem, or whether this was actually going to be an unusually violent event.

His model had always been a worry. The inaccuracies it produced were relatively small but he knew that simply predicting the wrong landfall site had cost lives in the past. His father had died in an extreme weather event and Jack had been there. So he knew what 'costing lives' meant.

To him the improvements Bill had made in his model

had been a godsend. Every day Bill had been coming up with improvements in his data model and the associated equations. So much so, that he was beginning to actually have confidence in his own computer model, something unheard of!

He was really rather pleased that everything was coming together at the same time; but was it time to be more worried? He thought not, but there was enough doubt in his mind to be a little bit more cautious than usual. So he'd asked Ollie to ensure his planes took double the stocks of seedpods they would normally take. Even though he had no worries about the original seedpod formula, he'd ensured that his planes were carrying the new formula. This consisted of a slightly more potent chemical reactant than the Hercules pilots had. He'd had the deep water pumps active for much longer than was technically required. The five Flettner ships were pumping salt water early. What the heck, it was worth being cautious just this once. Anyway, he needed to see if they would have any effect and pumping early would give him the best results with that variable.

No, it wasn't time to be more worried. Let's face it – the intention wasn't to stop a hurricane. It was just to calm it down a little, to reduce its potency, so that they could prevent most of the damage and loss of life that might ensue.

'So why am I still nervous?' he kept asking himself.

I suppose in the back of his mind there was a little niggle about the storm that was following Bonnie, Hurricane Colin. Colin didn't look to have anywhere near the power of Bonnie and most computer models, except his, were still saying that the two storms would diverge!

Again, Jack had found himself in front of the TV screen.

"We're now going over to Gus Denning at the weather centre. Gus?"

"Thanks, Francis. About an hour ago, Hurricane Bonnie stopped moving west and started to move north towards Tallahassee. She's currently a Category Five hurricane but is likely to weaken slightly as she passes over the western tip of Cuba. I've been informed by NCAR that the five research ships that were in the vicinity, in front of Bonnie, have now sailed westward to avoid the storm.

Citizens on the west coast of Florida and the coasts of Mississippi and Alabama have been told to evacuate ..."

Jack immediately switched the TV off. That was it! That was all the information he needed.

"Mary!"

"Yes, Jack?"

"It's time for you and Sarah to go north. The storm's headed right for this community and we don't want you two here when it strikes."

Mary and Jack looked at each other for a moment. They embraced.

"I'll get the baby's bottles made up. Can you get the car round to the front door?"

"I'm on it," Jack went to check the car.

North meant a visit to Jack's Mom Martha. For the next hour the Winters' house was mayhem but by the end of it the car was packed and Sarah was strapped into her baby seat.

Mary and Jack stood at the driver's door and hugged each other. "You look after our baby, you hear," he said.

"And you look after yourself, I love you!" They kissed again.

"I love you too." Mary got in the car and closed the door. The driver's window was down.

"Look Mary, you need to stay up there for a week. Don't be fooled by reports that the storm is dying down. Remember there's a second storm coming in. Stay up there and I'll come and join you when this thing has all blown over."

"OK. You're not especially worried about this particular storm, are you?" his wife was concerned.

"Not at all. Just best to be safe. You get going."

Jack pulled himself away..

Mary started the car and drove off slowly, blowing a kiss to him as she left.

Jack waved and shouted: "See you soon!"

Once Mary was away, Jack started on the list of phone calls he knew he needed to make.

First Mom: "Hi Ma! I've just sent Mary and Sarah up to you, Emma's fine, she's staying with a friend in Boulder. We're expecting a hurricane down here and I thought it best to get everyone out the area."

Martha knew the hurricane was on its way. Ever since her dear husband, Philip, had perished, she always kept a close watch on the weather forecast. In the beginning it was to protect Jack but now it was just habit. In fact, she'd moved north, away from the south and east coasts, for the same reason: to protect her boy.

She was absolutely horrified when Jack decided to move back south, but at least in his job he was always weather watching. She knew a rogue twister wouldn't sneak up on him. "And why aren't you with them?" she asked.

"You know why, Mom. I have a lot of people down here to protect."

Martha knew what the answer would be, she was very proud of the way her son had turned out. "Well, you take care now."

"I'll be fine. You just make sure Sarah doesn't keep you awake all night!"

"It'll be nice to see her, the only person that keeps me awake all night is her dad."

"See you, Ma!"

Jack's next priority was his neighbours and friends. By the time he'd finished that list he was feeling exhausted. In the end, he was comfortable that most of them would be evacuating. He knew John and Margaret wouldn't, they were both in their eighties and had decided long ago, "that it was time to stay put," as John would say. He hoped they would survive.

It was now time to phone Bill, to see if he had any updated news on the storm.

"The last report I saw, it was losing its ferocity. It was down to Cat.4 and looking like going to Cat.3, but I'm getting the family out, Jack, just in case."

"Wise move, Bill. Mary and the kids have just left. Once you've shipped everyone out, batten down the hatches and get down to the hangar for the pre-flight briefing."

"OK, I'll see you there Jack!"

Jack set to rummaging around the bottom floor of his house for what he considered to be the family valuables: photographs and documents being the highest priority. He took them upstairs and stored them on the highest shelf he could find. He'd managed to find a few watertight containers and stuffed as many photographs in there as he could. He took most of the light stuff upstairs also, just in case the storm surge came into the house, which was quite likely. When he'd done as much as he could inside the house he went to the garage to get the plywood sheets to cover the windows. Once they were hammered in place it was now time to get out and face the storm itself.

"Has he gone past yet?" Emma asked Scott for the ump-teenth time.

"Em! Just be patient, he ..."

Just at that moment Emma's dad passed where they were parked.

"You're OK now, you can get up."

Emma raised herself from between the seats, rubbing her back.

"Wow! That *was* uncomfortable, sheesh!"

"Do you think it's safe to go back?"

"Dad won't be back now until the hurricane has passed, let's go."

Emma thought the house felt quite eerie with the windows shuttered against the storm. While Scott made a couple of warm drinks she turned her laptop on and logged onto the site tracking the storm. She could see the obvious shape of the two hurricanes, but off to the west she noticed what looked like a gathering thunderstorm being dragged into the area. She couldn't be absolutely sure yet but it looked like there might be more than one or two tornados within it.

By the time Jack had got to the hangars all the staff were there, except for Bill. All their families were heading north and to be quite honest, if they hadn't been involved in try-ing to calm this hurricane, Jack would have had everyone else, including the three aircraft, moved north too.

Alexandria shouted: "The latest weather report's com-ing on."

The whole team gathered around the TV.

"We're now going over to Gus Denning for the latest from the weather centre. Gus?"

"Thanks, Jonathan. For the last few hours hurricane Bonnie has been moving northwards over the west coast of Cuba and into the area where the research ships had been spraying salt water into the cloud cover and you know, it looks like they've had some effect."

A huge cheer came from all over the hangar.

"Shhhh! Let him finish!" said Alexandria, gesturing with her hands for everyone to calm down.

"The strength of the storm has fallen to a Cat.3. Now we'd have expected that a Cat.5 would come down a little to say Cat.4, due to the increased drag over western Cuba but not all the way down to a Cat.3. You have to remember that the 53rd have only just taken off on their seeding mission.

Now even though this is good news, the National Hurricane Centre says that the evacuation should continue, since Hurricane Colin is close behind and is currently a Cat.3 storm and, unlike Bonnie, is currently building in strength, not decreasing."

Bill arrived. "I've just heard the news on the radio. The deep water pumps and Flettner ships look like they made a difference!" he sounded elated.

"Yes, we've just seen it ourselves, Bill," said Jack.

"What do you think, Jack? Should we take the planes up?"

"Absolutely. Sam, Charlie, Joe, Alexandria and you Bill, pre-flight meeting now. In the ops room."

The whole team assembled around the large table in the centre of the room. A map of the panhandle area, and the seas to the south, was laid out.

Sam addressed the assembled team. When it came to the flying, and not the science, Sam was in charge:

216

"Now look guys, this is the first time we've had to tackle something this big, so we need to be sure what we're doing before we go up there.

First of all, check your GPS to ensure you maintain a parallel flight path through the storm. Your weather radar will tell you where the eye is and if you overlay the radar from the TCAS, that will let you know that your altitude and spacing is good. Keep around three miles apart at fifteen thousand feet.

Icing up may be a problem. Your instinct may be to do a one eighty and come back, but only do that as a last resort. If the problem becomes chronic, try losing altitude first. If you *can* shake off the ice try to rejoin us in the eye."

Sam looked everyone up and down. "Good Luck! Over to you, Jack."

Jack didn't feel he could add to that. "Well, what are we waiting for? Let's do it!"

As the three WRI planes took off, Jack got on the coms to Ollie: "Ollie how long before you drop your pods?"

"We've dropped one load already, Jack. Just after we re-entered the eye wall. We're continuing our standard alpha flight path and we'll drop another load this time just before our second entry to the eye."

"Have you seen any reaction to your first drop?"

"Not yet, Jack, but this is not like a thunderstorm. I wouldn't have expected anything yet."

"Fair enough, Ollie. We'll be in the storm soon. We should be able to time our drop to coincide with your second drop."

"OK, Jack. Remember to keep your height. We don't want to meet each other head on – and let me know when you're about to deploy!"

What now seemed like hours passed, as both sets of planes made their way into the storm. The buffeting was something that Jack couldn't get used to and the occasional losses of altitude made him feel sick every time.

"We're nearly at the wall, Jack," warned Uncle Sam.

"Aero-One to 130J-01, come in Ollie?"

"Ollie here, Jack."

"We're about to deploy."

"Give us a count down, Jack. We'll deploy at the same time."

"Aero-Two and Aero-Three are you ready?"

"You bet!" said Joey.

"Affirmative," said Charlie.

"Don't forget everyone – heads up – there's gonna be a lot of airplanes in that eye!"

"Five, four, three, two, one, *deploy!*"

All of the seedpods were deployed successfully and the whole mass of airplanes entered the eye at the same time. The three WRI planes were at fifteen thousand feet and they could see the squadron of Hercules down below. It looked like Ollie had arranged them, so that five of the planes were at twelve thousand feet and the other five at around nine thousand feet. All well apart from each other.

The Hercules were already pointing homewards and heading for the eye wall, although the eye wall, from where Jack was looking, seemed to be a lot more patchy than when they'd first entered the eye.

The WRI planes had to turn for home, and as they did so they could see more and more of the land below. The storm was definitely breaking up.

Jack called home base. "Anything good to report, Lewis?"

"Yes, Jack. Bonnie is down to Cat.1 and is expected to drop quickly to tropical storm, as she comes ashore."

You could hear everyone on the other airplanes cheering. Even Jack allowed himself a little congratulation as he said, "Let's go home fellas."

Scott's camera work wasn't impressive at the best of times, but under these conditions it was next to abysmal.

"Emma, lean against the wind."

The wind noise was so intense that she could hardly hear Scott and she must have only been about fifteen feet from him.

"I *am* leaning against it, if I straightened up I'd be blown away!"

"No! I mean lean some more. See how far you can lean and it still hold you up."

"OK."

Emma was nearly at forty-five degrees before she felt the pull of gravity.

"Wow, awesome!"

"Let me have a go with that camera," she said.

They struggled closer to each other and Scott handed the video camera over to Emma. She panned around the street, showing the wild weather effects to the camera, then focused back on Scott.

"Watch out, Em!"

As she ducked, a large sheet of wood hurtled past.

"I think we need to go inside, Em. The winds are getting a little on the dangerous side now."

As they made their way back to the house the wind suddenly died down and slowly but surely the sun began to show itself.

"It can't be the eye-wall already," said Emma. "It's far too early."

She rushed inside to look at her computer screen, Scott following behind her.

"It's breaking up, I don't believe it. Well done, Dad."

The journey back to the airport was much calmer than the journey out and the whole team was feeling elated that they'd managed to significantly reduce the power of the storm.

The coms crackled into life. It was Lewis: "Jack, your model is saying that Bonnie isn't dead. She's allowing Colin to merge with her. If it's right, Jack ..." the coms went silent.

Bill from Aero-Two interrupted: "Jack, that's impossible! Remember The Fujiwhara Effect!"

"Bill, I trust this model. It's been right every time since the modifications you made. They've never let us down ... no, we go with that version of events."

The National Hurricane Centre came on line. "Hurricane Colin has just made a sudden change of direction and is swinging northwards. He seems to be merging with what's left of hurricane Bonnie and from what we can tell he's taking the same course.

- Chapter Sixteen -

Hurricane Colin

Lewis came on the coms, "Jack, the new trajectory for Colin takes it right over us and right over your house!"

There was no reply from Jack. He was watching what was happening on his monitor and was having trouble believing what his eyes were seeing. He was astounded at how accurate his model had been, but that held little consolation now. He was very pleased that he'd had the foresight to evacuate Mary and Sarah, but had no idea that Emma and Scott were back at the house. There was no doubt now that his house, and WRI's base, were about to become hurricane fodder and there was next to nothing he could do about it!

Jack recovered his composure, "Look fellas, we have at least four hours before Colin makes landfall, so let's get a plan together that will at least calm the thing down somewhat.

First of all, remember we have three research planes, still fully loaded, with the new seed mix."

Charlie came on the coms, "We need to get these planes home and refuelled fast, if we're going to try another run."

Jack didn't hesitate. "OK everybody, head for home, now! Lewis, can you get in touch with General Steven Grahams? His assets are near you, but he himself is in Fort Myers. Cynthia has the number. You'll need to use the code words: 'Extreme Weather Event'. I repeat 'Extreme Weather Event', or he won't respond to you. Tell him he'll need to assemble his forces roughly where his assets lie but on high ground and as near to the airport as possible. Lewis, it's important that he assembles his team on high ground. There will be a huge storm surge if we don't manage to calm the hurricane."

I don't know from which direction, Jack thought, but there *will* be a huge storm surge.

"Forgive the pun, Lewis, but let me know if you manage to get any of this off the ground."

"I'm on to it, Jack!" replied Lewis.

"Can anyone think of anything else?"

There was complete silence …

Lewis didn't waste any time and called the Fort Myers base immediately.

"Could you put me through to General Grahams' Office please?"

"Connecting you now, Sir." The General's secretary answered the phone.

"General Grahams' Office, who is speaking please?"

"This is Lewis Patton calling from the Weather Research Institute in Pensacola. Could I speak with General Grahams, please?"

"I'm afraid I have strict instructions from him not to be disturbed," answered the secretary.

"This is extremely important, Miss. I have a coded message for him. He'll be glad of the interruption, if you say exactly what I tell you to say."

"Very well." The General's secretary grabbed pen and paper. "Could you tell me what message I am to give the General, please?"

"Say that it's a WRI emergency and say the code words –'Extreme Weather Event'. After saying those words, tell him to assemble his team on high ground, as near to Pensacola

Airport as possible. It's vital that he assembles his forces on high ground. We can't be absolutely definite, but it's possible that he may only have around four hours to prepare.

The secretary was writing the message, repeating the significant bits as she wrote. "Extreme Weather Event... High ground... Near Pensacola Airport... Four Hours."

Lewis spoke again, "Oh! After speaking with the General would you please ensure that you immediately return my call? I need to know his response."

The General's secretary added "immediate response..." to her list.

"I'll do that, Sir. I'll contact him immediately and get back to you!" General Grahams' secretary knew that the meeting he was in was extremely important, but there was urgency in the voice that had just given her those code words. She knew she had to disturb the meeting.

As she neared the conference room door, she could hear snippets of conversation from the room. She knocked on the door; the chatter subsided to a murmur and the General shouted, "Come In! Come in!" She opened the door, strode over to the General and whispered the words 'Extreme Weather Event' into his ear.

The General's face suddenly became very serious. He looked around the table and addressed the men: "We have a serious matter to attend to gentlemen. The WRI have just issued their first 'extreme weather event' warning."

He turned to his secretary.

"Did they say anything else Gillian?"

His secretary looked down at her notes. "Yes sir, they said to assemble the forces as near to Pensacola Airport as possible, but on high ground. He also added that you need to be ready within four hours, if possible."

"God, that's tight! Right then! It's obvious that we have no time to lose gentlemen. You know exactly what to do.

We rehearsed the scenario only two weeks ago. Let's get to it! Gillian, return the call and let the WRI team know we are on our way."

"Yes Sir!" She was relieved that she had followed her instincts and disturbed the meeting.

Just as the three returning WRI aircraft were coming in to land for refuelling, Lewis came on the coms again.

"Jack, more bad news, I'm afraid. We've spotted a thunderstorm being pulled into the area and it looks like it has tornadic winds in it."

"This is getting silly. If I didn't know any better I'd say the weather has got it in for us today," Jack said jokingly, then more seriously: "Lewis, we can't help you with the storm. We have to save all our pods for Colin."

"I understand."

"Lewis, if the General responds, use his assets for your storm and leave the hurricane to us."

"The General has responded. He just said they were on their way."

Jack was comforted by those remarks.

"Excellent, Lewis. Good work!"

As all three WRI aircraft were refuelling, the sky was becoming darker and darker. They could see lightning and hear thunder in the distance. You could tell by the fact that the thunderclaps were getting closer in time to the lightning flashes, that the storm was headed directly towards the airport. By the time the aircraft were back in the air, the thunderstorm could only have been a few miles away.

"Isn't it worth tackling that storm before we go after the hurricane?" asked Sam.

"No, Sam. If we tackle that storm we won't have enough

time to meet the hurricane out at sea. If we kill the hurricane out at sea, the storm surge will be relatively normal. If we only manage to kill it when it's over land, then not only will there be a storm surge but there will also be a biblical downpour and if that happens the resulting floods would be devastating."

*

Jessica Jones, JJ to her friends, was a keen musician. She had quite a collection of stringed instruments hung on the wall but her pride and joy was her baby grand piano. It was a present from her husband, Dennis, to mark her thirtieth birthday. To accommodate it, she had to persuade her husband to extend the front left side of the house. So, even though her birthday had been some seven months earlier, the piano had only just arrived.

Jessica had the instrument carefully positioned within the extended room, so that when she was giving lessons she could see to the front of the property. Her idea was, with this arrangement, she could see if anyone was approaching the house while she was playing or teaching.

It must be said that a large number of her male students came mainly to look at her and only partly to learn how to play. She was a very attractive lady with beautiful nut-brown eyes and long, waist-length, dark-brown hair.

Jessica was standing at the window looking out at the view and listening intently to nine-year-old Katie, who was having her first lesson on the new piano. She was one of Jessica's more gifted students and the teacher had high hopes for her student's future development.

The view from the music room overlooked parkland. The house was probably positioned on the highest point of the surrounding area. A children's playground could be seen, some three hundred yards across the road and to the right of the window.

Suddenly there was a huge increase in traffic noise outside the house. Police sirens were sounding, loud hailers were announcing the arrival of the military, and all without any prior notice of an exercise, thought Jessica.

Katie stopped playing. Neither Jessica nor Katie had ever seen an artillery brigade. So as the army moved in front of the house and started deploying the big guns, both of them just couldn't take their eyes off the scene that was unfolding. The lesson was quickly abandoned and they both stood at the window watching the unfolding drama.

"They're making a real mess of that grass, Miss Jones," said Katie.

"Yes, they are, aren't they," said Jessica, calmly staring at the unfolding scene.

Of course, Jessica had seen these guns before, either in war films, or in news footage from conflicts in the Middle East. However, she had never seen them positioned near a children's play area before and she was quite surprised at how large the guns were.

The Pensacola Police had escorted the Army team onto the parkland and had cordoned off a large part of it, including the children's play area. Even though the police advised everyone to go home, a large number of children and their parents had assembled alongside the cordon.

No one, including Jessica, believed for one minute any of those guns would end up being fired. She, like the rest of the onlookers, thought it was just an exercise. So when the first salvo was launched, the watching civilians were severely shaken.

Jessica's instruments all sang out at the same time. The sound of the first salvo had made both girls jump and they quickly found themselves hugging each other for comfort.

The shock wave had also cracked and broken a number of windows in houses closer to the firing position, adding to the sound of mayhem outside the house.

The main effect on the gathered crowd was that of fright. Nearly all of the children were screaming, crying, and running away from the guns. The crowd dispersed so quickly that by the time the second salvo was launched there was hardly anyone left. The area was deserted, except for Jessica and Katie. They still couldn't take their eyes off what was happening.

General Grahams' forces had been fortunate. There just happened to be a platoon on site, doing routine maintenance, when the call came through to deploy the battery.

They were even luckier with their target. Now they were to engage a local thunderstorm rather than the approaching hurricane. The local commander had been told that the two combined events would be devastating and that the new target, even though smaller than the original, was just as significant.

The commander was quite pleased that their 'new target' could actually be seen and heard. It was the thunderstorm they had been watching develop in the distance, while they were seeking high ground in order to deploy their forces.

They would still use their Doppler radar to increase accuracy, since they had been told to aim for the centre of the storm or any tornadic disturbances within it. But they hardly needed help with their aim, since they could see the thing developing right before their eyes.

Hammerhead was over the moon with how his plan was going. The humans had never suspected that Colin was the real danger and that Bonnie was just being used to draw their fire. Colin's change of direction was also a masterstroke and now Hammerhead was on the scene with the Tornados Four. He was sure, this time, he could safely say goodbye to those interfering humans.

As usual, Hammerhead was far too overconfident and was totally taken aback when the first ground based shell hit. The Fluffies and their Windlets on his left side were immediately freed. Then he was hit by a barrage of shells on all sides and once again he was being torn apart by the humans.

The shells were also having a devastating effect on the Tornados Four: Lightening and Crime-Scene had been killed instantly and Notorious was down to Cat.2, hardly worth worrying about. The Commander, though, was still fully active at Cat.4 and he was heading as fast as he could towards the hangars.

He was only a few hundred yards from his target when the final barrage of shells hit. For all their fury, the Tornados Four were gone.

By this time, Hammerhead was too small to raise even a rain cloud, but his spirit was willing the last hurricane on: "C'mon Colin, do your stuff. They can't have much fire power left by now!" he shouted.

Hammerhead was spot on. The artillery unit had used all the reserve armaments. Ollie's team had used up all their seed pods in fighting Bonnie and the WRI team only had one set of the new type of seed pods left and Hurricane Colin wasn't even here yet.

"Base Camp to Aero-One, come in!" Lewis called with some excitement.

"Jack here, Lewis."

"General Grahams' forces seem to have won the day, Jack; thunderstorm and tornados gone."

"Fantastic, Lewis. Let's hope we have as much success in calming Colin down." His elation at Lewis' news was tempered with the knowledge that the only weapons left to calm Hurricane Colin were the remaining pods in the research planes.

"Base Camp to Aero-One, come in."

"Lewis, this needs to be more good news, not bad!" said an exasperated Jack.

"I'm not sure which it is Jack!"

"What do you mean?"

"Gerald Dayton has just been on the line saying he's taking the Flettner ships back over to Key West so they can help with fighting hurricane Colin."

Crikey! At that point Jack realised that in all the excitement and turmoil he had forgotten about the Flettner ships.

"That's bad news, Lewis, very bad news, they won't stand a chance in that storm. Can you get Gerald back on the line and patch him through to me?"

"Will do."

Jack put his head in his hands and waited for the patch.

"You're through," said Lewis quietly.

"Gerald, is that you?"

"Here Jack!"

"You can't be serious about going back in. It's going to be far too rough for the five untested experimental rust buckets you have."

"Too late, Jack, we're nearly in position."

"Do you really think those ships can stand the intensity of the storm? There's no way you'll get out of the way of the rough seas if you move back in." Jack's stomach was churning. He wanted to call the whole thing off.

"We need to test these ships in bad weather anyway, Jack."

"There's bad weather and then there's BAD WEATHER and then would you believe, there's REALLY BAD WEATHER."

"Look Jack, we only need to lower the intensity of the storm by one and we'll reduce the damage enormously. We've all talked about it and we all want to make the attempt."

It was obvious there was nothing he could do to persuade Gerald Dayton to change his mind. "OK Gerald, but if you do this you need to spray as much as possible, so start spraying *now* as you move in."

"Already doing it, Jack."

Jack smiled. Definitely my equal, he thought and added, "Good luck, Gerald!"

"You as well! We'll be fine, Jack. See you soon."

Gerald's decision had shaken Jack. It brought home the danger they were all facing and he wasn't at all convinced they were doing the right thing. He turned to his pilot, "What about you, Sam? Are you alright for going in again?"

"That's what I'm here for, Jack. I say we do it."

Jack got on the coms "Look lads..." He was talking to all flights of the research team. "We are now moving into the realms of the unknown here. We're about to fly into the jaws of hell and I'm not convinced that we can make any difference to the outcome anyway.

I've had a chat with Uncle Sam here and we've decided to go in and drop our pod contents into the eye wall. I would fully understand – in fact I'd be glad – if you guys wish to pull out. Anyone going in there may well not survive in these relatively flimsy planes."

"We'll not be pulling out, cobber!" shouted Joey.

"I say old chap, I'm quite looking forward to seeing an eye wall again. Never can get used to the power of nature; couldn't live with myself if I were to pass up such a chance," said Freddie.

Jack smiled "OK. Let's get in there, fellas."

And with that, all three planes headed for the hurricane.

- Chapter Seventeen -

The Final Battle

Fluff and Cindy had kept well away from the proceedings so far and had witnessed the early part of the battle in its entirety. They were well aware that the humans were losing. They knew that death and destruction, on a very large scale, was moving ever closer, but there was absolutely nothing they could do about it.

There was one thing for sure though. The Princess had told them to shout her name the moment the family home was in danger and not a moment sooner. This was their duty in this battle, and they would carry it out to the letter, even if it meant their own destruction.

Emma was upstairs in the house backing up her files to her flash drive. She felt more comfortable knowing all her work was on a small memory stick that she could keep by her side. It was just a precaution in case the laptop was trashed during the storm. A window opened up showing she had mail.

She logged on. The message was from Angela Lingstrom of the Pearl Institute. The message read:

"Hi Emma,
    There's quite a lot of weather going on in your neighbourhood at present."

You can say that again, she thought

"We are using your Laptop as a node to gather data from our data loggers in your vicinity. If you are able to, please keep a watch on the laptop. If you are on it at the moment press the download key below and run the program that is downloaded. It will present you with a display that has two buttons on it. The green button labelled SAFE (F1) should be pressed once the storm has passed. The red button labelled DANGER (F5) should be pressed if you and the laptop are in any danger."

This is just a precaution to ensure we have sign off data before shutdown.

Thanks for your help!

Angela

A bit cold that, thought Emma. Bothered about the data and not the person. "Mind you, I suppose they're from Iceland," she muttered to herself and smiled.

She finished backing up her laptop, downloaded and ran the program, then took the laptop downstairs to the kitchen to join Scott.

Jack, on the way into hurricane Colin, addressed the two other planes: "We're going to fly through the hurricane and into the eye. Once in the eye we need to synchronise re-entry to the wall and ten seconds after wall re-entry, we drop the pods. We must deploy the pod contents at exactly the same time or it won't work. Two planes won't be enough. Let's do it exactly as I say."

Moving into the hurricane together wasn't a big deal; *staying* together would be absolutely impossible and extremely dangerous without the electronics. Just prior to entry, Jack got on the coms: "Don't forget team, like Sam said in the briefing, we don't want to be bumping into each other: use your GPS and TCAS, let your weather radar tell you where the eye is, and keep around three miles apart at fifteen thousand feet. Once you're in the eye, stay there until the rest of the team join you."

The other two planes acknowledged the call.

As they moved in, the coms were on and off. Sometimes you could get one or the other planes but most of the time it was just garbled.

Lightning was all around them and to makes things worse at times, the clouds were so thick Jack couldn't even see the tips of Aero-One's wings.

The five Flettner ships had gathered off the eastern coast of Mexico, to avoid Bonnie. As soon as Bonnie had been calmed they'd set sail back to their designated spray points.

Because the reliability of the Flettner Rotors hadn't yet been proven, the converted craft's original engines were still operational, so they made good speed through the water.

The objective was quite simple: to get to their spray points before hurricane Colin could build significantly; and then start spraying again.

It was obvious within a very short time that this would be impossible. Colin had simply taken over where Bonnie had left off. Yes, there was probably about six hours in-between but that was far too little time for them to regain their positions or to have any reasonable effect on the ocean temperature.

Gerald's conversation with Jack had at least made him think more of the dangers they were facing and after a further conversation with Mike, in which neither of them was convinced that spraying during the hurricanes passage would make a difference, they decided on an early retreat.

The trouble was they couldn't retreat as fast as the hurricane was moving in and so they were now encountering mountainous seas.

Mike, on the Lancelot, had noticed a widening gap between his ship and the Julian: "Lancelot to Julian, come in Julian."

"We hear you loud and clear, Lancelot," said Gerald Dayton. "What can we do you for?"

Mike recognised the voice and the mixed up phrase: "Gerald, you're falling behind. Is there a problem?"

"Rudder trouble I think. The Captain's gone to have a look." A loud bang was heard over the coms, as the Julian hit the bottom of the wave.

"I've sent Barnard, Lucia and Stinger packing but we're going to stay with you. Can you keep us informed of progress?"

"Will do, Mike."

Mike was on the bridge of the Lancelot and his only sailing experience was this posting, so he had no feel for what he was currently going through. He didn't realise that seas could be this rough. One minute they were looking at the rain sodden skies and the next they were pointing down this mountain of sea and could only see a chasm of frothy water. The noise was just awesome. Each time the boat hit the bottom of a wave there was a tremendous bang, as if they'd hit something solid.

He turned to the Captain of the Lancelot. "Are they in any danger, Brad?"

"I'm afraid so, Mike. If they've lost their rudder then they're lost. It will only be a matter of time before the boat gets a huge broadside wave and they'll be over."

"What, you mean sunk?" Mike said incredulously.

"I'm afraid so."

Mike hadn't realised that the loss of a rudder could

be so catastrophic. He waited for what seemed like an eternity, but was probably around ten minutes, before he called back.

"Lancelot to Julian, do you read?"

"Still here, Mike"

"How is it with the rudder?"

"It's a goner."

Mike had a sickening feeling in the pit of his stomach. "Repeat?"

"It's not operational, Mike."

"Turn the Flettners on. They'll give you some control over your direction."

"Captain's already thought of that, Mike; he's just gone to find out why they haven't come on."

Mike turned to his Captain "Will we know if he's OK?"

"Look at his forward deck; if it's pointing in our direction he should be OK. If that start's to drift south, he's in big trouble."

And slowly but surely the forward end of the ship started to turn and there was absolutely nothing anyone on either ship could do about it. With the rudder gone they were powerless to change direction. Within a very short space of time, the next big wave hit them and they were over. It only took a few minutes for the ship to completely disappear.

Mike just stood there, stunned; he couldn't believe what had just happened.

The Captain said, "I'm sorry, Mike, but we need to get out of here!"

"OK, Brad," Mike wasn't for arguing.

The ride in Aero-One was extremely bumpy and the rain incessant. It must have been hours before Aero-One reached the eye-wall and boy was this sight something to behold. The calm and the beautiful sunshine contrasted so abruptly with the mayhem and the grey goo that had gone before.

Just the fact that they'd made it through to the eye was elation enough but seeing this awesome sight of nature was absolutely breath taking.

The eye must have been two miles across and a good 50,000 ft high. Aero-One was at 15,000ft and the eye wall absolutely towered above him. Jack and Sam were so awestruck that the plane nearly entered the opposite eye wall. Jack noticed it first: "Sam!" he shouted. Sam banked the plane sharply and they just avoided going back in.

"Aero-Two should be coming into the eye soon," said Jack, as they both peered into the clear skies.

"There he is!" said Sam.

A little dot of an aircraft was just apparent a few thousand feet below them, on the opposite side of the eye wall.

"Don't get too high, Sam."

"We must be in an updraft. It's a bit like a giant thermal, I didn't realise we were so high."

"He's spotted us. He's coming up," said Jack.

Aero-One and Aero-Two were more or less flying in formation now, waiting for Aero-Three to join them. "Shouldn't be long now," said Sam.

Jack couldn't help thinking that Joey's plane was the weakest of the three and if any of them were to fail, then the battering that Joey's fuselage had got during the last flight would surely make him the favourite to break up."

With that thought still dangling in his mind, he heard the very loud buzz of two propellers pass right overhead.

"Sorry to be late lads. It got a little hairy in there."

It was Joey's plane coming out of the eye wall, right on

top of the other two planes, missing both by a matter of a few feet.

"Good Grief Joey! You nearly took us all out."

"No, I could see you; stop acting like a Sheila, you're alright, aren't you?"

"Why are you so high?"

"The lightning took out our instrumentation for a while. I'd just got it back on as we approached the eye wall. There wasn't time to lose height."

Jack thought he'd better bring the conversation back to the reason they were all there: "Listen fellas, we need to ensure that we don't hit each other on the run out, so we'll fly in a star burst. It'll be a little bit tricky with the space we've got but it's the safest exit strategy.

Aero-Two, you take northeast.

Aero-Three, you take southeast.

And we'll take due east.

We need to enter the wall at the same time and launch the pods ten seconds later. Copy that?"

"Copy that," came twice over the coms.

"Then let's do it."

Fluff and Cindy had waited long enough. The weather over Jack Winter's house had deteriorated so badly that slates were starting to come off the roof. Cindy was finding it extremely difficult to keep Fluff in place and the two of them had started to drift away from Jack's house.

"Fluff, I can't hold position much longer," Cindy shouted over the tremendous noise of the storm.

"I can see that Cindy. We're losing ground. We'll not know when to call for the Princess if we move much further away."

"I can't hold us, Fluff. The storm winds are too strong."

"Keep trying, don't give up."

Suddenly Fluff was pushed back to his original position.

"Well done, Cindy, I suppose you found your second wind," Fluff said jokingly.

"This is no time for jokes; it wasn't me that got us back here."

"Eh!"

"It was I!"

Cindy and Fluff recognised the voice immediately.

"Scraper! What the heck are you doing here?"

"Heard a rumour, on the wind, that you might be in a spot of bother. So me and some friends thought we'd come and give you a hand"

"Friends?" said Cindy, who had stopped pushing as soon as she realised that she'd had more than one helper. She needed to rest. "So who are these windlets?"

"My pupils! I was giving lessons on how to carve ice flows, when I heard about your problems."

"Very impressive," said Fluff.

"Well I have a few years experience."

All three of them laughed.

With Scraper and his friends joining in the fight, Fluff was feeling quite upbeat, even though the circumstances were still dire. That is until he glimpsed the twister heading directly for the house. He immediately shouted the Princess's name, as loudly as he possibly could.

"Emma!" Scott was looking out the window. A rather large twister had come into view.

"Where the heck did that come from?"

"We need to get in the cellar, now!."

"OK! Let's go," and they both headed for the stairs. Emma suddenly realised she hadn't got the laptop. She ran back to the window and pressed the F5 key. Then quickly ran down to the cellar with Scott.

240

"Ten, nine, eight..." Jack was counting down for the launch of the seedpods. He didn't think for one minute this would work but it was their only chance. The only card they had left to play.

"Seven, six, five..." Funny though, as they entered the eye wall and back into the mayhem, he had glanced up. He was sure he'd seen the distinct mother of pearl colour of a nacreous cloud. He shrugged the thought off. No, not this far south, he thought.

"Four, three, two, one..." he pressed the button. The pods deployed.

"Good grief! What's happening?" It was as if the eye wall was expanding at an incredible rate, moving out away from the airplanes. In front of the wall was wind and mayhem, behind the wall sunshine and calm. Within a few minutes there was no trace of the hurricane whatsoever.

Everyone, in the air and on the ground, was shouting and celebrating. Everyone that is, except Jack.

Jack knew there was no way his seedpods could have caused what had just happened. He was stunned. His only hope of understanding what had just happened was if there had been enough scientific instrumentation trained on the hurricane during its collapse.

If that was the case, then the recordings of the events of the last few moments, and the details they contained, were vital evidence.

That thought would have made him more cheerful if the news from Mike hadn't been so dire.

- Chapter Eighteen -

Fluff and Cindy Get High

Hammerhead had decided, after two run-ins with Jack Winter, that it was definitely time to move on. He thought maybe he should keep going west, or how about all the way around the world – why not?

There was the thought in the back of his mind that maybe he should get friendly with some other thunder-heads, take a look at the Ethiopian Highlands, somewhere near Hurricane Control. The thought of being part of a hurricane sounded rather exciting. Times they were a changing and he wasn't at all sure he liked the future for a mere thunderstorm.

"They were good people, Mike," said Jack.

Mike was standing in front of the memorial to the crew of the Julian. The memorial service had just ended. Mike had spent time talking to Scott and his Mom and the other families of the dead seamen and was feeling their pain.

He'd really got attached to Gerald and the rest of the Boulder team and he just couldn't get over how quickly the whole thing had happened.

"It could have been me Jack," said Mike.

"I know; its just fate, Mike. Any one of us could have taken a hit that day. Now global warming is on the in-crease it's becoming the nature of our jobs."

Mary, carrying Sarah, came and stood along with Emma, Scott and his Mom beside the two men. Mike stroked Sarah's head.

"That's what it's all about, Mike. Having a safe future for the kids," said Jack.

They all stood there in silence for a time, looking up at a little Fluffy cloud passing slowly overhead.

As they were walking away from the memorial, Emma turned to her dad and said quietly: "I think we should have a break, Dad."

"I agree, but I don't think your Mom would be too pleased at giving you a holiday after what you've just put her through."

Emma ignored the feedback and said, "Iceland, Dad. That would be a real break for us all. Completely different scenery, a place you can stretch your legs and have time to think. A place far away from the hustle and bustle of everyday life. A place we can get to know each other again."

Jack smiled to himself. He was being set up, but he didn't mind; it sounded like an excellent idea and he was always ready to forgive Emma's adventurous spirit.

"I'll have a word with your Mom."

Emma grabbed his arm and hugged it tightly.

"Do you think Scott and his Mom would come too?"

"*Em!*"

Fluff and Cindy were just glad to be moving on again. They'd just said goodbye to Scraper and his students, who were on their way back north to do some more carvings.

"It was very good of Scraper and his friends to come and help us," said Fluff.

"It's a good thing he did!" said Cindy, "There was absolutely no way of keeping in position without their help. If they hadn't turned up, I dread to think what would have happened."

"Fluff!" Fluff knew that voice. It was unmistakably royal and a voice he loved to hear; he looked up.

"Hello Princess, it's lovely to see you again."

"It's lovely to see you too, Fluff. You do realise that you and Cindy are heroes up here?"

If clouds could go red in the face, Fluff would be red.

"We only did what you asked us to do, Princess."

"*No*, you did much more than that. In fact, if you hadn't been brave enough to come so far north, Jack Winter's world would be very bleak by now."

"Thank you," beamed Fluff.

"Not only that, but you also helped us to have a little more respect for the human population of the planet. Not at all an easy thing to have done. I thought as a reward I would bring you an old friend. He has a present for you."

"Hi! Fluff, it's me."

"Equation!"

"That's right lad."

"And what brings you here?"

"The Princess Pearl, Fluff! She just told you."

"No! Why have you come?"

The Princess joined in the conversation, "I talk to Equation quite regularly and during one of our conversations he told me that you would like to meet me properly one day. Face to face, so to speak."

Fluff was embarrassed. There's no question that she was right but he couldn't remember telling Equation this. Ah! Yes, he'd told Cindy but... of course, it was Cindy! Windlets don't keep secrets.

"The Princess has allowed me to tell you and Cindy a secret, a secret only I know," said Equation.

"What's the secret Equation?" asked Fluff.

"Well exactly, *that's* the secret!"

"What is?"

"It's a secret *equation*."

"Oh! I'm confused!" Fluff sounded exasperated.

"You're confused! Anyway have you ever heard of the equilateral triangle?"

"Yes, it's a shape. I've never seen it but I've heard about it. It's said that if you can attain this shape, then the Royal Family will reward you by allowing you to join them. But that's just a story – fiction."

"It's not fiction, Fluff," said the Princess, "but there is something you need to know."

"What's that?" Fluff was getting quite excited at the prospect. He didn't think for one minute he would ever have the chance to actually be with the Princess, some thirty thousand feet higher than he'd ever travelled before.

"Neither you nor Cindy could ever get closer to earth again."

Fluff looked at Cindy. As far as Fluff was concerned it was a 'no brainer', but there was no way he would force Cindy to do it against her will.

Cindy, on the other hand, knew what Fluff wanted and her loyalty to Fluff was boundless. If Fluff was going, she certainly was. She needed to keep a watch on this Princess to make sure she didn't toy with Fluff's feelings. Also, the more she thought about it, the more she was excited herself with the thought of seeing a different realm.

"Well, what are we waiting for?" said Cindy.

"Then let's give it a try," said Equation.

"I can't do it," said Fluff, "I've no idea how to!"

"That's because you're not a windlet."

"What's it to do with a windlet?" asked Fluff.

"Have you ever wondered why thousands of clouds, some of them with brilliant minds, have never figured out how to create a simple shape like an equilateral triangle?"

246

"Well, no!" said Fluff.

"It's because with that particular shape, you need a windlet to do one of the sides – the cloud can only do two of them.

Fluff, make a 'V' shape," said Equation.

Fluff obliged.

"Now bring the two sides in a little ... stop. That's it."

Equation then whispered to Cindy.

Cindy flew around Fluff in a pattern that cannot be passed on to humans; needless to say, an equilateral triangle was born.

Suddenly a beam of light shone down and engulfed Fluff and Cindy. They started to ascend into the Royal Domain. As Fluff was ascending he shouted to Equation:

"Thanks, Equation, thanks for your help!"

Cindy also shouted goodbye.

Equation turned for home. He still had a few problems to work out for the Pearl Institute and time was of the essence.

THE END

A Word Of Warning

Remember, and remember well. You are the ones living in the age of global warming and it's going to take an awful lot of hard work and dedication to reverse the damage already done.

*You **can** make a difference, and you really **do** need to **make** a difference, otherwise it won't be stopped.*

And if it isn't stopped?

Well, I have one last thought for you.

Just as a thundercloud goes through a metamorphosis as more energy is brought into its system and becomes vastly different from the little Fluffy it once was.

Just as a hurricane goes through a metamorphosis as more and more energy is pumped into its system and is vastly different than the collection of thunderstorms it once was.

So will the atmosphere one day go through a metamorphosis and be completely different than it now is – unless we stop pouring more and more energy into its system!

Just imagine you have never seen a thunderstorm, that you have only ever seen a Fluffy. Could you tell that it would turn from the small little white cloud it once was into the monster it turns into, just simply by adding more and more energy?

Just imagine you have never seen a hurricane, that you have only ever seen a thunderstorm. Could you tell that this little thunderstorm would turn into a hundred mile wide storm with winds so violent that they could raise the sea level by four metres or more?

And have you noticed the most worrying fact of all?

That in each case, when a metamorphosis does take place, it leads to an enormous leap in the amount of violence that takes place.

If you do not act quickly enough then no one knows, not even the best scientists in the world, what will happen.

May your God be with you!

Appendices

Appendix A

Cloud Characters

The Fluff character is based on the cloud type Cumulus Humilis, which roughly translated from the Latin means 'humble heap'.

This is the one cloud type that really does cheer me up. Where I come from they are called 'Cotton Wool' clouds. They are generally accompanied by an otherwise clear blue sky.

© Serg64 (shutterstock41922018)

Bright white cauliflower shaped clouds. Their home, so to speak, is between two thousand and three thousand feet (although when I look up at them they seem to be only a few hundred feet away).

I think these have to be my favourite clouds.

The Lenticular clouds, shown below, are the ones that Sparkle encountered on his last trip to earth.

© Cindy Landry (istock000007974034)

Layers of these can often be found on mountaintops.

I always find it hard to believe that just a few of those friendly Fluffs can turn into a thunderstorm like the one below. Hammerhead is based on a typical thunderstorm, or to give it a more precise scientific name, the cloud type Cumulonimbus. Growing from a base of two thousand feet to sometimes over sixty thousand feet (eleven miles high) these clouds are extremely powerful.

© David Falk (iStock000008485774)

Thunderstorms are definitely not my favourite characters, especially when I'm underneath them. The higher the cloud the darker it is underneath, which can be a good guide to how powerful they are.

Yet again, it's hard to believe that just a few thunderstorms, with a little help from a warm moist ocean, can be turned into a hurricane and the gigantic structure you can see below – one that threatens everything in its path.

© Matt Trommer (shutterstock4906567)

I wonder what transformation awaits us when we put a little bit more energy and moisture into these structures? Maybe we're about to find out?

?

The nursery and the fine drizzle has to come from the cloud type Stratus, what else! Home for Stratus is anywhere from zero to six and a half thousand feet. When it's at zero feet, we call it mist or fog.

© Christophe Testi (shutterstock9960199)

The Inspection Team characters are based on the cloud type Mammatus (from the Latin for breasts).

© Nicholas D Haan (shutterstock307215)

The 'Play Twister' or dust devil:

© Bruce Rolff (shutterstock19468144)

This is a good representation of the standard twister. Waterspouts are much less powerful than full-blown tornados.

© Dark o (shutterstock12328546)

The hardened twister, the killer:

© Jeff Smith (shutterstock18723787)

The Princess Pearl character is based on a cloud type called 'Nacreous' Clouds.

© Jamie Marland (iStock000001440879)

These are rare clouds, sometimes called mother of pearl clouds. They exist 15 to 25km high (9 to 16 miles high) and well above normal tropospheric clouds.

They are iridescent but exist at much higher altitudes than ordinary iridescent clouds. They are normally seen at high latitudes in places such as Scandinavia, Alaska and Northern Canada, whereas low-level iridescent clouds can be seen anywhere.

- - - - -

Reading: The Cloud Spotter's Guide by Gavin Pretor-Pinney

Internet: http://www.cloudappreciationsociety.org

Appendix B

The Fujiwhara Effect

Sakuhei Fujiwhara was a Japanese meteorologist who experimented with cyclonic structures. After much research he noticed that when two cyclones merge, they first rotate around each other. This dance that cyclones do was duly called the 'Fujiwhara Effect'.

When two tropical cyclones rotate around one another, they do this about their geometric centre. The centre need not be the middle of the axis. The stronger cyclone tends to have a dominant effect on the track of the weaker one. It is generally thought that cyclones will only merge if the distance between them is less than 750miles.

Fujiwhara Interaction (NOAA)

The above is an actual satellite image of two hurricanes interacting. The image was taken on the 24th August 1974 by one of NOAA's satellites. The image is of hurricane

Ione (left) and Kirsten (right). The image is from the NOAA photo library, the 'NOAA in space' collection.

FACT: Hurricanes don't tend to run into each other, although sometimes two storms will begin moving close to one another. When this happens the winds around the storms begin interfering with one another. Usually this will weaken one or both storms. No matter what they do, two hurricanes never come together to form a stronger storm.

FICTION: The hurricanes in this book know better than that! Of course they come together and form much stronger storms. It's more dramatic that way.

- - - - -

Internet: http://en.wikipedia.org/wiki/Fujiwhara_ effect

Appendix C

Storm Chasing

Hurricane Flights

Since the sixties, weather satellites have ensured that hurricanes don't take us by surprise. These 'pictures' of the weather do not, however, provide enough information about the storm itself. To know exactly how strong it is and to better estimate where and when landfall might occur, aircraft reconnaissance is used. These guys basically take a closer look at the storm, which also helps science learn more about the inner workings of these violent events.

The United States Air Force has a Weather Reconnaissance Squadron (the 53rd), who fly WC-130J turboprops (see below) to collect data from hurricanes in the Atlantic Ocean, the Caribbean and the Gulf of Mexico.

WC-130J

The National Oceanic and Atmospheric Administration (NOAA) also have two WP-3D turboprops (see below) for scientific research on hurricanes and other weather events. The turboprops collect data from inside the storms. NOAA also has a Gulfstream jet, which often flies around and over storms. Reports from all of these airplanes, combined with the satellite data, give hurricane forecasters the ability to predict storm strength and landfall data.

WP-3D

Fatal flights

You may well ask the question, "Isn't it dangerous flying into hurricanes?" The truthful answer is 'yes'. Since the first hurricane flights in 1944, four storm-chasing airplanes have gone down in storms. All of the men aboard the four airplanes were lost.

Oct. 26, 1952: An Air Force WB-29 was lost in Typhoon Wilma over the Pacific with 10 men aboard.

Sep. 26, 1955: A Navy P-2V-5F disappeared in Hurricane

264

Janet over the Caribbean Sea with nine Navy men and two Canadian journalists aboard.

Jan. 15, 1958: An Air Force WB-50 disappeared southeast of Guam while flying into Super Typhoon Ophelia with nine men aboard.

Oct. 12, 1974: An Air Force WC-130 went down in Typhoon Bess over the South China Sea with six men aboard. Search airplanes picked up signals from a crash-location radio beacon and reported seeing seat cushions and oxygen bottles, which could have been from the airplane, in the water.

But when you consider all the flights that have taken place and the fact that no aircraft have been lost since 1974, then many pilots think it's a risk worth taking.

- - - - -

Internet: http://www.hurricanehunters.com

Appendix D

Flettner Rotors

We need to keep things simple here since this is not a science book – it's a storybook. Here we go:

An airplane flies for the simple reason that engineers have designed the wings so that when the plane moves forward there is less pressure on the top-side of the wing than there is on the bottom side. This difference in pressure between the top and bottom sides of the wings is called a pressure gradient. Engineers named the shape they discovered an Aerofoil.

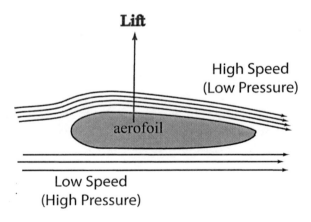

The principle of the pressure gradient can be demonstrated very easily by having two people push, with exactly the same force, on each side of a piece of card. One person is to push up and the other person is to push down. You'll know if they're pushing with the same force because, if they are, the card will remain stationary. If the person pushing down decides not to push as hard, but the person pushing up pushes exactly as before, then the card will move up.

In essence the Flettner Rotor does exactly the same thing that an aerofoil does. It creates a pressure gradient.

Just as the airplane must move forward to provide lift, that is air must be moving past the aerofoil, so the Flettner Rotor must be spinning and have air moving past it to provide propulsion (to provide its pressure gradient). Once spinning, if wind travels past the spinning rotor then the pressure on one side of the rotor is less than the pressure on the other side of the rotor. Thus the rotor, and whatever is attached to it, is pushed from the high to the low-pressure side.

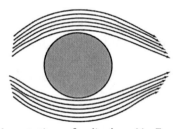

No rotation of cylinder - No Force

Above is the inaction, so long as the cylinder is not rotating. As soon as the cylinder rotates, a force is generated.

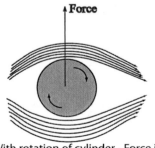

With rotation of cylinder - Force is perpendicular to direction of wind.

This Flettner Rotor ship, the Buckau, was built in 1923.

The Buckau

- - - - -

Internet: http://en.wikipedia.org/wiki/Flettner_rotors
http://en.wikipedia.org/wiki/Magnus_effect